Willow Grove

Martha Rodriguez

 Under supervision of
Scotchwood Hill Publishing Services

DEDICATION

My love and respect to the ladies who seek shelter from abusers and the children who depend on those who listen to God and help them. My love and respect to those who allow God to put in their hearts the love and wisdom to help those who need someone a time of need.

ACKNOWLEDGEMENT

I'm forever grateful to those who listen to my ramblings and ideas and help me. I'm so thankful for NEA Writers Inc, my editor, Patricia Blake, beta readers Debbie Archer, Beth Beck, and Brenda Rawls. I'm surrounded by encouragers, and I love you all.

Martha Rodriguez

ONE

At last, it was ready. And just in time. As David and Sadie stood on the wide porch at the front of the newly remodeled shelter, a large speedboat docked at the landing not far away. Three passengers boarded the golf cart to travel the short distance to the shelter. At the same time, a young woman—a stranger—approached from the opposite direction.

David and Sadie, followed by the stranger, hurried to the cart to help the driver, Jerome, with a bleeding woman and a crying child. The child clung to the woman as the group entered the building.

"Tashina!" Sadie called. A woman in scrubs ran out to meet them. She led them into the clinic they had set up, and David helped her lift the bloody woman onto the examination table. He turned to comfort the child while Sadie filled out paperwork on the new clients. The stranger was on her knees, talking to the little girl. David watched and listened to the exchange.

"My name is Wren," the young woman said as she used a tissue to wipe the child's tears. "What's your name?"

The child sniffed. "Micah." She tried to look around

Wren. "Where's my mama? What are they doing to her?" she asked.

Wren pushed the girl's blonde hair back from her little round face. "Your mama is gonna be fine," she said. "Nurse Tashina will take good care of her." She led Micah to a chair. "Let's sit here and wait for her, okay?" She pulled the child into her lap and hugged her.

"Jack hit my mama," Micah whispered. "Why does he always hit her? She didn't do anything bad."

Wren looked into the child's face. "Is Jack your daddy?"

"No. He's her boyfriend." Micah lowered her head. "My daddy went to heaven. Jack says now he will be my daddy." She scrunched down. "But I don't want him to."

Wren held the child close and rocked her, wiping a tear from her own eye. "How old are you, Micah?"

Micah held up four fingers.

"Four? Wow. You're a big girl. Can you tell me when you'll have a birthday?"

Micah brightened. "I just had my birthday. Mama made me a pink cake with a four on it. I have a new bed, too."

"Oh, my. Do you have your own room?"

"Now I do, 'cause we moved to a new 'partment with Jack."

Sadie came to stand beside David, and they both watched as the young woman comforted the child. "She's good with her," Sadie said.

"She is." David grinned. "Maybe we could use her around here."

"Probably be a good idea to find out who she is first."

"You're right. Wonder what she's doing here?" David walked over to Wren. "So, you're Wren? I don't remember seeing you around here."

Wren looked up at him and continued rocking Micah. "Yes, I'm Wren. Are you David Kingston? You run this place?"

David nodded. "This is my wife, Sadie. This is our

establishment, just opened today."

Tashina came out of her office and gestured to Micah. "Your mama wants to see you, sweetie." Wren took the child to her mama, and Tashina turned to Sadie. "The woman's name is Iris. She's beaten badly, but she'll be okay."

Wren returned and spoke to David. "Mr. Kingston, I live on the west side of the island. I worked at the casino until it closed, and now I need a job. I don't have a way to work off the island. Think you'd have a position open I could fill? I'm a fast learner, and I'll do about anything if you hire me."

David looked at Sadie, who nodded. "Well, Wren, looks like you came just in time. Sadie and I saw how well you handled Micah. We'd be glad to have you work with us." He extended his hand, and she grinned as she shook it, then went with Sadie to fill out some paperwork. The new shelter for abused women and children had its first clients and its first employee on the first day it opened.

David walked back to the porch and looked toward the river.

Things had changed so quickly, and he hoped for the good. This was a considerable project. Would it succeed? Oliver Crandall, who had built the casino they had turned into a women's shelter, had set up the finances to run the place, and donations were already coming in from various places so that part should be good. But what if it didn't succeed? He had given up his shipping business to open this place. Could he go back if things didn't work out here? Would he ever want to go back? He turned to go inside. This had to work. It had to. He'd make it work no matter what.

Meanwhile:

Blood oozed from Nora Langdon's nose and mouth as she leaned against the brick wall in front of a city apartment. She tugged on her bloody, torn shirt to cover her exposed breasts and the red scratches on her chest and arms.

"Ma'am. Ma'am. Are you okay?" A police officer leaned over her as she slumped to the ground. She lifted her red, swollen face and stared at him through blackened eyes. Scrapes covered her arms, and blood ran from cuts on her legs.

"You need some help. Who did this to you?"

She tried to get up, but the policeman motioned for her to stay down. "I'll call an ambulance," he said.

She grabbed his hand and pulled herself up. She moved her head to look around him, her eyes wild. "No, please. I'm fine. I gotta go."

"But, ma'am, you're hurt. Please let me help you."

She leaned toward him with a pleading look. "I have to get away from my husband," she murmured. "He'll kill me."

"What is his name? Where is he now?" The officer looked around, positioning his body to protect her.

"Oh, no," she said. "I don't want him arrested. I just wanna get somewhere he cain't find me."

The officer pulled out a tablet and pencil. "Yes, ma'am, I know some people who will help you. Can you tell me your name?"

"Nora. My name is Nora."

"Okay, Nora. There's a mission nearby where you can wait until I contact someone who can give you the help you need. It may take a little while, so just be patient." He walked a few feet away and pulled out his phone.

After the call, he returned and led her toward the police car. She looked confused, then panicked. "Are you arresting me?" she cried. She tried to run and fell, face-planting hard on the concrete. Fresh blood gushed from her nose and face. She wept as he helped her to her feet.

"Nora, I'm not arresting you. I need you to get into the car to take you to a shelter." He handed her a handkerchief and helped her in. He watched her in the rearview mirror. She held the cloth to her nose as she stared out the window.

He tried to make conversation. "So, have you lived in the city long?"

Her eyes jerked to look at him in the mirror. "All my life." She kept watching him in the mirror. "Do you think I deserved a beating?"

A gasp came from the front seat. "Oh, no! Of course, I don't."

She seemed appeased. "He beats me a lot. Lately, it's anytime I look at him."

He glanced back at her. "Do you have children?"

"No. I got pregnant once. Griffith beat me so that I lost the baby. Now the doctor says I cain't have kids. Then he beat me for that."

His silence encouraged her to continue. "I tried to run away. He said if I did it again, he would beat me 'til I wished I was dead. I told him I already did." She looked down at her hands a moment, then leaned forward. "Sir, do you have a wife? Kids?"

He nodded. "Yes. A wife and two kids."

"My dad was mean, but not as mean as Griffith."

The officer pulled the car into a parking place in front of a brick building and opened the door for her.

"What's this place?" Nora asked as she limped toward the door.

"It's a community building where people look out for the homeless and such. Sort of a mission, I guess. They'll watch out for you until my friend Jerome gets here. He'll take you to the shelter I told you about. He's a real good guy, so don't be afraid. The people here know him." The room was large, with couches, chairs, and tables scattered around, and a kitchen area was visible. The officer introduced her to the people inside the building and left.

The workers gave her some clean clothes and showed her the bathroom. When she returned, they offered her a bowl of soup and a glass of iced tea. A couple stood talking while four others sat at a table in the center of the room. A little girl came over to stand beside her.

"Are you okay, ma'am?" she asked. Nora smiled at her.

"I am now. Thanks for asking. You're very pretty. What's your name?"

"Milly." The little girl pointed to a frightened-looking woman scrunched in a large armchair. "That's my mama over there."

Nora looked at the woman. "Is she okay?" she asked.

Milly nodded. "She's scared. Memaw and Papaw died, and a man came and told us we had to leave. So, they let us stay here since yesterday."

"That's really nice of them," Nora said. She looked around. Through an open doorway, she could see beds in another large room.

"This looks like a nice place," she said. "The soup is good."

"Are you gonna live here?" Milly asked.

Nora smiled at her and shrugged. Where would she live?

TWO

David and Sadie held hands as they walked together to Willow Grove early in the morning.

"I have some calls to make before lunch," David said. "I'm trying to catch up on some paperwork."

She pecked him on the cheek before she went into her office. When he started to close his door, she called to him. He turned and smiled when she threw him a kiss.

About mid-morning, she carried a file into his office. "I hired a cook this morning, and I think we'll need a housekeeper."

"A young woman named Mandy came in a while ago looking for work," David answered. "She's waiting in the dining room. I wanted you to talk to her." He rubbed his forehead. "This is all happening fast."

"I know. Isn't it exciting, though?" A large smile covered Sadie's face as David answered a telephone call.

He jumped up and headed for the door. "Gotta go. Jerome needs me. Said something about picking up a package in the city. We may be a while."

She laughed and planted a kiss on his cheek. "Oh, no," he said. "You're not getting away with that." He grabbed her and bent her over backward. A passionate kiss made her catch her breath.

"Oh, wow!" She flung her arms around his neck and returned the kiss. The sound of a cough made them turn.

"I'm sorry. I didn't mean to interrupt." A blushing

young woman stood outside the door.

David laughed and stepped back from his wife. "Sadie, this is Mandy." He winked at Mandy and flipped Sadie's ponytail. "You need to stop flirting with your husband and see if you can find her a job around here. I'll see you later."

Jerome was gassing up the blue speedboat when he got to the dock. "We have to go to the city for a pickup," he said. "Sadie said she ordered some things, and a guy called saying he has some packages ready."

While they were picking up the packages, Jerome answered a call. "That was Officer Jim," he said. "They have a lady at the mission who needs our help."

David and Jerome drove the short distance to the mission. A man who seemed to be in charge greeted them. They talked awhile, and then he nodded toward Nora. David stood to converse with the man, and Jerome walked toward her. She rose as he approached.

"Hello. Nora?" He extended his hand. "I'm Jerome from the shelter. Officer Jim called and said you need help."

Nora offered a weak smile as she shook his hand. "The police officer said you'd help me." Nora smiled and nodded to the staff, then turned back to Jerome. "Thank you for comin'. I hope you're takin' me to a place where my husband cain't find me."

"Yes, ma'am." Jerome put his hand under her elbow. "We need to get started. It's a few miles upriver. When Officer Jim called, we were in the city. That's how we came so fast."

"Wait a minute, Jerome." David motioned. "I think there's someone else here who needs our help."

Nora watched as the men talked to a frail woman hunkered down in the armchair. Soon David and Jerome led two women and a child, June, Milly, and Nora, to an SUV. They would be added to the client list at the shelter.

David drove through the city streets, dodging traffic until they reached the river where they had anchored their boat. Before long, the blue speed boat skimmed along the top of the water.

While Jerome steered the vessel, David sat with the passengers. "Have you ever heard of Crandall Island?" he asked.

Nora glanced at the frail woman, but she turned her head away. Nora shrugged and answered. "I've heard of it. Ain't it got a big casino on it? I think my husband mentioned it once."

"Has he ever been there?"

She shook her head. "I'm sure he ain't. He never was much of a gambler." She turned her head away. "His vices are drinking and women."

The women and child held on as the speeding boat bounced across the waves of the Mississippi River. David's jaw tightened. "I'm sorry, ma'am. I don't know why some men have trouble doing the right thing, especially to those they're supposed to love."

She lowered her head. "Yeah," she murmured. Then she looked back at him. "Please call me Nora."

He smiled. After a moment, he asked. "Do you have children?"

"No."

He nodded. "Then you have only yourself to take care of." He glanced at the other woman and her child. "Do you mind if I ask your names, ma'am?"

The woman pulled her blanket closer, and the child leaned against her. "I'm June, and this is Milly."

"June, we're taking you and Milly to the shelter. The folks there will take care of you. We'll be there in a few minutes."

Before long, floodlights revealed a landing on one side of the river. Jerome slowed to guide the vessel into a dock beside three other boats. A lady in scrubs ran to greet them as the men helped the passengers from the boat and up the ramp. They climbed into an ATV and rode to the front of the shelter.

The nurse ushered them into a large room inside the building. She directed June and Milly to sit there while she led Nora into the clinic. She helped Nora up on an examination table.

"Nora, is it?" the lady asked. "I'm Tashina. I will check you over, and then we'll get you settled."

While Tashina inspected the cuts and bruises, her soft, reassuring voice offered comfort and hope to Nora. She treated the cuts and administered mild pain pills. Then she took June and Milly into the examination room. After that, she led them up a wide stair to rooms furnished with beds, armchairs, and tables.

"You'll stay here as long as you need," she said. "There's a bath through that door. You'll take your meals with other clients and staff in the dining hall. If you need anything, please ask any of the staff whom you'll meet a little later." Tashina smiled, and Nora hugged her. June and Milly had a room with two beds across the hall.

"Thank you," she said.

"I feel safe now. I ain't felt that way in a long time."

Nora looked around her room and rested awhile, then decided to look around the shelter. A laundry room sat across from a kitchen where a couple of women chattered as they clanged pots and stirred something that smelled wonderful. She glanced out at a patio where inviting lawn furniture sat on the concrete around a large pool.

She went back inside and soon heard voices coming from a lounge area. A look into the room revealed several comfortable-looking couches and chairs scattered around the room. A TV sat on one side, and a tall bookshelf on the other. A couple of women were playing a board game at a table by a large window. One laughed and yelled, "I beat you!" When she turned, Nora jerked back. She did not expect to see her in this place.

Meanwhile:

Eight-year-old Elfi watched ripples push a wadded gold-colored paper up to the bank from her roost in the fork of a willow tree. It floated like a yellow flower among the twigs and leaves in the shallow water. Minnows darted below it, and a noisy blue jay swooped down to inspect the bright object. Then the current pulled it out to the deep where it would be swept away.

If only she could wad herself up and float away on the current like the yellow paper. Maybe it would take her to a place where love ruled. Perhaps someone would find her and take care of her. Was there such a place?

She was a nobody. Unwanted. It was written on the paper. All her short life, she had longed for love. Inside her heart, she knew there had to be such a thing. When she found the crumpled paper this morning under her mom's intoxicated body, she had read it over and over, trying to comprehend. "Someone please come get this kid. I can't do this anymore." That's what it said. She had taken care of her mom since she could walk. What did she mean, 'I can't do this anymore.'?

THREE

"Sadie, where'd you put my briefcase?" David shuffled down the hall into the bedroom, where Sadie rocked Benjamin. "We've got real trouble."

"Shhh. You'll wake Benji. Your briefcase is right where you left it when you came home yesterday." She nodded toward an armchair in the corner and lifted her face for a kiss.

David leaned over to kiss her and touched the child's blond hair. "He's asleep. Want me to put him down?" He lifted the chubby one-year-old from Sadie's shoulder and lay him in the crib, patting him back to sleep when he stirred.

Sadie rose and stretched. "I was almost asleep myself. I sure could use a nap."

"I know this has been hard on you." David rifled through his case and pulled out some papers. "That woman from the Department of Human Services is coming this afternoon. She seems determined to close us down before we start. I don't know who is feeding her information, but I wish they would get it right. I'm ready to clear this mess so we can concentrate on our clients."

"How many do we have now?"

"Six so far. Jerome says some of the law enforcement in the city has heard of us, so we can count on getting more." He sat the briefcase on a table. "We've tried to work things out so we wouldn't have to deal with government agencies, but here they are, trying to knock us down. All we want to do is help women and children who are being abused."

"I know," Sadie said. "We don't have time to deal with the bureaucracy while women and kids are beaten to death."

David sucked in a deep breath and blew it out slowly. He placed a hand on her cheek and pushed her hair back. "I promised you a day off, and tomorrow is it. Sophia and I will handle things at the office."

"I really appreciate that. I need a day to relax and spend time with Benji." Sadie started toward the kitchen. "I'm going to fix a sandwich. Want one? I have some ham and cheese."

David shook his head. "No, you sit down. I'll fix us both a sandwich." She watched as he worked. Then she yawned and stretched. "I'm going to check on the laundry while you do that."

Before long, two sandwiches and glasses of iced tea were on the table. He loved the kitchen in the new home they had built close to the shelter so they would be near work. Sadie designed the house with an open floor plan so they could watch Benji play while they prepared meals. It was much roomier than the house they had in the city, and the shady yard was ideal for a growing boy to play with his dog.

When he turned to call Sadie, he found her curled up in her recliner, fast asleep. He looked over the papers he'd pulled from the briefcase as he ate his lunch, then moved to the bedroom door to watch his son. He walked over to kiss the baby and then returned to kiss Sadie on the top of the head. He made a quick trip to his woodshop to check on a shelf he was building.

As he approached the tall building, he marveled at

the beautiful structure. The upper rooms that had been a hotel now served as a perfect shelter for abused women and children. The building sat back from the river, accessed by a broad drive that led to the landing.

David entered the front doors and turned left toward his office. A frustrated Sophia, the shelter attorney, and his sister-in-law saw him from her office opposite his. "David, the DHS agent will be here soon, and we still have some issues to deal with."

"What are you talking about?" He took the paper she shoved at him. She pointed at a section, and he peered at it.

"You mean we can't call this institution a women's shelter? Why not?"

"It's complicated," she said. "The women we want to help need protection from those who abuse them. It's our job to make sure this place can't be identified as such by those people. We must call it something that won't reveal what it is."

"That shouldn't be so hard. We can call it Crandall Island Garden Club or something."

"Humm — then we'd have gardeners from all over the city coming here to join."

"How about Crandall Island Refuge? No, don't need to use that word. How about Crandall Island Women's Group?"

Sophia grimaced. "How about let's deal with these other matters, and maybe a name will pop up later." She reshuffled the papers. "We must decide how to manage the budget so we won't have to accept federal or state funding. The government is already trying to tell us how to run this place. I received two letters this week wanting us to fill out a form, make an appointment with DHS, or some such nonsense. I don't know how they discovered we're even here."

They disappeared into David's office and spent the

next hour working on the legal documents until a knock on the door warned them that Ms. Woods had arrived.

A tall, slender woman with wheat straw-colored hair piled high on her head barged into the office. Her eyes scanned the room, and her lips pursed as though she found the whole experience distasteful. She pushed aside a pile of papers, planted her briefcase on Sophia's desk, opened it, and then removed a manilla folder. Green eyes peered over the file at David and Sophia, reminding David of a cat waiting to jump on unsuspecting prey.

"According to my records," she sneered, "this establishment doesn't meet our standard codes. You cannot have clients here until certain modifications are made."

"And exactly what would those modifications be?" asked David. "You haven't even seen our building. You have no idea what we're doing here."

"Ma'am, we are not registered with the government, so why are you here?" Sophia scowled at the lady. "We are a private organization."

Woods' mouth opened and shut, and she ruffled through the papers in the file. "Uh, we received word that you are taking on clients without the necessary credentials. Who is in charge here?" She looked at David. "You, sir? What credentials do you have to run a drug rehabilitation center?"

"First of all, this is not a drug rehab." David gave her a look that made her step back. "Can you tell me what credentials are required for a person to shelter abused women?"

Sophia moved to stand between Woods and David. "Ma'am, I am an attorney licensed in Tennessee and Arkansas," she said. "I can tell you we are breaking no laws or codes. I don't know who is sending you reports, but I can tell you they are giving you the wrong information. This is a private establishment on private property. I don't understand how you even know about us."

Woods' eyes were wide, and her face red. "We — uh --I was sent here by DHS in Tennessee. We were informed that women and children were being forced to come here and were being abused." She backed toward the door, her eyes darting around the room. "I'm sorry if I have offended you, but as a government agency, we must check out any report we receive of abuse. You understand, right?" She continued stepping back until she was against the entrance. David reached around her to open the door, and she fled. A man at the wheel of a speedboat awaited. David hoped that would be the last they would see of her.

Meanwhile:

On a cloudy Sunday morning, fourteen-year-old Emmie looked out the apartment complex window where she lived with her mom and eight-year-old brother, Randall. Emmie hoped her mom, Tina, would return soon. She had been gone since Thursday, and the little bit of food that was in the cupboard had disappeared by Friday evening. Randall had been crying all morning, hungry and scared. The last time she had left them alone was for only two days, and when she had returned, Randall asked her where she had been. She yelled at them for messing up her life.

Emmie spent her evenings after school with a friend until she arrived home one day to find Randall alone. He had dropped a glass of milk, leaving broken glass and milk spattered all over the floor. Blood dotted the kitchen rug, and a shard of glass was sticking in his foot.

"Where's Mom?" Emmie had asked him.

"I don't know. She left when I got home from school, and I haven't seen her since."

Emmie looked at the clock on the stove. "That was five hours ago. You mean she just left you here alone?"

Randall sniffed. "So what? She does it all the time. You're always at Julie's house. What do you know? You don't care."

After that incident, Emmie came straight home after school, and Tina started staying out later and later until she didn't come home at all.

One day when Emmie rounded the corner a couple of blocks from home, she saw a woman talking to a man in a car. Thinking it was her mom, she started to run, but the woman jumped into the car, which pulled away from the curb. Emmie hurried home to find Randall alone again. She was sure it was her mom, but why would she get into a car with a man? Maybe it was a friend. Perhaps she would come home soon. But she didn't.

She pulled herself away from the window and went into the kitchen. Knowing she would find nothing but still hoping, she rummaged through the cabinets and the refrigerator. Her rumbling stomach would have to wait until she could figure out how to get some food. She tried to comfort Randall.

"Tell you what," she said. "I'll go out back to see if anyone has put some leftovers in the trash cans. Maybe I can find something edible."

She found a few ends of pizza crust, which was better than nothing. Maybe it would stop Randall from crying for a little while. She ate a small one and gave the rest to her brother.

A little later, Emmie heard a knock on the door. A neighbor lady stood there holding a covered dish. "I made too much lasagna for me and Tom," she said. "I don't want it to go to waste and thought you might like some." She handed the warm dish to Emmie and looked over her shoulder. "Is your mom home? I'd like to say hi to her. I used to see her a lot, but not lately."

"S—s—she isn't here right now," Emmie stuttered. "I'll tell her you said hi when she gets home. Thanks for the food."

The lady smiled. "Just leave my dish beside my door when you finish. And you're more than welcome."

The two hungry kids grabbed forks, and soon the lasagna disappeared. Emmie smiled at Randall as he wiped his mouth on his sleeve. They would sleep well tonight, and tomorrow they would have lunch at school to satisfy their hunger.

The following two nights, the same neighbor brought them pizza and spaghetti and always asked to see Tina.

"I don't think she believes me," Emmie told Randall. "I think she knows Mom isn't coming home."

A few days later, a lady came to the door with the neighbor. When she questioned Emmie and Randall about their mom, they told her the truth. They knew she wasn't coming home.

FOUR

In her short career as a registered nurse, Tashina had witnessed various types of wounds and bruises, but she winced when she looked over this patient. The woman's eyes and lips were swollen, and blood ran from wounds on her head and mouth. Both old and new bruise marks and scars covered her back, sides, arms, and legs. Fresh cuts covered her stomach and breasts like the abuser had cut her with a dull kitchen knife. This abuse had been ongoing for years and looked to be increasingly worse over time. She threw a blood-soaked towel onto the white-tiled floor with the others. Next time, this woman would not survive.

"Don't be afraid—I'll take care of you." Tashina's soothing words seemed to calm the trembling woman. Refusing to allow memories of her past to distract her from the job at hand, she pushed aside the images that flashed across her mind.

"What is your name, love?" The woman responded to the caring touches and words.

"Juliet." She winced when Tashina touched a spot on her neck.

"Do you have children?" Juliet tried to rise, but Tashina shook her head and admonished her to be still. "Are they in danger?"

Juliet shook her head. "Not now, but they will be when he wakes from his drunken stupor in a few hours. I

19

need to go to them."

"Don't worry. The officer will take a statement from you, and someone will go after them."

Tashina cleaned, medicated, and bandaged Juliet's wounds, and in a few hours, the woman's seven-year-old twins, Jax and Jamie, were clinging to their mom.

Tashina completed the examination and introduced the clients to Sadie, who assigned them two rooms with a bath. To dispel their fears, she took Juliet and the children on a tour where they could see the armed guards on all sides of the building and the alarms on every door, which could be opened only by those in authority. Jax and Jamie were excited when they saw the indoor playground and pool.

"Can we play here?" Jamie asked.

Sadie tweaked the girl's nose and laughed at Jax's wide eyes. "Yes, you may play here when you want and as long as you are here."

"How long will that be?" asked Jax.

Juliet's eyes darted toward Sadie. "Well," Sadie answered. "As long as you and your mom need a place to stay. We'll not worry about that now."

Jax looked at his mom, and she ruffled his hair. "This nice lady is letting us stay here where we'll be safe. Is that all right?"

He nodded and ran to swing with his sister.

"I know I've already said it, but thank you again. Rafe has already hit the kids a few times, and I know it will only get worse. They are afraid of him. I feel safe for the first time in a long while, and I know they do, too."

Sadie smiled and took her hand. "I'm just glad someone found you and brought you to us before it was too late." She turned to leave as Juliet watched her children laugh and play. "Supper will be served at six. After that, we'll discuss the routine around here. I'll see you then, okay?

Sadie smiled and waved at Juliet as she returned to her office. What nice kids. Pushing back her thick amber hair, she picked up her briefcase and stuffed some papers she might need to look at later. She agreed she needed a day off, and she looked forward to spending it with her son Benji, her pride and joy.

She walked the short distance to the shelter daily and enjoyed the warm sunshine on the walk back home. She would go to her parent's house to pick up Benji, then prepare supper before David came home.

She loved the narrow, tree-lined walkway between the shelter and her house. She walked around the back of the house to enter the kitchen, and when she reached for the door, it was open. She stopped. She had closed it when she left this morning. David left before she did. He couldn't have been there later because he went to the city to take care of some errands. She hesitated, then crept through the open door. Nothing seemed amiss. Tiptoeing through the kitchen, she peeked into the living room but saw nothing. Breathing a sigh of relief, she went into the bedroom.

There, in the middle of her old-fashioned patchwork quilt, lay a man. A big man. A naked man. Grinning from ear to ear.

She screamed and ran. But he was quick and caught her. He dragged her back into the bedroom and slung her onto the bed. She jumped off the opposite side before he could grab her. He threw himself over the bed and snatched her. She pulled as hard as she could, but he held on. His stink made her retch. She struggled to breathe. His breath was worse than his body odor. Matted hair covered his chest, arms, and back. Gagging, she grabbed a handful of chest hair. He yelled and slapped her hard across the face. He straddled her and jerked her thin blouse up, popping off the buttons and ripping the seams. He worked to pull up her skirt. Fighting panic, she grabbed a pillow and pushed it against his face. He pulled it from her, threw it onto the floor, and slapped her again. She grabbed another handful of dirty chest hair, yanking it as hard as possible. He yelped and recoiled, allowing her to slip out from under him. Rolling off the bed, she remembered something David had told her earlier. She pulled open the nightstand drawer. Her hand closed around a small handgun, and she aimed it at him.

"You won't shoot me." He smirked. Just as he lunged for her, she pulled the trigger.

Meanwhile:

In the visitor's area of the state prison, a woman held the phone to her ear as she listened to the man on the other side of the screen.

"I told you what to do, Caroline. Now just do it." His voice was harsh, and the guard looked at him and shook his head. He knew the attendant would take him back to his cell if he didn't calm down.

Caroline swiped at her eyes and shook her head. "Cosmos, I don't know if I can. There are guards stationed on the island, and I'm scared. If I get caught, you know I'll go back to prison."

Cosmos scowled and swore under his breath. "You'd better stop whining and get the job done if you want your precious fix every week. One word to Carp, and you're done."

"Please, Cosmos. Don't do that." Caroline wiped her eyes again and gritted her teeth. "I'll do it. Just give me some time." She slammed the phone into the cradle and jumped up. "I'll never forgive you if I get caught."

Cosmos rose, and the officer opened the metal door. On the way out, Cosmos brushed his hand against the guard's hand as he passed through the door, and a smile flickered across the guard's face as he stuck something into his pocket.

FIVE

David sucked in his breath as he drew close enough to see his house. Security people were everywhere, and Jerome paced in the yard.

"What's going on?" David asked. "What happened?" He ran toward the house with Jerome close behind.

"I'm not sure," Jerome answered. "I think someone broke into your house. Sadie's in there."

The police officer stationed on the island stood in the hall talking to a white-faced Sadie. Inside the bedroom, blood covered the bed and the floor. When Sadie saw David, she threw herself into his arms.

Officer Jason explained. "That man broke into your house, David, and assaulted Sadie. She shot him."

The man lay on the floor, partially covered by a sheet. He moaned and writhed, and when he saw David, he yelled. "I need a doctor. I'm bleeding to death."

"Shut your face," Officer Jason said. "You're not going to bleed to death." He turned to David. "We'll load him on the ranger and have him out of here shortly. I have all the information I need from Sadie. We'll be charging him with assault."

"You need to charge her with attempted murder," the man on the floor yelled. "She tried to kill me."

Sadie whirled to look at him. "I should have. You don't deserve to live."

Officer Jason smirked. "Livin' won't be nearly as fun

for you now after that bullet." He turned to David. "She shot him right you-know-where no man ever wants to be shot." He snickered, and the man moaned and turned his face toward the wall.

They loaded the man on the ranger, and Officer Jason threw his clothes on top of him. They would take him to the dock and boat him to the city.

David took Sadie to her parents a half-mile down the road to stay until he had the house clean.

A few days later, David decided to boat to the shipping office to check on Kade. Since Kingston and Crandall Shipping merged to become Crandall Shipping, Kade ran the company while David helped Sadie with the shelter. Even though Kade and Sophia had moved to the island, David hadn't seen much of Kade. If he wasn't out of town taking care of shipping clients, he had his head in the business ledgers or was home with Sofia and their infant son, Jonathan.

David hopped up the steps and entered the outer office. "Kade around?"

The secretary, Emma Clancy, hung up the phone and turned to David. "Sweet boy, where have you been? You never come around anymore, and I miss you."

David laughed and hugged his dear friend. "Bless you, Ms. Emma. I love you. You're one of my favorite people. You know I was here just a couple of weeks ago."

"I know, but that's too long. You need to come see me every day. Or at least every week." She patted his arm.

"David! What are you doing here?" Kade came out of his office and extended his hand. David ignored the hand and threw his arms around his friend.

"Man, you must be working out." David punched Kade's shoulder and poked his stomach. "Feel those abs.

I know sitting at a desk hasn't done that for you."

Kade laughed. "I do run every morning, but these…" he patted his stomach. "These are from hefting that chunky baby boy of mine." He picked up a photo from Ms. Emma's desk. "Just look at this kid. Did Sophia give you a photo?"

"Oh, yes. She's as proud of that boy as you are."

Kade sobered. "I know you didn't come here to brag on my Jonathan. What's going on, David? Is everything all right? My sister still doing okay? That was a rough experience for her."

"Yeah," David said. "She's a tough one. I'm amazed she thought fast enough to lower that gun before she pulled the trigger."

Kade laughed. "She taught that dude a lesson he won't forget." He motioned for David to follow him into his office. "Sophia says there are some areas of conflict at the shelter."

"Yeah, but nothing major. Just the DHS nosing around. Seems like someone is feeding them lies about us, causing trouble. We don't want Uncle Sam telling us what we can and can't do."

"That means no government funding."

"Right. Oliver set us up so we can run mostly on the interest from the trust fund, and we have a few business friends who donate regularly. Also, some of the islanders help us out."

"Yeah, Dad set us up pretty good."

"It keeps us all afloat," David said. "The only thing that concerns me is the way some of the islanders have struggled since the casino closed and they lost their jobs."

Kade adjusted his collar. "I guess some of them have reverted to jobs they had before the casino."

"Do you remember the Simms family on the east side?" David leaned back in his chair. "You know, the house built on stilts right on the river?"

"I remember them. Don't they have about four girls?"

"Yes. I remember them being excited that they were having a boy."

Kade squinched his eyes. "What about them?"

"Doesn't seem like it's been thirteen years ago. Their son, Lyric, came to the office the other day looking for a job. I hired him for a few hours a couple of days a week in the afternoon. He seems like a nice kid."

"Good. I'm glad we can help the island families. I've hired several to work at the resort."

David nodded. "Looks like the resort is doing well."

"Business has been booming since I hired Leroy and Clara Sears as managers. We have so many requests for reservations we can't fill them all. People love the golf course, even if it is rather small."

"The island has sure changed since we grew up there," David said. "A few of those who left when Oliver built the casino and hotel have returned. That makes me happy."

"Like Jerome? Seems like he's doing a great job."

"He sure is." David pointed upward. "That man is a godsend. He not only runs back and forth from the mainland, but he pitches in around the shelter. Keeps an eye out, you know. And he's great with the clients he brings in. I was glad to assign a boat to him. I'd trust him with my life."

"Doesn't his daughter Angie attend a high school off the island?"

"She does. She helps us out, too. Great kid."

Kade took a cup of coffee and offered David one. "I have an idea for the buildings on the north end of the island," Kade said. "They're empty now, and we don't need to waste them."

"That's true. We need to find a use for everything. What is your idea?"

"There are some islanders who need work, and since

27

they already live there, why don't we allow them to use the buildings to sell their crafts and wares? You know, many of those folks are great artisans. Some of the women make quilts, some make jams and jellies, and …."

David interrupted. "Yeah, and old Jeb builds the most beautiful furniture. His son makes bowls and vases on the lathe. They do great work."

"That's true. They need a place to sell their crafts. Why can't we let them use the buildings?"

David stared at the floor, thinking before he answered. "You mean like a craft village or something?"

"Something like that. You know how crazy city people are about hand-made furniture and crafts."

"Hmmm. That may be a genius idea. With the ferry landing on the island's northeast end, visitors would have to pass it on the way to the resort. The shops would draw them."

Kade nodded. "With the line of trees separating the resort from the shelter, we won't have to worry about anyone bothering the clients."

"Right. And there's no major road from the east side to the west side. We can make nice streets around the north buildings and a sort of wall with a gate as a barricade to discourage anyone from traveling down the middle to the south end. We'd still have the road around the perimeter of the island."

Ms. Emma peeked around the door. "Sounds like you two have a great plan for that island property. Oliver will be proud of what you're doing."

Kade laughed. "I sure hope so. I'm glad the old man saw the light and changed his ways."

"Yes," said David. "God sure did a work in him. He's a different man. Benji sure loves him."

"So does Jonathan. He makes a great granddad for our kids. He and Mom love to spoil them."

David turned to leave. "That reminds me. I need to

get home. They're coming for supper tonight, and I'm helping Sadie."

He hugged Ms. Emma, and Kade walked him to the boat dock.

"When are you coming over?" David asked. "You can't be too busy to spend time with your sister and best friend."

"We'll show up at your door one evening, and you can feed us." Kade shoved the boat away from the dock when David started the motor.

When David reached the island, he steered the boat toward his favorite thinking place since childhood — the willow grove. He would do a little meditating before going home. He frequently visited here, enjoying the breeze that whispered through the willow branches above his head. He shared the place with various birds, turtles, and lizards that seemed to accept his presence.

His mind drifted to the shelter. Sadie told him the clients were doing well, although some feared being found by a husband or an ex. He would do everything in his power to prevent that. And that included finding a name for the place.

He loved the willow grove. It was where he came when he felt burdened with an issue or when he wanted to feel God's presence. Here he had first realized he was in love with Sadie. Here, he felt God's approval to buy Pruitt Shipping, which became a prosperous company. Many decisions in his life had been made right here in this spot. Through the years, wind and rain from storms had shifted the sand and uprooted some trees, but new trees had grown, and the grove withstood everything that came against it.

That's it! That's the name of the shelter. Willow Grove Shelter. If only Sadie and Sophia would agree.

Meanwhile:

"Brent, you know Mama isn't awake yet. Don't bother her. I'll try to find us something to eat."

Ten-year-old Sage rummaged through the kitchen cabinets, finding only an empty cracker box and some stale buns. She pulled a plastic glass from under a pile of dirty dishes and rinsed it. Roaches crawled out of a pan and up the wall.

She filled the cup with water and handed it to her eight-year-old brother along with the crackers and bun, keeping one bun for herself. She moved dishes from the sink, ran the water until it was warm, then put in the sink stopper. She would clean up the kitchen, and maybe her mother would be proud of her. The dish detergent bottle was empty, so she found a sliver of a bar of Dial soap in the bathroom. It would have to do.

Loreen stumbled into the kitchen. "Baby girl, what are you doing?" She swiped at red, swollen eyes and winced when she bumped against the door facing. Three years before a car accident had damaged the nerves in her right arm, making her unable to work. The doctor prescribed Hydrocodone for pain, but after a few months he refused to renew her subscription. She started drinking to alleviate the depression that had set in. Even after the pain subsided, she craved the drugs and found a dealer.

Her live-in boyfriend soon left, tired of trying to raise her kids and keep the house while working late hours. Her disability check was barely enough to keep her supplied. Could she help it if she didn't always have enough money for groceries? Her foggy mind told her she was doing the best she could. After all, she'd had to provide for the kids alone since their father ran out soon after Brent was born.

"I'm going to wash these dishes and clean the kitchen, Mama." Sage smiled at her mom. "You can lay back down."

Loreen sniffed and rubbed her nose. "Oh, sweetheart, I'll get that done. Just let me get a drink and rest a minute." She picked up a whiskey bottle, drank the last swallow, and then staggered back into the bedroom.

SIX

David returned home to find Sadie and Benji playing in the backyard with their new Golden Retriever puppy, Gus. He smiled when the baby stretched out his hands.

"Da-da." Benji babbled as he patted David's face and poked at his eyes. David blew under his chin and loved on him before he sat him down. Benji toddled over to Gus and babbled at the dog, who licked his face. "Dus." He patted the dog's head and leaned over to give him a slobbery kiss. David and Sadie laughed as the dog and child ran off together.

Sadie rose from the lawn chair and reached for David's hand. "Let's go start supper. My parents will be here soon." David called Benji, and together they went into the kitchen and chatted as they prepared the meal. Sadie belted Benji into his highchair and gave him a bowl of cereal.

"Have you met the new client yet?" Sadie asked. "She has a set of twins, a boy, and a girl. They seem to be happy considering what they've been through."

"I was there when Jerome brought them in," David answered. "He picked the mom up at the police station and then had to go back later to get the kids. A neighbor saw them standing in the street. Said they were locked out of the house and were hungry. They had seen their dad beat up their mom, so they hid in an alley. They were scared."

"Tashina says he beat her badly. She says the woman wants a divorce as soon as possible but fears what her husband will do when he finds out. I'm meeting with her tomorrow." Sadie picked up the spoon Benji dropped on the floor.

"I'm going to Memphis in the morning to meet with a guy from a shelter there,' David said. "He'll advise me on some issues that can be sticky. We sure want everything to be legal and above board, so we don't have problems later. It's a good thing we have Sophia here."

She handed him a spoonful of sauce to taste. "Maybe he can advise you on a name for the shelter."

"Yum, that's good. May need a pinch of salt." He wrapped his arms around her and kissed her on the neck. "I thought of something this afternoon that might work. What do you think of Willow Grove for a name?"

She tested the words. "Willow Grove. Willow Grove." She turned to return his kiss. "I think it's perfect."

"Do you think Sophia and Kade will like it?"

"I'm bettin' they will. We'll call them later tonight." She pulled some breadsticks from the oven and poured pasta into a bowl. "I made the salad earlier, so I think everything is ready. And just in time, too."

Oliver and Kathleen came through the door and headed straight for Benji, who waved his hands and kicked his feet in excitement.

Sadie laughed as the older couple unfastened the child and lifted him from the chair. "He loves you both so much."

"We love him, too," Kathleen said. Oliver pulled a toy from his pocket and gave it to his grandson as they moved into the living room to play with him.

"Look at that," David said. "Not even a hello or how are you. They only have eyes for that baby."

"Say," Oliver came into the kitchen. "Do you have someone guarding the upper east point? I thought I saw someone pulling a boat in there."

David frowned. "No one should be docking there. It's too rocky. Even island fishermen stay away from that area. I'll check it out tomorrow." Oliver shrugged and returned to play with his grandson.

—✧—

When they called Kade and Sophia later that night, they all agreed Willow Grove would be the perfect name for the shelter.

"It's subtle and doesn't reveal the true purpose of the building," Sophia said. "Now I can finish the paperwork and wrap up the legalities of this thing. I knew you'd find a name. It's perfect."

—✧—

Jerome let his boat drift into the dock with a bedraggled woman and a small child the next day. He had called the shelter, and Tashina met him at the pier.

"Jeff Wilson found a paper floating on the water and took it to his wife," he told Tashina when he stepped out of the boat. "You remember Jeff and Dora, who run the grocery and bait shop on the chute. Jeff said the message on the wet paper was hard to read, but they could make out that someone wanted to get rid of a kid."

He pulled Tashina away from the boat so the passengers couldn't hear. "Jeff said later that he saw this girl wandering outside and took her into the store. She was dirty, and her clothes were ragged, so they knew something wasn't right. When he showed the girl the paper, she said she threw it into the water. She told them her mama was sick and they needed food, so Mrs. Wilson took some groceries to the house. They found the woman passed out on the couch. There was no food, and the house was infested with mice and fleas."

"Has she aroused enough to agree to come here?" Tashina asked. "Does she know what this is?"

Jerome nodded. "She has, and she does. Of course, her brain has pretty much been fried, but she asked for help, so I brought her here."

They turned back to the boat, and Jerome helped the woman to the bank. The girl, who looked about seven, clung to her mother. "What are you going to do with her?" she asked. Tashina wrapped the woman in a blanket and lifted the child from the boat.

"Sweetie, we'll care for her and help her get better. Can you help me with her?" The girl nodded. Tashina continued to murmur to them as she drove them to the shelter. "What is your mom's name?" she asked the girl.

"Grace."

"And what is your name?" Tashina's soft voice gave comfort to the frightened child.

"I'm Elfi."

"What a lovely name," Tashina said. "Elfi. I don't think I've ever heard that name before."

The girl smiled. "Mama says I reminded her of a little elf when I was born because I was so tiny."

"I'll bet you are a great help to her. How long has she been like this?

"As long as I can remember. I have tried to take care of her since my daddy left a while ago. But I didn't know what to do when the food ran out."

"Well, now everything will be better for you and your mom. If you'll open that door, we'll get her onto that examining table so I can check her over."

Grace roused and reached for Elfi. "Baby?" she whispered. "Are you okay?"

"I'm fine, Mama. This nice lady is gonna take care of us." She swiped at her eyes. "Aren't you, Miss....?"

"Ms. Tashina. I'm a nurse, and I'll give her the best care I can. You're not to worry, Elfi." A teenage girl came to the door. "Now, if you go with Angie, she will help you bathe and show you to your room. After I examine your mom, she'll be in a room with you."

Later that evening, Sadie and David met with Tashina to discuss the new clients. "The mom is in pretty bad shape," Tashina said, "but the little girl is already making friends with Jax and Jamie. She's a courageous little thing. I guess because she's acted as an adult most of her life."

Sadie nodded. "Children who are adultized early in life are forced to become self-sufficient."

"Do you think Grace will be stable enough for us to talk with her in the morning?" David asked. "Sadie will have to evaluate her, and then we can get her processed into the system."

"She should be ready," Tashina said. "Of course, until we get her dried out some, she will be in and out, but she should be able to talk to you."

A loud noise came from the kitchen, and David jumped up to see what was happening. The others followed close behind.

Jax, Jamie, and Elfi stood before the opened refrigerator, and a sheepish Angie cleaned a spill on the floor. The twins ran to hide behind the door.

"We spilled some milk," Angie said. "They wanted some cocoa to go with the oatmeal cookies I made. I'm sorry."

Sadie laughed. "It's okay, guys. Don't feel bad." The twins cowered, sniffling and holding onto each other. "Come on, guys," Sadie said as she knelt before them. "You're not in trouble. Anyone can have an accident." She started to wipe their tears, but they drew back, still clinging to each other. She rose and continued to speak softly to them.

A movement in the other room caught David's attention, but the room was empty. Then the door that led to the patio closed. He hurried to look on the patio, but no one was there. He scratched his head and went back inside.

Meanwhile:

Marleigh picked up her six-month-old infant and sighed. "Aiden, you sure are getting to be a big boy." He grabbed the bottle from her hand, and milk oozed out one side of his mouth as he lay back against her. Marleigh leaned her head back on the rocking chair and was dozing off when heavy footsteps on the porch awakened her. She leaped to her feet, almost spilling the baby on the floor, when the door flew open.

"What have you been doing?" Elliot leaned toward her until his face almost touched hers. "There are tire tracks in the drive. Who has been here today? What are you hiding from me?"

Marleigh pulled back and stuttered. "N—N—no one has been here. I've been here all day with Aiden. I don't have anything to hide from you."

"Don't lie to me, you tramp. You're just like your mother."

"I am not like my mother." Her face reddened. "Elliot, I promise I haven't done anything wrong. I've cleaned house and made you supper like I do every day."

"Yeah, right. I see the way you look at James Wheatly every Sunday at church. Has he been here?" He shoved her against the wall.

"Elliot! Watch out for Aiden. You'll hurt him." She pushed around him and put the baby in the playpen. He backhanded her as soon as she stood, knocking her to the floor. He kicked her in the back, ignoring her screams. Then he stormed out of the house.

She dragged herself to a chair and pulled up. She raised her shirt and inspected the red bruises layered over old, yellowed ones on her sides and arms. She jerked her shirt down when she heard him returning.

He walked to her and cupped her face in his large hand. "I'm so sorry, sweetie. I get angry when I think you might be cheating on me. I can't help it if I love you so much. I can't stand the thought of you wanting someone else besides me."

He leaned over and kissed her. "I hope you aren't hurt. Can I rub some liniment on you? Will that make it all better?"

She shook her head as he wiped the tears from her face. When Aiden started to cry, Elliot threw up his hands.

"What is wrong with that brat now? Can't you make him stop crying?" He wrapped his arms around her, pulling her to her feet. He started kissing her neck and moving downward until she pushed him away and picked up the baby.

SEVEN

The list of clients was growing, and David, Sadie, and Sophia kept busy making sure everything ran smoothly. David hired islanders Louisa as a cook and Mandy as a housekeeper, and a couple reopened the church Max Shepard had started before he left. It was within walking distance for the clients and shelter staff to attend on Sunday mornings.

The Craft Village on the northeast side was about ready to house crafts and other wares from the island dwellers. Old Jeb was placed in charge of the village and organized crafters so that everyone was excited to start selling their goods.

Sadie met with the clients daily to discuss issues bothering them. Some of them had been arguing over trivial things, like who does what chores. Others were experiencing fear that former abusers would find them. Most complied with the shelter rules, but a few complained and outright rebelled. A client named Caroline seemed to enjoy stirring up trouble and was often at the root of the conflict when fights broke out among the clients. Sadie reasoned with them and talked to Caroline privately about the situation but to no avail. Finally, David asked everyone to stay in the dining area after the meal. Kade and Sophia joined them for dinner and stayed to support David and Sadie.

"Folks," David said, "we are here to help you, so give us a chance before you find fault. If you have a problem, come to me or Sadie, and we will try to help you work it out. Meanwhile, be there for each other. Encourage each other.

And be kind. That's always a good thing."

Sadie and Sophia sat nodding their heads, but Kade stood. He scowled and looked over the group until David gestured for him to speak.

His voice matched his scowl when he finally spoke. "Listen, people, these folks are trying to help all of you. They give their time and energy to help you—the care they offer costs you nothing. So BE GRATEFUL. For heaven's sake, just show some gratitude. They do care for you, although—at this point—I'm not sure why." He turned toward his chair, then turned back around. "You're welcome!" He sat down, and the room was quiet.

All over, heads were nodding as the clients looked at one another. "He's right," some murmured. Then Elfi stood.

"Thank you, Uncle Kade. May I call you that?" She looked at him, and he smiled and winked at her. "Thank you, Mr. David and Mrs. Sadie. We all love you. We're sorry we're so much trouble." She looked around and pointed at herself. "I want to make up for the complaints by helping more around here."

"You dear child," said a client named Marleigh. "I've never heard one complaint from you, but I will join you in being more grateful. Thank you all."

The rest agreed and rose to shake hands with David and Kade and hugged Sadie and Sophia. Everyone was smiling as they went to their rooms. Sadie stood by the door into the hall and overheard a conversation between some girls.

"I don't know why y'all can't just get along." The voice belonged to Emmie.

Then Caroline spoke. "I know they blame me, but I can't help it if some people around here are jealous of me and try to get me into trouble."

"Jealous? Who's jealous of you?" It sounded like Wren. "You still get your highs, and you'll be in trouble when you're caught." She snickered. "Why would anyone be jealous of someone who puts water in their cereal?"

Laughter filled the hall until the sound of a slap followed by a grunt silenced it. Sadie listened, but the altercation seemed to dissolve, and they moved on down the hall until Sadie could no longer hear them.

When they were all gone, David turned to Sadie. "I still say you're too easy on them. They've got to learn to face their problems head-on and stick up for themselves without fighting."

"Seriously, David, you think being hard on them will help? They've been through a lot already. I don't think the answer is being stern with them. I think they need love and compassion. They'll come around."

"I hope you're right," he said. "By the way, are you getting any negative vibes from Nora?" he asked.

"Yes, something is going on with her. Lately, she's been talking like she wants to leave. Something about a sister who lives down the river on the city's outskirts. I understand, and I've warned her to be careful."

"Well, no one will make her stay." David finished the last of his sweet tea. "That goes for all of them. This program is for volunteer clients. I think they feel safe here, so they'll work together after tonight."

"We need to keep a close eye on Caroline," Sadie said. She relayed the conversation she'd overheard.

David jumped when his phone rang at 2:00 a.m. "HELLO?" He didn't mean to yell. It was Jerome.

"David, can you come at once? We need you."

"What's wrong?"

"Just hurry." The phone went dead.

David jerked on a pair of jeans, slipped a tee shirt over his head, and ran out the door. He tried to answer Sadie's questions on the way out, but the lack of information made it impossible. "I'll call you," he said.

When he arrived at Willow Grove, blazes were shooting out a small window in the laundry room, and smoke boiled from under the rafters. Jerome ran to meet David.

"What happened?" David asked.

"I'm not sure," Jerome said. "Tashina said something woke her up, and she felt the heat when she passed the laundry room on the way to the bathroom. She called the fire department, and then she called me."

Tashina appeared from around the corner. She had a blanket wrapped around her shoulders and looked shaken. "It had to be started by one of the clients," she said. "I think I know who it was."

She pulled David away from the crowd that had gathered. "Since she has been here, she has been nothing but rebellious. I told her she could go anytime, but she said she has no place to go and wants to stay."

"Why is she here? Who sent her?"

"It's Caroline. I took a call from a shelter in the city, and the man said she came to them one day high and asked for help. She told them she needed a place away from her friends and family. The guy said he didn't think much about it when she mentioned Crandall Island, but later he thought it seemed odd that she would even know about this place. He called Jerome and sent her here."

"Go over there close to that bunch and see if you hear anything. I'll walk around the building." David motioned for Jerome to go around the opposite side of the building.

He walked far enough from the building to stay in the shadows, and when he was well behind it, he saw two figures hovering close to the wall. He watched them for a while. Then they went through the back door, which he knew should be locked. They came back out in just a few minutes and moved further around the structure. He followed, moving closer. He closed the distance between them when they appeared to head toward the river. He took a flashlight from his pocket and shined it on them, and when they turned, he was shocked. He did not expect to see the faces that stared back at him.

Meanwhile:

In the dark, a water vessel rounded the end of the island where the chute separated from the river to form the island, causing a raccoon to skitter in anger when it dropped a big fish. Paddles dipped into the water, turning the boat toward the mainland. A flashlight flickered toward the shore, revealing a man sitting under a cottonwood tree. When he saw the light, he stood and waved. Those in the boat waved back and paddled harder as they glanced back at the shore.

"What took so long?" the man yelled as the boat neared.

"Oh, Jase here almost got caught when he had to stop for a pee break."

"Shut up, Sully. Nobody asked you."

When Jase and Sully jumped out of the boat onto the shore, the man smacked Jase on the head. "Boy, cain't you pee on the run? You cain't afford to get caught. You'd best pee your britches before you end up in jail again."

"I saw her, Dad. She's there for sure."

"I know, son. She's the one who set up this job."

"Oh. I thought Cosmos set it up."

"He ordered it done, fool, but he cain't do ever'thing from prison. Someone here is needed to put feet and hands to the job. That's us. And her."

"So, what are we gonna do now? How long's it gonna take to take these people down?"

"You jus' keep an eye out and wait. We got people in place to make bad things happen over there. Now git back in that boat and hide where you can see the dock. And don't git caught."

Jase and Sully jumped into the boat and started the motor. Sully kicked it. "You idiotic motor, you do this every time." He continued to swear and crank until it sputtered off down the river.

EIGHT

"What are you guys doing here?" David guided the teenagers into a room in the back of the shelter. "Don't tell me you had something to do with this trouble."

Lyric and Angie stared at him, mouths open. "No—oh, no, sir!" Lyric's head swung back and forth, and Angie's face reddened.

"Sir, we thought we saw someone running behind the building," Angie said, "so we came back here to see who it was."

"Yeah," Lyric said, "that's all. Sir, we would never do something like this. We love it here."

David looked from one red face to the other. "Okay," he said. "I believe I can trust you both." He hesitated. "Did you see who it was?"

The kids glanced at each other, then Angie spoke. "We first thought it was Grace, but it was too tall to be her. So, I don't know."

"Okay. Let's go around to where the others are." David ushered them around the building, and they joined Tashina, where she watched the firefighters roll up their hoses and prepare to leave. David patted her on the back. "Go get some rest," he said. "We'll clean up tomorrow."

Jerome stood at the dock, looking for anyone who might be out of pocket. He motioned for David.

"A boat left the dock right before I got there," he said. "It was too far away for me to see who it was. I didn't recognize it, so it wasn't from around here."

David grimaced. "We'll have to post a guard by the dock at night. We can't take a chance on someone coming here to cause trouble."

Sadie sat at her desk, trying hard to maintain professional composure. The young woman sitting across from her spilled out vile, bitter words from her mouth while her eyes blazed with hurt and anger.

"I know you're hurting," Sadie started, but Grace cut her off.

"No, you don't know." She pounded her fist on the desk. "Have you ever been beaten by the one supposed to love and protect you? Have you ever had to hide because you're afraid you won't survive another hit in the head? Have you ever been so hungry you thought you shrivel up and die? Not just for food but for love. For support. For someone to know you're there." Her tear-filled eyes searched Sadie's face until Sadie felt like the woman could see into her soul.

"No, I have never been there. I've never suffered what you have. I can't know how that feels, but I care about you, Grace. I'm here for you."

"Every man I have ever known has been mean to their women. My dad beat my mom, When I was twelve, he started slapping me around. Accused me of being a whore. 'Just like your mom,' he'd say. My uncles did the same thing. Then what'd I do?" A scornful laugh escaped her mouth. "I married one just like them. No — worse."

She looked down at her trembling hands. "I didn't want Elfi to grow up like that. Then look at me! I started drinking." Another laugh. "Then he put me down for that. Called me a failure as a wife and mother. Didn't matter what he did, whatever I did was worse. So, he left." She rose and started pacing. "How could I do that? How could I stay so drunk I neglected my baby?" She swiped her eyes. "She could have died, and I wouldn't have known." She collapsed to her knees on the floor and wept with her hands covering her face.

Sadie took a tissue for herself and one for Grace and then she went to her. She knelt beside her and wrapped her arms around her. She rocked her like a baby until the sobbing turned into sniffs. As Grace wiped her face with the tissue, Sadie helped her to her feet and back into the chair.

Grace lifted her head and stared at her. "I'm sorry, Mrs. Sadie. I didn't mean to yell at you. I'm sorry I cursed at you. You don't deserve that. I know you're trying to help."

"It's okay for you to pour out your anger," Sadie said. "It's better than keeping it inside. You can cry on my shoulder and fill my ears with your pain any time. Please know that."

Sadie was glad to see a weak smile on Grace's face. "Thank you, Mrs. Sadie," Grace said. "I know you've been caring for Elfi when I couldn't. She loves you so much, and she loves it here. You don't know how much we appreciate your help. You and Mr. David have saved us."

She rose to leave, and Sadie squeezed her hand. "Elfi and I are pretty good buddies. And Grace, I want you to feel free to talk to me any time."

Sadie headed for the kitchen to see if Louisa had anything for a snack. She and the cook were pretty tight, and Louisa often kept some chocolate or bacon crackers because she knew Sadie needed something to munch on in the afternoons.

Louisa greeted her with a cheerful laugh when she stuck her head around the kitchen door. "Right here, girlie. I had a feelin' you'd be comin' around soon wantin' something to eat." She held a container with crackers and dip and a dark chocolate bar.

"Oh, Louisa, you're the best. You know just what I like." Sadie sat at the counter and dug into the crabmeat dip. "Ummm...this is soooo good!" She wiped her mouth with a napkin. "What's for supper?"

Louisa laughed. "You always thinkin' about food, ain't cha, girlie? Be careful, or one day you'll be like me." She patted her large belly as she lifted a lid from a pot. The smell drifted right into Sadie's nostrils.

"White beans and ham," Sadie said, neglecting her professional language and picking up the southern dialect shared among the shelter staff. "I betcha there'll be cornbread, too."

"You know it." Louisa sat beside Sadie while she finished her snack. "Fergive me, Mrs. Sadie, but I need to bring something to the front."

Sadie raised her head to look at the older woman. "What's that, Louisa? Something bothering you?"

"Well, it's just that...and mind you, I ain't tryin' to cause no trouble, but it's been kinda flyin' around that the state is takin' over this shelter, and soon everyone will be asked to leave. They gonna close it down."

Sadie pursed her lips. "Now Louisa, you know David and me well enough to know we'd tell you if anything like that was going on. It's just a rumor someone started, and there's no truth to it. Don't you worry none. You're here to stay as long as you want."

Louisa drew in a deep breath and let it out. "I shore am glad to hear that, Mrs. Sadie. Some of us have been real worried. Ever since the casino closed and we lost our jobs, me and Mandy and some others have been so happy to work here for y'all."

"And we're happy with you and Mandy. You're a wonderful cook, and she's the best housekeeper ever. We want you both to stay with us." She popped another piece of chocolate bar into her mouth. "How's Wren working out? Is she a good helper for you?"

"Oh, yes. She's a hard worker and a quick learner. Soon I'll have her doing some of the cooking. Her mama taught her real good."

"I'm glad to hear it. I think she's torn between working with children or becoming a chef. She can learn a lot from you."

"There's another thing." Louisa stood and picked up a dishcloth. "That Bob from over at the Craft Village — he done tol' us that he don't like y'all bringing all these hoodlums and delinquents from the city over here, and he's gonna do something 'bout it. I'm afeared he's gonna cause y'all some trouble 'for it's over."

Sadie's fist clenched. "Louisa, don't believe everything you hear. I'm sure Bob is just spouting off. We can't allow his big talk to make us afraid, can we?"

Walking down the hall toward her office, Sadie heard angry voices from the dining room. She stopped and listened, then stuck her head around the corner to see who was talking. Iris and Nora were standing toe to toe. Sadie couldn't determine what they were saying, but they looked and sounded angry. When they turned and headed off in different directions, Sadie shrugged. The issue seemed resolved, and she was too tired to deal with it now.

Meanwhile:

Lacy grabbed the hand of her kindergarten teacher, Miss Ginni. "Please don't make me get on the bus. I can't go home."

"Sweetie, put on your coat. The bus is leaving."

"Noooo! Please don't make me go."

Miss Ginni watched as the bus filled with children pulled away from the school. She knelt in front of six-year-old Lacy and wiped her tears. "Lacy, why don't you want to go home?"

The brown eyes filled with tears.

"You can tell me, sweetie. What is wrong?" Miss Ginni pushed the black hair out of the round face and peered into the sad eyes.

Lacy looked up into Miss Ginni's face for a moment. "Because my mama will hit me," she said.

Miss Ginni drew back. "Your mama hits you?" She tried not to appear shocked. "You mean she hits you when you do something bad?"

"I try to be good. I help her fix supper and do the dishes all by myself. But she hits me anyway."

"Do you have a brother or sister?"

Lacy wiped her nose on her shirt sleeve. "No. It's just me."

"Oh." Miss Ginni patted the girl on the back. "Does she hit you when she gets angry?"

"I guess. I think she's angry all the time. She hits me with her fist." Lacy started sobbing. "I don't like it when she hits me. It hurts so bad."

"Okay, Lacy. Will you look at these books to see if you can find one about a cow? I'll be right back." Miss Ginni stepped outside the door and called Mr. Gareth, the school therapist. "Do you have time to come to my room a minute?" she asked. Mr. Gareth often came to her room to see one of his clients. Soon he went down the hall.

"Hello, Lacy," he said. "Did you miss the bus?" He glanced at Miss Ginni and back at the child. He picked up a book. "Say, have you read this? It looks so interesting. Do you think I'd like it?"

Lacy nodded and pointed to a different book. He picked it up and read the first page. "I think you don't really want to look at a book right now," he said. "I think something else is on your mind. Am I right?"

"Mr. Gareth, Lacy didn't get on the bus because she doesn't want to go home today." Miss Ginni knelt again in front of Lacy. "Can you tell Mr. Gareth what you told me, Lacy?"

Lacy raised her fists to her eyes and sobbed. Miss Ginni handed her a tissue, and she wiped her face. She looked from Miss Ginni to Mr. Gareth, then nodded.

"I don't want to go home because my mama will hit me with her fists," she said. "She hits me every time when I get home."

The adults were silent for a while, and then Mr. Gareth spoke up. "Do you think we need to call your mom and tell her you'll be late coming home?"

Lacy drew in her breath and burst into tears again. "Then she'll be more mad." She buried her face in her hands and sobbed. "I don't want to go home."

Miss Ginni handed her another tissue. "May I look at your belly?" she asked, and the little girl nodded. Her eyes blazed when she pulled up Lacy's shirt, and she motioned for Gareth to look. Old and new bruises covered the child's torso and shoulders.

Gareth grimaced. "I'm making the call," he said. He stepped into the hall and soon motioned for Miss Ginni. "They say we have to take her home. They don't have room for her right now."

Miss Ginni's mouth flew open. "What? I can't believe that. How can we do that knowing what will happen to her?"

"I know. What are we going to do? I can't bear the thought of taking her home, but what choice do we have? If we don't, the mom could yell kidnapping."

Mr. Gareth scowled and shoved his hands into his pockets, and tears ran down Miss Ginni's face as they turned to face Lacy.

NINE

Sadie stood at the door of David's office and watched his back as he scrolled through information on his computer. "David, what did you do with the money bag? I can't find it anywhere. I'm going into the city today to make a deposit."

David whirled around to face her. "What do you mean? I never had the bag."

"But you had it yesterday when we were leaving. Didn't you put it in the safe? It isn't there now."

"No, I didn't have it. I thought you locked it up." He jumped up and followed her to the next room, where the safe sat open in a corner. He rifled through some papers inside it, then turned to look through the drawers of a large desk in the middle of the room. "Let's ask Sophia. Maybe she knows something about it," he said.

Sophia shook her head. "What monies were in the bag?" she asked.

"Some cash donations from some of the Island Village folks and a couple of checks from donors from the city. About five hundred dollars cash."

Sophia picked up her phone and made a call. Soon Angie and Lyric appeared at the door.

"Have the two of you seen a bank bag anywhere?" she asked. "We're missing one."

The teens shook their heads. "What does it look like?" Lyric asked.

"Yeah," said Angie. "We'll help you look."

Sadie showed them a bag. "It's like this except blue," she

said. "And it had some checks and cash inside. We need to find it."

They scattered and began looking in every room, searching through drawers and closets. They met in an hour with nothing.

"Maybe we should meet with the clients to ask them," Sophia said.

"No." Sadie sat down at her desk. "We can't do that. It would make them feel like we don't trust them."

"And they might think we're careless," David added. "They don't need to know anything about the business end of the shelter. We want them to feel safe here." He looked at Lyric and Angie. "You're to keep mum, guys. You're important around here, and we need to know we can trust you to keep quiet about things you know."

The teens glanced at each other and nodded in agreement as they left the room.

"Do you think they'll say anything?" asked Sophia.

"No," Sadie answered. "They're good kids. They care about the clients and respect what we're doing here."

"They sure do," said David. "They help out around here so much with the chores and things. I know I can count on them."

"They help so much with the children," said Sadie. "They've really pitched in around here."

"So, what will we do about the bank bag and the money?" Sadie bit her thumbnail.

"I'll ask Jerome if he has seen or heard anything. He's always around here and hears more than people realize." David headed for the door and met Jerome down by the dock.

Jerome scratched his head and frowned when David told him the situation. "I heard something that could be related," he said. "When I was having lunch earlier, a couple of gals giggled in the hall. I heard one say, 'Enough to buy a dress and matching shoes I've been wanting.' Something along that line."

"Do you know who the girls were?" asked David.

"I couldn't be for sure, but it sounded like Caroline. I know she pals around with Emmie, but I can't say."

"Thanks, Jerome. Maybe someone will know something without us making accusations. We'll have to keep our eyes and ears open." David rubbed the back of his neck. "I hate this. I've never liked confrontations and even less with people who've already been through so much."

Later in the afternoon, Sadie found him in his office gazing through the window.

"Why don't you visit the willow grove?" she asked. "You'll find some peace and maybe some answers there." She leaned over and kissed him on the neck. He turned his chair and pulled her into his lap.

"Sweetheart, you may be right. I sure could use some peace right now."

His arms encircled her, and her face turned to receive his kisses. After a moment, he rose, and soon he was sitting on a log in the grove of willow trees, watching the wildlife creatures skitter along the banks of the river he loved.

Remembering the last visit to the grove, he looked up at the branches waving above his head and then moved to another log. He picked up a handful of sand and let it sift through his fingers.

His mind drifted back to another time when things were simple. He and Kade spent many days playing along the river, building forts, fishing, and once, they even built a raft after they read Huck Finn at school. That was almost a disaster, and they would likely have drowned had FBI agent Max Shepherd not rescued them when he was after a criminal.

"Dear Lord," David prayed, "I want to help these women and children learn to make right decisions so their lives will be better. I want to understand them and their pain, their needs, and their dreams. How can I when my life has been so good — so sheltered? I have never suffered as they have. I have never experienced betrayal as they have. I have always been surrounded by people who love, support, and care for me."

He put his hands over his face, shaking with deep sobs. When the tears subsided, he raised his head. A quietness settled over him, and he leaned back against the log. An eagle soared below a single, fluffy white cloud that decorated the blue sky above, and a scripture ran through his mind.

"But those who wait on the LORD Shall renew their strength; They shall mount up with wings like eagles, They shall run and not be weary, They shall walk and not faint."

A smile spread across his face. "Thank you, Lord." As he drove home, an idea came to him, and he laughed out loud. He'd have to talk to Sadie and Sophia, but it felt right.

Meanwhile:

Nora hunkered down and clung to the side of a small boat as the wake from a passing speedboat pushed it under the willow branches at the bank of the river. What was she thinking when she sneaked out of the shelter and headed to the mainland in the stolen fishing boat? She only wanted to reach her sister's place downriver. Mr. David would be so angry with her. That is, if Griffith didn't find her first. If that happened, no one would have to worry. Her life would be over.

Her own father was a wanderer, and she'd watched her mother suffer the price a woman paid when she married the wrong man. She'd seen it time and time again in other homes along the river. A drinking man was bad enough, but he was a gambler and a womanizer, the mixture was like bore worms in a pine grove. The results were destruction and hurt.

She started the motor and guided the boat across the expansive stream toward the mainland. She looked in both directions, hoping to make it before another boat knocked her over. A large barge hauling grain bags drifted downstream, and she motored beside it. Her ex worked on the river, but he was a mechanic on a riverboat, not a barge. She peered down the river and relaxed. It was an excellent hiding place until she reached her destination a mile or so further down.

"Nora? Is that you?" She grabbed the tiller to guide the boat out of his reach, but it was too late. Griffith jumped from the barge and landed beside her, snatching the tiller from her hand. He revved the motor, and they sailed past the barge and down the river. She hadn't planned to meet him this way.

TEN

"Sadie, where are you?" David hurried into the kitchen in time to see Sadie carry a large basket of clothes into the laundry room.

"I'm here," she called. She stuffed baby clothes into the washing machine and added detergent. "What do you need, my love?"

He waited until she set the basket down, grabbed her around the waist, and twirled her. She caught her breath and giggled.

"What are you doing? Put me down, you goofball."

"I have an idea I think you'll love. I think it just might be the solution to our problem. We can try it if you and Sophia are willing."

"Well, what is it? Are you about to make Sophia and me do something we'll regret?"

He pulled her into the kitchen to sit at the table. "This idea just popped into my head, so I think the Lord put it there. I'm not smart enough to think of it on my own."

Sadie thumped him on the head. "Tell me now."

"How about we take all the clients on a picnic and then go shopping at the Island Craft Village? They have all kinds of shops over there, and I think the ladies will enjoy it."

"I'm all for that!" Sadie clapped her hands. "Have you been there in a while? They have some nice boutiques with clothes fashioned by the islanders. They also have shops selling perfumes, makeup, hair products, purses, and such." She jumped up and grabbed the phone. "Oh, David! I'm so glad that thought popped into your head, whoever put it there. I'll tell Sophia, and we can start planning it immediately."

A few days later, a group of women and children carrying baskets walked along the path that led to the Craft Village. Sadie and Sophia allotted each client a certain amount of money to spend. They would eat a picnic lunch in a tree grove before arriving at the village.

"We can leave the picnic basket there," Sadie said, "and pick it up on the way back. No one will bother it."

"Yes," agreed Sophia. "Let's visit the shop that has purses and wallets first. Then we can put money in their wallets. They will pay for their items instead of us doing it."

"Good idea. That will give them a sense of independence. I think that will be good for them."

They purchased wallets and stuffed money into each one. They divided into two groups, one with Sadie and one with Sophia.

"Mommies," Sadie said, "you're in charge of your little ones, and those who don't have children will help keep the children without adults corralled. This can be a productive and fun excursion if we all work together. Understood?"

Mommies and children alike nodded, and off they went, each group in a different direction, to visit the shops.

Sadie was rummaging through a clothes rack in a boutique with one eye on her charge when someone tugged on her shirttail. She looked around, and Emmie stood there with her eyes filled with tears.

Sadie peered into the child's face. "What's wrong, sweetie? Can't you find anything you like?"

"Mrs. Sadie," Emmie whispered, "I'm sorry. I did wrong. I'm so sorry." She held out a handful of money.

"What's this?" Sadie asked. She noted that it was more than had been put into the girl's wallet.

"I took this money from your office. I know it was wrong. I'm so sorry." Tears flowed down her cheeks.

"Oh, Emmie!" Sadie pulled the girl behind the rack out of sight of the others in the store. She pulled a tissue from her purse and wiped the girl's face. Then she put her arms around her and squeezed her tight. "You did that by yourself? No one helped you?"

Emmie's face reddened, and she hesitated. "She — oh, yes, I did. Mrs. Sadie, are you going to send me away?"

"No, child. You did the right thing coming to me. That's called repentance, which means you are truly sorry for what you did. Will you do it again?"

"Oh, no! I will never steal anything ever again! I keep having bad dreams until I can't sleep at night. It's been awful!"

Sadie smiled. "That's good. Your conscious has been telling you what you did was wrong, and you listened to it. You'll be okay if you listen to your conscience." She handed the girl a clean tissue and led her back to a clothes rack. "Think now you can get your shopping done without guilt?"

Emmie grinned. "Yes, I believe I can." She hugged Sadie. "Thank you so much, Mrs. Sadie." She trotted off to join Angie, who was looking at sandals.

The group shopped on one side of the street and met the other group as they swapped sides. Sadie and Sophia exchanged a thumbs-up as they met. All was going well.

But that changed in a moment.

Meanwhile:

Bob stepped out of his wood shop and motioned to Frank, the leather shop owner next to him. The two men had been friends since childhood. They had discussed what they considered the island's plight since they changed the casino into a shelter for what they called lower-class scum.

"What we gonna do about Kingston and his pet project? He's gettin' that place filled with those low-lives." Bob kept his voice low. The last time he complained aloud about the shelter, some of the other crafters defended the Kingstons.

"I know," Frank said. "When that Yarrow girl came the other day, she said it's awful how the riff-raff are taking over that place. She said David and Sadie let them do whatever they please. Said the women are lazy and the children run wild."

"I don't doubt it." Bob's mouth matched the downward curve of his shaggy eyebrows. "We gotta figure out some way to close that place down."

"Yeah. The Yarrow girl is one of us and is loyal to the island. She'll keep us informed."

ELEVEN

A commotion toward the end of the street caught the attention of the shoppers. When Sadie left the store, she saw Sophia's group in the middle of the fray. She gathered her group, and they went to see what was happening.

"You need to git these delinquents outta here. They don't belong. That girl was stealin' from me, and I don't aim to have it." A shop owner shook his finger and yelled at Sophia, who sheltered Elfi from the man's ire. "I don't know why you Crandalls wanna bring all this scum from the city here to our peaceful island. We don't want them here."

The rest of the wide-eyed group gathered around Sophia as she attempted to reason with the man.

"Sir, she wasn't stealing from you. She was only looking at the item. These children are not delinquents. They're just shopping."

Elfi swiped at her eyes and nose. "I wasn't gonna steal anything, Mrs. Sophia. I promise. I wouldn't do that."

"I know you wouldn't, sweetie," Sophia said. She turned back to the man. "Sir, we'll leave your establishment. You won't see us in here again. Ever." She herded her group away from the front of the store.

Sadie whispered for her group to go with Sophia and faced the man. "Sir, how dare you treat these ladies and children like that. We came here to shop in your stores instead of going to the city." Her face was red, and her fists rested on her hips. "We believe it's our responsibility and pleasure to patronize our island businesses."

A fellow shopkeeper stood by the man with a scowl, but one merchant stepped up by Sadie. "Bob," he said, "you know the Kingstons are good folks, and they are doing a good thing bringing these people here to shop."

"Well, I don't like it one bit," Bob said. "Next thing ya know, they'll be takin' over the whole island jus' like Oliver tried to do. Guess y'all forget 'bout all the gamblin' he brought here and all the kids that disappeared."

"All that is in the past," a man said. "Oliver changed his ways and did a good thing by makin' it possible to help people in need. Besides, it wasn't Oliver that took those kids. You know that. You can blame one of our own folks for that mess. Cosmos Rouge is responsible for that."

"Yeah, Bob," another spoke up. "Guess you forgot how Oliver helped us when the flood took our homes. He helped us rebuild and then built levies so's it won't happen again."

"That's right," a younger man said. "He helped us find our Ginger when she disappeared. These people helped us all when times were rough."

Another merchant stepped forward. "Guess y'all forgot who made this village possible for us. Without the Kingstons and Crandalls, we'd have no place to sell our goods 'less we go into the city. An' we cain't all do that." He gestured toward the group of women and children. "I want them to shop at my store. I'll gladly take their money. In fact, I'll give them a discount for coming in and spending their money on my goods."

The crowd started to disperse, and comments in support of Sadie continued. "Ma'am," a female shopkeeper said, "you can bring these young'uns to my store any time. We appreciate this craft village y'all gave us and your work at the shelter."

Sophia had been listening, and now she stepped up. "Which is your store?"

The vendor pointed to a place with various clothes, hand-carved toys, and home decor. "Just over there," she said.

Sophia gestured to her group, and they followed the woman into her store. Sadie led her bunch into the building.

"Oh, look!" The ladies moved from one item to another, pointing out those they admired. They paid for their purchases, and when they left the store, other vendors waved them to their businesses. They visited all those who supported them.

When they finished shopping, they stopped at an ice cream parlor to enjoy a treat from Sadie and Sophia before they headed home. Laughter arose as they discussed their purchases and swapped stories about their experiences. Sadie told Sophia about Emmie's confession. "She says she did it alone, but somehow, I doubt that. If someone helped her, she isn't telling."

"I agree," Sophia said. "I don't think she did it alone. I wonder why she won't tell. Guess she doesn't want to be a squealer."

"I'm sure. If we can't get these girls to make better choices, we've failed them." Sadie looked around when someone grabbed her hand. She smiled at Randall, who held up a toy he had bought. "Look at that!" She took the toy, looked it over, and then held it up to Sophia. "Look at the quality of this toy. Such intricate details. Those crafters are so good. I'm glad the village is doing well."

"Kade says the village is popular with the city people," Sophia said. "He said the ferry is busy daily, and they've had to make a schedule to keep everything running smoothly. It sure has provided the islanders with good incomes."

"David and I took a little trip the other day through the island, and the homes have obviously improved. The folks seem happier."

When they arrived at the shelter, the clients went to their suites and met back at the lounge. They compared their purchases, oo-ing and ah-ing over the bargains they'd found. Sadie and Sophia grinned at each other. They couldn't wait to tell their husbands how successful the shopping excursion had been.

Later when Sadie started home, she decided to take a detour around the shelter and along the river. It was such a lovely day, and she wanted to pick a bouquet of lilies that grew down the river a little way. She hummed as she walked along and laughed at a pair of ducks that dipped their heads into the water to catch fish. She stopped to look at a horned beetle climbing over a twig when she heard what sounded like sobbing.

She approached a river birch surrounded by ostrich ferns beside the path. The sound grew more distinct as she drew closer. She pushed back a fern, and a girl sat on the ground, hands over her face, sobbing. Sadie touched her shoulder, and the startled girl looked up and gasped.

"Mrs. Sadie!"

"Caroline, what is wrong? Why are you hiding here? Why are you crying?" Sadie knew her social work professor would disapprove of her method of responding to the girl.

The girl hung her head and sniffed. Sadie knelt on the ground beside her and put an arm around her shoulders. "Can you tell me why you are crying?"

The saddest brown, tear-filled eyes searched Sadie's face. Caroline raised a hand and let it fall onto her lap. Her head moved back and forth, then hung even lower.

"Sweetie, you can tell me whatever it is. Would you like to go somewhere more comfortable where we can talk?"

She nodded, and Sadie helped her to her feet. She led her down the path to a bench where people often sat to watch the ducks. She sat beside her and leaned over to peer into her face.

"What is it, lovie? Can you talk about it now?" She pulled a tissue from her pocket and handed it to the girl.

Caroline wiped her eyes and nose and stammered. "I'm so sorry, Mrs. Sadie. I—I—I...."

"It's okay. Take your time. We aren't in a hurry."

After more weeping and wiping, Caroline straightened

and looked at Sadie. "Mrs. Sadie, I haven't been honest with you. You've been so good to me — to all of us — and I...."

"What is it, sweetie?"

"You see, my mom has been in jail for selling drugs, and my dad is an alcoholic. He does nothing but drink. Mom gave me drugs from the time I was four years old, and Dad thought it was funny to get me drunk in front of his friends when I was seven. They all laughed when I stumbled around and said stupid things."

Sadie didn't realize she wasn't breathing until she felt faint. "I'm so sorry, Caroline. I'm sorry your life has been so hard. But I'm glad you came to us at Willow Grove. Here you can get well and start a new life."

Caroline fiddled with her fingers. "It's just that--I don't know--I don't think I can start a new life. I need a fix right now so bad I can't stand it. Don't you see? My dealer was meeting me here, but he didn't show." She rose and paced, wringing her hands. Sweat ran down her face, and her eyes darted back and forth.

Sadie took her arm. "Come on, sweetie. We'll get you back to Tashina so she can help you. Soon you'll be good as new."

Meanwhile:

"What happened? Why didn't you give it to her?" The man with a bulbous nose raised his fist above the head of the younger man, who held out a small plastic bag containing pills.

"I told you my boat broke down. I couldn't get to her in time. By the time I borrowed a boat and got there, she was gone."

"This is the last time you'll have an opportunity to make a bundle. He won't trust you to make a drop for us again."

"But, Carp, I couldn't help it. It wasn't my fault."

"I done told you she has to have her fix every day or she'll quit us. We cain't afford to lose her. Cosmos is counting on her and us."

TWELVE

Tashina worked with Caroline while she sweated through the drying-out process. Tender-hearted Grace sat with the girl for hours, reading the Bible to her and tending to her every need. Considering what she had been through, she understood the needs of a person going through withdrawals from drug dependency. She also knew that God's Word would help to change her focus and make the process easier and quicker.

The room Grace and Caroline occupied was on the third floor at the end of the hall. Women who had screamed in their own pain, whether it was withdrawals or the pain of being beaten and alone, prayed for the girl. Tashina checked on the shivering, drawn girl and her constant companion, Grace. Afterward, she'd sit on the edge of her bed crying and praying.

"Will you please give me something?" Caroline asked Tashina. "Anything. Please?

When Tashina refused, Caroline screamed and slammed her fist into the wall. Then she collapsed into a ball on the floor and wept. "Why won't you help me?" she pleaded.

Tashina and Grace dragged her to the bed, where she immediately fell asleep. When she awoke, she smiled. "I'm sorry for all the trouble I've caused," she said. But later during the night, the pleading for a fix started again.

"You hate me," she yelled. She went around the room, pulling out drawers and looking in every vessel she could find. She ran to the door, but Grace jumped in front of it to hold her in. She flopped down on the bed.

"We don't hate you," Grace said. "You're just afraid. You haven't been clean in so long you think you can't do without a fix. But you can."

Tashina patted the girl's arm. "Caroline, don't give in to the fear. Here, listen to this." She read from Psalms 91. "Because you love me, I will rescue you. I will protect you because you know my name. When you call to me, I will answer you. I will be with you when you are in trouble. I will save you and honor you. I will satisfy you with a long life. I will show you how I will save you."

Grace turned the pages of the Bible and read another one to her from Second Timothy. "For God gave us a spirit not of fear but of power and love and self-control."

Caroline lay still and closed her eyes. Grace put on some soft music, and soon, the girl was asleep.

One night, Caroline left the room while Grace slept in a chair. She ransacked Tashina's office, waking Tashina. When Tashina attempted to return her to her room, she fought hard, scratching and biting. Tashina managed to get to her phone and called David. He helped her drag the girl back to her room, where she cursed and screamed.

Sometimes, Grace read the scriptures to her, but mostly, Caroline read them herself. Her days became more peaceful, and she blended in with the other clients, taking on more responsibility until she no longer felt afraid. Then the flu hit. Tashina quarantined her upstairs until she recovered. Grace stayed in the room next door. Caroline slept off the fever, and when the cough subsided, she was ready to join the others downstairs.

Tashina came in to check on her. "Morning, sunshine. How are you feeling today?"

Caroline blinked, smiled, and sat up. Grace handed her a glass of water, and she drank it all.

"Think you're ready for a shower and some clean clothes?" Tashina asked.

"Then some breakfast," added Grace.

Caroline nodded. "I sure am." She looked around the room, then at Grace. "You've been here with me all this time, haven't you?"

"She sure has," Tashina said. "This woman is a marvel."

Grace grinned. "I don't like to see anyone sick. Especially after what you've already been through."

"I'd hug you, but I'd better wait until I'm sure I'm germ-free and smell better." Caroline laughed and waved a hand in front of her face.

When she had showered and appeared in the dining room for breakfast, the clients applauded to welcome her back. They formed a line to make her feel loved with hugs and words of encouragement. The girl soon laughed as she sat among them at the table with a plate of eggs, gravy, biscuits, and bacon. Grace and Tashina knew she would still have some rough days, but she was well on her way to complete recovery.

Later, Caroline stuck her head in Sadie's office. "Mrs. Sadie?" Sadie smiled at the girl and motioned for her to enter.

"I have something for you," Caroline said. She held out a fistful of money. "This is yours. That day you found me on the river, I was waiting for a fix. I intended to pay for it with the money I stole from your office. I'm so sorry."

Sadie rose and took the money.

"That's most of it." Caroline looked at the floor. "I gave some to Emmie. She saw me take it, and I gave her some to keep her quiet. She didn't want to take it, but I insisted."

Sadie frowned and nodded. "That explains it," she murmured.

"Huh?" Caroline's forehead creased.

"Never mind." Sadie moved around her desk to hug the girl. "Oh, Caroline, I'm so glad you've made this step to correct a mistake. This wasn't easy, was it?"

Caroline blushed. "It sorta was when my head cleared up so I had right thinking. I realized how you've helped me. The Lord also helped me, and I want to do the right thing, so that made it easier."

David kicked back in his recliner and turned the TV on while Sadie rocked Benji to sleep. He flipped the channels until he found a Western, watched it for about ten minutes, and then flipped to another channel where rough-looking hairy men restored old vehicles. After a few minutes, he changed it to a cooking show, and Sadie nodded her approval. But that didn't last long. Soon, he was back at the western, then to a detective show.

"Can't you find anything you like?" asked Sadie.

He glared at her, then moved to an old *Walker, Texas Ranger* rerun. Sadie rolled her eyes. She put Benji in his bed and returned. "Can't you find a good movie we can both enjoy?"

"I'm not in the mood for a Hallmark kissy movie," he answered. "I'm around all those women at the shelter all day, so I need something manly to watch."

Sadie's eyes sparked, but she held her peace.

He kept switching the channels from one show to another, finally landing on a rated R violent show with blood, exploding body parts, and vulgar words that would hurt the ears of Judas Iscariot and torch Saint Peter. His scowl showed he was unhappy, but Sadie didn't know what bothered him. She flipped through the pages of a magazine, glancing at him periodically.

"Want some ice cream?" she asked.

He shook his head.

"How about some no-bake oatmeal cookies? I can have some whipped up in a little while."

"No."

"I have some ranch potato chips. Want —"

"NO! I don't want anything." He flipped the channel back to the hairy men restoring old cars. Sadie went into the kitchen to clean the refrigerator, and while her head was stuck in the crisper pan at the bottom, she felt warm hands moving over her back. When she raised, she bumped her head on a rack, and a jar of dill pickles rocketed toward the tile floor, splattering pickles and juice everywhere.

"Oh, my word!" She exploded. "What a mess. What are you doing? I thought you were still watching those hairy men play with their greasy tools."

"Excuse me," he muttered. "I was going to apologize, but I guess I'll go back to finish watching the show you hate so much." His scowl deepened as he whirled to return to his recliner.

Sadie fumed as she cleaned the mess. "Lord, give me patience," she whispered. "And help him with whatever is bothering him." She pitched the soaked dishrags into the washing machine, lit a candle to dispel the smell, then headed into the living room.

David had turned off the TV and stood staring out the window. She stood beside him. "You sure do keep our yard pretty. I love the dogwood and redbud trees you planted."

"Thanks."

"Are you ready to talk about it?"

"What?"

"Whatever is bothering you."

"Oh." He turned to look at her. "It's just that — well — I think you coddle the clients too much. I think they should be pulling their weight."

Sadie backed up. "What do you mean I coddle them?"

"You let them by with too much." He fiddled with the window curtain. "Some of them are lazy, and they fuss with each other. I know you're the therapist, but you're also in charge of them. I think they'd do better if you tighten the reins more." To emphasize, he jerked the curtain, almost pulling it down. "Oops." He plopped into his recliner.

A red-faced Sadie pushed the curtain back into place, then turned. "You're right about one thing—I am the therapist." She looked down at him. "Might I ask who you think is lazy? As far as the fussing, I assume you mean the children. David, they are children."

"Tell me one thing. Are the clients doing the chores they're assigned?"

Sadie hedged but finally answered. "Some of them try to get out of doing them. The other day, Judith did the laundry when Iris didn't show up to get it done. Wren fussed when she had to help in the kitchen. She says she isn't a client, and her job is only to work with the children. This is true, but I want her to work in the kitchen occasionally. I think it's good training for her, and Louisa says she's a good cook. Then Grace and Marleigh fought over who would clean the dining room after lunch."

"Then it isn't the children."

"Well, actually, they have been quarreling, too. Over the swings, over the pool, over the toys. It's always something. I talk and talk to them, but they can't seem to get along."

"See what I mean? You need to come down on them hard."

He reached for her hand, and she withdrew it and sat on the couch.

"No, I can't do that. People in their lives have been so mean to them. I can't see that me being hard on them will help." She turned her head away. "I'll figure something out. That's my job."

David jumped to his feet. "Well, then, you figure it out. I'm just trying to help. I'm going fishing." He stomped out the door. He returned later when Sadie had finished cooking supper.

"You've already made supper?" He held up a bucket. "I caught a mess of fish, and I've already cleaned them."

"It's too late for fish tonight," Sadie said. "We can have them tomorrow. Hurry and get cleaned up. The bread will be out in a few minutes. Benji is hungry, and so am I."

When David returned, Sadie had finished setting the food on the table and put Benji in his highchair. David put his arms around her and nibbled her neck.

"I'm so sorry," he said. "I thought about it while I waited for the fish to bite. Honestly, what the clients do isn't what's bothering me."

She turned to face him. "I thought not. Then what is it?"

His lips lowered hard on hers as he cupped her face. She waited while he pulled her close and continued to kiss her.

He finally pulled back and gazed into her eyes. "I miss you, sweetheart. I feel like you're always so busy that I hardly get to see you alone. Even when we are alone, you think and talk about the clients and the shelter. It's like you're consumed by it, and there's little left for me."

She lifted a hand to his cheek. "I know you're right, my love." She tiptoed to meet his lips for another kiss. "I'll try to do better. Why don't we schedule some time for us? Get away a while."

He grinned. "That's a great idea. Let's go fishing for a couple of days. We can take the big boat downriver. Jerome can keep an eye out here, and Kade can come over to check on things."

Sadie laughed. "I think they can manage a couple of days without us. Tashina is capable of running things, and everyone will help her."

The next day, they packed some clothes and food and headed downriver. They caught several fish, and the scenery was entertaining. Sadie laughed at a fisherman in another boat who was having trouble landing a large fish.

"Hey!" David yelled. "Need some help?"

"I think I can handle it." The man laughed as he netted the fish and held it up for them to see.

They floated up a small tributary until they found a good place under a grove of trees with branches overhanging the water. It looked like an excellent place to fish, so they would moor the boat there for the night.

Soon, the smell of grilled steak floated to the top of the trees and out into the forest along the river's side. As David set up a small table on the deck, Sadie made a salad to go with the steak. They would enjoy the outdoor meal. They failed to see the weather-beaten house and sagging barn that blended with the huge sycamore trees not far from where the boat bobbed on the water.

Meanwhile:

"You know they ain't legit." Bob put a receipt into the bag with a leather belt and handed it to a customer. The man stuffed a wad of bills into his wallet.

"What do you mean, not legit? What is not legit about it?"

"DHS has been there several times to check them out, but they can never catch them."

"What are they doing?"

"They got these women and little kids doing hard work. They make them do chores all day long. I hear they won't let them eat hardly anything. Some say they're starving them to death."

"Have you seen that for yourself?"

"Nah. The Yarrow girl keeps us informed on what's goin' on over there. She says they work those little kids long hours. You know that's against the law."

"So, why are you telling me? What do you expect me to do?"

"You're a lawyer, ain't ya? You can sue them or something."

The man rubbed his bald head. "Why do you dislike them so much?"

"It ain't that I dislike them," Bob said. "I just don't like the idea that they've opened a place on our island and filled it with those hoodlums from the city. They got no right to do that."

THIRTEEN

They finished the steak and salad and cleared the table. They would put some hooks out in hopes of catching a catfish while they enjoyed the sunset from the deck. Sadie set out lawn chairs and fixed drinks while David baited the hooks. Soon, they held hands, watching the sun go down behind the line of trees along the riverbank.

"Benji was so happy to spend the night with Grand-Mamá and Poppa," Sadie said. "He loves your parents so much."

"I know." David laughed. "They spoil him rotten just like your parents do."

"They all have been lifesavers for us." Sadie squeezed David's hand. "We are so blessed to have such wonderful, involved parents. I don't know what we'd do if we didn't have them to keep him while we're working. Mom and Dad like the schedule that allows them to take turns with Jesse and Melody."

"Mom and Dad are happy with the arrangement, too," David said. "Of course, they also have little Jonathan. Did I tell you they want to take Benji to the zoo?"

"That's a great idea. He's old enough to enjoy that. I'll bet my parents will want to go, too." Sadie said. "I'm so glad our parents are close again. They were apart too long."

"Yeah. Since Dad cleaned up his act, it's almost like old times when they did everything together. And I'm glad they moved back to the island." His mind drifted to Max Shepherd, the federal agent who ended child trafficking and gambling on the island when he captured Cosmos Rouge and his cronies. "Mom and Dad hated seeing the Shepherds leave but were happy to return to their old house. Max said they were sad to go, but he had to do something else since his cover was blown. I think the agency promoted him to a higher position."

Sadie yelped. "I think I have a bite." She jumped up and jerked her pole. "Must be a big 'un." She struggled with the line and soon reeled in a big channel catfish. David took it off the hook and put it on a stringer. "That'll make a good supper when we get back."

"Now I have a bite," David said. He pulled in a nice fish, then another, until the stringer was full. "We'll have to invite Kade and Sophia for a fish fry."

Sadie pulled up the stringer. "I think we'll have enough for the whole family."

They worked together to clean and store the fish on ice in a large chest. Sadie lit a candle to diffuse the smell of fish, and then they nestled together in the soft bed as the boat rocked gently in the quiet of the night. David nuzzled Sadie's neck, and she responded with gentle caresses. After a time of tender loving, they settled in for the night and were about asleep when David sat straight up, listening. He nudged Sadie awake. "Did you hear anything?"

She pulled his arm. "No. Lay back down. I was about to start a good dream."

He lay still a while, then sat up again. "I know I heard something." He moved to the door and peered out to the deck.

"It's probably night critters," Sadie murmured. "We're at the edge of the river and the woods. There're all kinds of creatures out there. Come back to bed."

While they were sound asleep, a banging on the deck woke them both. "I know that was something," David whispered.

Sadie squeezed his arm. "Be careful," she whispered back.

He eased out of bed and tiptoed to the door. Opening it a crack, he peeked out. Something was moving on the deck. Why didn't he bring his gun? Kade had warned him about keeping one ready in case he had to defend himself. After spending so much time fleeing for his life when he ran the shipping company, he hated to even think about it. The running from speeding vehicles and ducking from gunshots were over when Oliver's repentance changed him from an enemy to a solid friend.

"Here. Take this." Sadie handed him a skillet and a big spoon.

"Want me to cook it?" he asked.

She snickered. "That, or hit the spoon on the skillet to scare it away. Whatever works."

He peered out again, and tiny lights stared back at him. He sucked in his breath. Since he had lived all his life on the island, he was familiar with all kinds of animals that lived along the river, and he realized a nursery of raccoons had climbed from the tree along the rope and into the boat. He and Kade had argued over a group of raccoons being called a nursery until he used Google to prove it. He didn't often win arguments with Kade and was happy to add one victory to his record.

The skillet and spoon would work. He jumped out the door and beat the skillet with the spoon. He and Sadie laughed at the skittering little animals as they spilled over the side of the boat. When they investigated, they guessed that the animals had followed the smell of their supper and had found the tank where they had stored the fish. They almost had it opened when David and his skillet spoiled their supper.

They were in a deep sleep when another sound awoke David. This time it was no raccoon. He could hear footsteps on the deck. He put his lips next to Sadie's ear.

"Sadie, Shhh, don't make a sound." He put a hand over her mouth.

When she was awake enough to understand, he removed his hand from her mouth and whispered. "Someone's on the boat."

"You sure?" she whispered back. "Maybe it's another animal."

He felt around for a flashlight he had forgotten about earlier. He eased to the door and inched it open. Someone flashed a light around the deck. Maybe it was only one person. No, there were at least two. Sadie handed him the skillet, and he moved out the door and along the wall furthest from the intruders. She held onto the back of his shirt and walked so close she almost tripped him. He pushed her with his elbow and gestured for her to get back.

"Who's there?" He made his voice deep. "Stop where you are."

He shined his light at the same time theirs flashed toward him, but his light was much brighter. Two soggy, wet boys gaped at him. The larger one had a fishing pole and tackle box in his hand.

"Please don't shoot," the larger one said. "We're sorry. We'll leave."

"What do you want?" David walked toward them. "How'd you get up here?"

"Oh, David, they're just boys," Sadie said. She started to step around David to walk toward them, but he pulled her back.

"Stay back," he ordered. He circled to one side, and they kept their eyes on him. He repeated. "I asked you what you wanted."

They looked at each other, and one started to walk toward him. "Stay where you are," David held the skillet up threateningly. They looked sturdy, so he couldn't afford to misjudge their abilities.

Sadie stood back while David prepared to fight. The bigger one leaped toward him, but David was ready and smacked him in the face. The kid fell back, and the other one headed in. Sadie jumped forward and stuck out her foot to trip him, causing him to faceplant on the hard deck. She jumped on his back and pinned his arms under her knees while David pulled zip ties from the fishing tackle box to tie the culprits to the deck railing.

"You have some explaining to do," David said. "Why are you stalking around our boat in the middle of the night? What do you want?"

"Nothin'," the smaller boy said.

"Oh, nothing, huh? Law enforcement might be interested in two boys invading private property." David pulled out his phone. "We'll call them right now and see what they have to say."

The larger boy looked at David. "Please, don't. Our folks'll be sore if they find out. We didn't think anyone was here. We didn't bother anything."

"Oh, is that right?" David stalked around them. "Then what were you going to do with my fishing tackle? First, you invade our privacy, then you steal from us and attack us."

The older boy hung his head. "I'm sorry. I was scared. I didn't know what to do."

"So you attacked me?" David scoffed.

"Sir, I'm sorry. We've never been on a nice boat like this. We just wanted to take a look at it."

"Do you boys live around here?" David asked.

They both nodded, and the older one motioned with his head. "Just over there a piece. Behind those trees."

"Do I need to pay a visit to your folks? Tell them about how you trespassed on our boat?"

The smaller boy wiggled and whimpered. "No, sir. Anyway, they'll be asleep right now."

David cut the ties with his pocketknife and pulled them to their feet. "I think we need to wake them up. They might like to know what their boys have been doing while they sleep."

Meanwhile:

Two men stood outside the general store in a small town not far from the island. One of them spat brown juice on the ground and kicked dirt over it.

"Yeah, we'd be rakin' in the money if Crandall and Kingston would've kept their noses out of our business."

"That's true," the other said. "I'd like to git ahold of them. Now I hear they've started some kinda business on the island. Probably rakin' in the money for theirselves."

"Sam said it's some kinda shelter for women." He snickered. "I cain't imagine why women would need a shelter. What they need is ...."

The second man interrupted. "Yeah, they need a good thrashing once in a while. At least mine does."

"Rakes me when I see Kingston steering that big blue boat up and down the river. Guess he has nothin' else to do."

"Bet that thing cost him a bundle. Of course, he has a bundle. One day, I'm gonna drive a boat like that."

"Nah, you won't. You'll never have enough dough for that."

The first man spat and kicked the dirt again. "Yep. I will one day. I git my business up and running good. We gotta git a better boat so's we can start running drugs and women. Then we can git a boat like Kingston drives."

"Then I'll run him over. Peel off some of that blue paint. Maybe put a bruise on that woman of his while I'm at it."

"I jus' wanna get my hands around his neck."

FOURTEEN

He fastened the zip ties around their wrists and escorted them down the ladder and to shore. They struggled, but with David holding them by their shirt collars, shallow water was close enough for them to get up the bank safely.

When they reached the bank, David could see a light at the house in the middle of the trees. The smaller boy's sniffing turned into bawling, and the older one scolded him.

"Stop crying, Bucky. We got ourselves into this trouble."

David looked down at the little guy. "Bucky, was this whole thing your idea? Or did your friend here talk you into it?"

"He's not my friend." Bucky stumbled and righted himself. "He's my brother."

"Oh! Your brother, then." David pointed his flashlight at the narrow trail they were on. "Does your brother always get you into this much trouble?"

Bucky sniffed. "No. I mean, sometimes he does." The older boy pushed him with his shoulder. "Quit, Allen. You do get us into trouble sometimes."

Allen grunted. "No more than you do."

"So," said David, "you both are troublemakers. Do your parents know that? What will they say when I tell them what you've done?"

They approached the porch, and David pushed the boys to the door. "Go ahead," he said. "Call your parents out here."

Allen pushed the door open and called. "Dad."

"A little louder," David said.

"DAD!"

From inside the house, they could hear movement and muttering. Soon a bearded man appeared. His hair stood on end, and his face was red with lines where he had been asleep.

Behind him, a wild-haired woman rubbed her eyes. "What is it, Rud? Who's out there?"

"Who's that with you, Allen? What's goin' on?"

"Dad, this is Mr. Kingston."

David stuck out his hand, and Rud looked at it like he didn't know what it was. David drew it back. "Sir, are these your sons?"

Rud nodded. "Yeah, they're mine. What's goin' on?"

"Well," David continued. "Your sons trespassed on my boat, were stealing my tackle box, and then attacked me. I thought it best if you knew, so I brought them home."

The woman stepped from behind her husband. "My boys wouldn't do anything like that. You're lying."

"Get back, woman." Rud pushed her back behind him. He looked at the boys before he spoke to Allen. "Is what he's tellin' me so, Allen? You'd better tell the truth, boy."

Allen shuffled his feet. "Yes, sir. But we didn't mean any harm to anyone."

"Yeah," said Bucky. "We just wanted to see inside the big boat. We didn't want to hurt anything."

Rud grabbed Allen and pulled him close, hauling Bucky with him. "You boys have really done it this time," he growled. "I'll whoop your butts until you look like you're walking back'ards." He turned to David. "Thank you for bringin' 'em home. I'll take care of this right now." He dragged them through the door and slammed it.

As David walked back down the trail, he could hear the yelling from the house. He recalled a good thrashing his dad had given him once when he teased a hog until he made it tear up a fence.

When he returned to the boat, he showered to remove any

ticks he may have picked up in the woods and the silt from the muddy water.

"I think we'd better pull out a little further," he said to Sadie. "Two times is too many in one night for unwelcomed critters to come onto our boat."

They boated further upriver the next day to view the magnificent homes and buildings along the shore. They would turn back at noon, spend one more night on the river, and return home the next day.

When the sun lowered behind the trees, the owner of a docking pier granted permission to moor the boat for the night close to a fishing area. They would be far enough away for privacy but close enough to be safe. No more unwanted visitors on this trip.

Deciding to take advantage of a small restaurant not far from the pier, they ordered and ate as they watched a few locals move onto a small dance floor to sway with the music coming from a jukebox.

David grabbed Sadie's hand and pulled her up. "Come on, sweetheart, dance with me."

Sadie laughed and obliged. They first moved to a slow song and joined a line dance next. David spun Sadie around when a popular song played. They were determined to enjoy their last night out on the river.

But the enjoyment halted when a man insisted that Sadie dance with him. She kept her eyes on David as the man whirled her around a few times, then David grabbed her hand and pulled her away from him. The man pulled her arm, and the two men juggled her back and forth. Finally, David forced himself between her and the stranger.

"I just wanna dance with the pretty lady," the man stammered.

"Sorry, bub, but she's mine." David led her back to their table, and the man followed. "Go find yourself another partner," David said.

"But I don't want another partner. I want her." The man

tried to pull Sadie back up.

David was gentle at first. "She's tired. She wants to rest." But when the man persisted, David lost patience. "Look, man, get it through your head. She doesn't want to dance with you. Find someone else."

The man shoved David and tried to hit him. David grabbed his fist and pushed the man into a chair. "Look, man, you're drunk. You need a cup of coffee." He motioned to the waitress. "Here." He placed the cup in front of the man. "Drink this. You need to sober up."

The man picked up the cup and spilled coffee all over the table, getting some on David. David jumped back and raised his fist. Then he thought better of it. Sadie cleaned the mess with a wad of napkins, and they left the restaurant.

As they walked toward the pier, they realized someone was following them. They stopped. It was the troublemaker.

"What do you want?" David asked.

The man was completely different. "I'm sorry about that mess inside, but I need to tell you something," he said. "I heard a couple of fellas talking, and I know it was about the two of you. Something about taking you down. One guy said you wrecked his friend's chances to get rich. The guy instructed them to make sure you pay." The man looked around like he thought someone was listening. "I don't know, man, but it's serious. I had to get your attention without them knowing. They know I heard them. Again, I'm sorry for the trouble I caused. I may have overdone it a little. Thanks for not decking me." He put a hand on Sadie's arm. "I'm sorry, little lady." He turned back to David. "I'd advise you to leave as soon as possible. You're in danger here."

Meanwhile:

A frail woman wrapped a blanket around herself and watched her five-year-old daughter, Susan, play at her feet with a ragged teddy bear. It had been two months since she lost her job, and with no paycheck coming in, she knew the landlord would be around any day to ask for rent. She had already been behind on the rent. She knew the landlord was kind and patient, but she knew her time was up. She had no clue what she was going to do.

A year ago, her husband died, and when she checked on his life insurance, she found out that another woman was named as the beneficiary. Who was this other woman? She learned that he had been married and had a family across town. How could he do that to her? Actually, he had done it to the other woman since she was his first wife.

Things went downhill from there. A nervous person already, her mental health had declined so much that she lost her job as a receptionist at the Holiday Inn. She worked as a bar waitress for a while but couldn't take the flirtatious men who considered it their right to touch, grab, and rub her body in private places. When she slapped one, her boss told her she should find another job. So she sat, day after day, wrapped in her blanket, looking out the window. She kept Susan home from school rather than leave the house to take her, even though the child begged to go.

Sure enough, the landlord knocked on the door.

"Mrs. Talley," he said, "I'm sorry, but I can't continue to allow you to live here without paying rent. I have a couple who can move in immediately, and I need the money for the upkeep of my buildings. I'm sorry, but you understand, right?"

She nodded. "I'll be out by tomorrow." She hated the sad look on his face as she closed the door. She hated the hardships she caused other people. He didn't deserve to suffer because she couldn't cope with life. Neither did Susan.

For the next week, she and Susan lived on the street, sleeping in abandoned buildings and under steps or where there was enough space to huddle together. She found scraps of food from trash cans behind bars and restaurants, at least enough to nourish her little girl. Sometimes they had to compete with dogs for food, but it kept them alive.

"Claire!"

She turned to see who had called her name. A woman pushing a cart walked toward her. "Claire, what are you doing out here?"

"Eva. Eva Malone. I haven't seen you in so long. What happened to you?"

Eva's grim smile showed blackened teeth. "Ah, you know. I got tired of fighting with Will and left him. I had nowhere to go, so here I am, livin' on the street. How about you?"

Claire looked around, and her face reddened. "I—I—I lost the apartment. I don't have a place to go."

Eva looked down at Susan. "Must be harder with a child. Glad I ain't got one. It ain't so bad for me by myself." She stared for a moment at Susan. "Hey, I heard there's a place for women like you. Ever heard of Crandall Island? It's downriver a piece. I hear they started a place there to help people like you and your girl. Interested?"

Claire's eyes brightened. "Sure am. How do I get there?"

"Well..." Eva stuck a dirty finger in her mouth. "I think I can hook you up. Might take some time, but I'll do my best. 'Til that happens, why don't you go to the mission on Fourth Street? They'll let you stay there for a while. Give you some food. Come on—I'll take you."

Claire took Susan's hand, and together they followed Eva. Maybe things would be better soon.

FIFTEEN

Traveling on the river at night wasn't as pleasant a trip as during the day, but David and Sadie enjoyed the full moon that flooded the river with light and lit up the beautiful homes along the shore. They arrived a little after midnight, tired enough to fall asleep as soon as they crawled into bed. They opted to unload the boat the next day.

"DAVID!" The yell woke David from a peaceful slumber. He rolled over to look at the clock.

"Sadie, it's already 9:00." He nudged her as he rolled out of bed. "Kade's here."

"Son, what are you doing sleeping all day?" When he exited the house, Kade slapped David on the back, rubbing his tousled hair. "Don't you know we have work to do?"

"What are you talking about?" David yawned and stretched. "What work?"

"Dad has a job for us—something about a roof on his shed," Kade said. "Say, man, how'd the fishing trip go? Did you catch many?"

"We did. Sadie wants to have everyone over for a fish fry soon. And that reminds me, we've got to unload the boat. Come on. You can help me."

"I thought you weren't getting back until later today. Why are you back early?"

David filled him in on everything that had happened. Kade's brows rose when David relayed the story of the man at the restaurant.

"Do you think you were in danger?" Kade asked.

"I did believe the man was serious." David led the way to the dock. "Enough that we came home last night. Arrived about one."

They unloaded the boat, carrying the luggage and fish inside. Sadie put the fish in the freezer and loaded the washing machine.

"Hey, sis." Kade pulled at her ponytail. "Heard you ran into some trouble. Sorry your trip turned out to be less than restful for you."

"Yeah," she said. "It could have been better. Still was good, though. We needed to get away."

"Maybe you can schedule a real vacation and go off somewhere later. You deserve it."

Sadie grabbed her keys. "I have to go pick up Benji," she said. "Whatever you guys are doing, be careful. That guy at the restaurant scared me. I think something is going on we don't know about."

Kade pressed his lips together. "Don't worry about us, sis. But I think you're right." He hugged her. "That goes double for you. You keep an eye out and take no chances."

Sadie kissed him on the cheek and left. She stopped at the shelter to check on things before she went to her in-laws to get the baby. When she entered Sophia's office, Sophia looked up from a pile of paperwork on her desk.

"About time you get back," she said. "Just kidding. Did you have a good time?"

Sadie relayed the details of the trip to her gasping sister-in-law.

"Oh, my lands!" Sophia said when Sadie finished with the story of the man at the restaurant. "Do you think you're in danger?"

Sadie nodded. "I'm afraid so. I think the man was telling the truth."

"Do you think David will take it seriously? I know how he and Kade are when they get together."

"Yes," Sadie agreed. "They think nothing will happen to

them. You'd think that after what David went through the past few years, he'd be more concerned about his safety."

Sophia nodded. "I sure am glad Oliver had a major heart change. He sure made it hard on everyone for a while. Thank the Lord that's over."

"For sure. He's my dad, and I love him dearly, but when it comes to him or my husband — well, you know how it is. I'm just glad both of them survived the ordeal."

The door burst open, and young Angie ran into the room. "Mrs. Sophia! Please, can you come? We need you."

"What's wrong, Angie? Who needs me?"

"Mrs. Tashina." Angie turned and saw Sadie. "Oh, Mrs. Sadie. I'm so glad you're back. I've needed to talk to you."

Sophia and Sadie both rose and followed the blubbering girl. "It's a new client, Mrs. Sadie. Mrs. Tashina said you'd have to talk to her. She's in a panic."

They arrived in Tashina's office to find a young woman and a little girl crying. Tashina met them in her outer office. "This woman is a mental wreck," she said. "She has major problems and is terrifying her child."

"What can we do?" asked Sadie.

"Sophia, if you could take the little girl — her name is Susan — and show her around, let her meet some of the other children, maybe it would get her mind off what's going on with her mom," said Tashina. "Then, Sadie, you can deal with Claire. I've cared for her physical wounds, but her mental wounds are greater, and that's your department."

Sophia knelt in front of Susan. "Mrs. Tashina says your name is Susan. Is that right?"

Susan sniffed and nodded.

Sophia smiled at the little girl. "Will you go with me? I have something cool to show you." She stood and held out her hand to the girl. Susan leaned against her mom, who was lying on the examining table.

The woman grabbed the child's arm. "No! You can't take my baby away. She's all I have."

Sadie tried to soothe the woman. "We're not taking her away from you. We want to take her somewhere safe until we get you both settled in. Can we do that? She'll still be close."

The woman's eyes were wild as they darted around the room. "Where am I? What is this place?"

"Ma'am, we're here to help you and your child. In this shelter, you'll both be safe." Sadie eased the woman's grip from Susan's arm and motioned for Sophia to move her away. Sadie positioned herself between the woman and the child and spoke softly. "Will you let us help you and your little girl?"

The woman leaned back on the table. Tashina put a warm cloth on her brow and covered her with a soft blanket. The girl took Sophia's extended hand, and they left. Sadie sat across from the woman, leaning toward her. "What's going on, sweetie?" she asked. "So, your name is Claire?"

Claire nodded. "I'm sorry," she said. "I know I'm a mess."

"You're going to be all right." Sadie spoke in soothing tones. "We're going to take care of you and your daughter. Can you tell me what's going on?"

A big sigh escaped Claire's lips, and her shoulders heaved. "We didn't have the money to pay rent, so we lost our apartment," she said. "We've been on the streets for the last few weeks. Then we stayed in a mission until someone called that man, Jerome. He came to get us."

"I'm glad he did," Sadie said. "He's a good guy. We're glad that you're here now. I know it was hard for you to live like that."

"I just feel so bad for Susan, you know? She's sad that her daddy died. She doesn't understand why we don't have money for the rent."

Sadie hesitated. What was this woman's story? "Was your husband sick? Maybe he had a lot of medical bills?"

Claire drew in her breath. "No, it was sudden. I knew he had a nice life insurance policy. I didn't know he gave everything to his other wife."

"His other wife? You mean his ex-wife?"

"No, his other wife. I knew he never seemed to have much money and was gone a lot. But I didn't know he had another family across town. He put them as beneficiaries of his insurance. He left me and Susan with nothing."

"Did you work? I mean, outside the home?"

"I used to," Claire said. "I worked at a hospital as a CNA for several years. I had some medical issues, so he told me to stay home with Susan and that he would take care of everything. And he did until he passed. He left us with nothing but heartaches." Her tears fell again.

Sadie handed her some tissues. "Let's get you settled in, and then we'll talk again. We'll figure something out, okay? I don't want you to worry about anything."

Soon, Claire and Susan were settled in a room. The other clients surrounded them with kindness and compassion. Sadie knew healing would come. She had to start thinking about a future for these ladies and permanent homes for the children.

Meanwhile:

The guard raised his eyebrows as a large man with a bulbous nose, a rope tattooed around his neck, and snakes tattooed down his arms and to his hands walked into the prison door. The guard had seen many piercings, but the chain from his nose to his eyebrow and then to his ear looked painful.

"I'm here to see Cosmos Rouge," the man said.

The guard showed him into the visiting area and instructed him to wait. Soon, Cosmos appeared on the other side of a thick glass. The men nodded to each other and picked up the phones.

"Hey, Carp. What's going on?" Cosmos asked.

"Man, that gal, Caroline, ain't showed up in two weeks. I cain't find out anything about what's goin' on."

Cosmos cursed and slammed his fist against the glass, causing the guard to scold him. "I ever get outta here, I'll get that wench." Then he frowned. "Wait a minute, you mean she hasn't showed up for a fix in that long? That's odd."

"No, man, that's what I'm sayin'. I ain't seen her. She must be getting her stuff from somewhere else."

"Who could supply to her on the island? Is there a dealer there now?"

"I don't know, but I'm thinkin' you cain't count on her no more."

Cosmos jumped up and cursed until the officer came to stand behind him. He grinned and said something, then the guard moved away.

"Ok, here's what we'll do. You get an islander to go to the shelter and pretend to be a relative of Caroline. Say you need her right away. They can take her to the river, and you can meet her there. See what's goin' on with her."

Carp agreed. "So what if she's out so's we cain't count on her anymore? Then what?"

"You got somebody else we can use? Remember, they have to get into the shelter by pretending to be abandoned or abused. It has to look real."

Carp snickered. "Oh, don't worry. I know one who won't have to pretend. It will be real."

SIXTEEN

David and Sadie were on their regular early morning jog down the island road when they were surprised by a visitor. One of the islanders stopped them as they jogged by his house.

"Hey, Kingston," he yelled. "We don't appreciate you bringing those low lives over here from the mainland to live among us."

David stopped and turned toward the man. "I'm sorry, Dan. I didn't know you were so concerned about a small group of women and kids who just need a little help."

"A lot of us 'round here are concerned. Who knows what that bunch will do. The druggies are prob'ly thieves. Most druggies are."

"I guess you should know about that," David said. "Tell you what. You keep an eye on your questionable activities, and we'll keep an eye on our clients. Then we'll all be happy." He and Sadie jogged on.

Amid the everyday chores, disruptions caused by differences of opinion and the job of keeping the children busy, David, Sadie, and Sophia managed to govern the shelter's business without outsiders' involvement. When some islanders complained that the shelter clients were low lives, David convinced Jeb and others at the craft village to step up their influence to shine a positive light on the shelter. Sophia handled the legalities, while David ran the business of keeping the buildings maintained and the employees happy. They were caught off guard when a man appeared on the island with an order for them to appear at the courthouse in the city. The husband of one of the clients was suing the shelter.

Kade and Sophia boated over a few days early so Sophia could consult a lawyer friend to help prepare her legal defense. David and Sadie followed, arriving in the city in time to confer with the lawyers. The four were surprised when Nora Langdon and her husband entered the office behind a lawyer carrying a large briefcase.

Sadie gasped and stood. "Nora! We wondered what happened to you. Are you all right?"

Nora ducked her head and moved to stand near her husband. Mr. Langdon, a large man with black hair, narrowed his dark eyes and grasped her arm, causing her to wince. "She's fine," he said. "In fact, she's more than fine since she got away from you guys."

Nora's face reddened as she looked sideways at her husband. He put an arm around her, pulling her close to his side. She stiffened as a look of terror covered her face.

Sophia's lawyer friend spoke. "Please be seated." He and Sophia sat on one side of the large conference table while the Langdons and their lawyer sat on the other. Mr. Langdon squared his shoulders and threw out his chest, reminding David of a WWE wrestler after he'd won a match. Except this man hadn't won anything yet.

After she pulled some documents from her briefcase, Sophia leaned forward. "Exactly what are you wanting, Mr. Langdon? What are your claims against Willow Grove?"

Mr. Langdon's lawyer smirked. "Your errand boy — I think his name is Jerome — picked up my client, Nora Langdon, from the Fourth Street Mission and boated her to your island. Is that correct?"

Sophia nodded. "Our employee, Jerome, was called by a law officer to help a distressed woman. Upon her request, he took her to our shelter for help."

The lawyer leaned back. "We maintain that Mrs. Langdon was in shock after an accident. She had fallen down some stairs and was badly hurt, rendering her incapable of making a rational decision. We contend that your employee, Jerome, took advantage of her incompetence when he took her from the mission."

Sophia looked at Nora. "Nora, is this true? Did you fall down some stairs?"

Nora looked from Sophia to her husband and back. She appeared to draw as far back into herself as possible. She first shook her head, then nodded it. Pain-filled eyes darted around the room to each person there. Then she looked down.

Sophia straightened. "What is your request, Mr. Langdon? Exactly what do you want?"

The lawyer cleared his throat. "We don't have to take this to court, Mrs. Crandall. We can settle here. All Mr. Langdon wants is one hundred thousand dollars to compensate for the pain and suffering of him and his wife. After all, he suffered extensively when his wife was held captive at your shelter, and she also suffered."

Sophia pulled in her lips and nodded. She leaned over to speak privately to David, Sadie, and Kade. The four of them stood and faced the Langdons. "We are not prepared to give you any compensation," Sophia said. "Once we have interviewed the officer who found Mrs. Langdon beaten up and bleeding on the street, we will interview your neighbors and family to get the whole story. I'm sure we'll have no problem finding those who will confirm our suspicions of domestic violence in this case."

Mr. Langdon jumped up. "Wait. You can't do this." He turned to his lawyer. "Wilson, you can't let them get away with this. I need that money. Come on, man."

Before they exited, Sadie turned to Mr. Langdon. "We'll have our people watching you. If we find that you have beaten your wife again, we'll charge you with assault. You can count on that, sir." They walked out the door.

Kade and Sophia wanted to stay in the city for a while, and David and Sadie returned to the shelter to find things in an uproar. A pale Grace met them when they came in. "Something is wrong. It seems like everyone is hallucinating. We think it had to be the spaghetti because everyone has been affected except a few who didn't eat it. Tashina and I ate only some salad, so we're okay."

"Where's Tashina?" Sadie asked.

Grace pointed. "She has them all in the lounge to keep an eye on them. It's bad, Mrs. Sadie. Real bad."

David and Sadie ran to the lounge. Wild-eyed women and children were stretched out on the sofas and chairs while others staggered around the room, batting at invisible bugs or fighting invisible varmints. Tashina was trying to keep a semblance of order, but was losing the battle.

"Here, kitty kitty." Angie crawled around on the floor, meowing while Loreen stood in a corner holding a dustpan like a microphone, singing *Can't Help Falling in Love* at the top of her lungs. Caroline sat in Marleigh's lap, sucking her thumb while Marleigh rocked her viciously, trying to sing *You Are My Sunshine* to the tune of *I Want to Hold Your Hand*. Lyric chased fire-breathing dragons through the house with a mop and broom, yelling, "Take that, ye dirty-rotten creatures. I'll learn ya to scorch me with your fiery stinkin' breath," and leaving a path of broken lamps and knocked down furniture.

While David helped Tashina, Sadie ran to the kitchen to find Louisa collapsed in chairs while Wren walked the floor. A teary-eyed Louisa raised her head. "Oh, Mrs. Sadie. I jus' don't know what happened. I was here all the time, so I don't know how anyone could've put something in the food. No one was here but Wren and me." She burst into tears.

Sadie looked inside the pots on the stove but could see nothing amiss. "Louisa, compose yourself and go over the morning events with me. Step by step."

Louisa raised her head and wiped her face with a towel. She stood looking around. "Let's see," she said. "Our menu for today was spaghetti with meat sauce, salad, and yeast rolls." She walked around as she spoke. "Wren got out all the ingredients. I started on the yeast rolls while she cooked the meat for the sauce." She burst into tears again. "Oh, Mrs. Sadie. I jus' don't know what to do. How could this happen? I jus' know you're gonna fire me for shore."

Sadie patted her on the back. "Now, Louisa, I'm not going to fire you. You're the best cook I've ever known. Now stop crying and tell me what happened next. Did either of you leave the kitchen even for a little while?"

"No. Wait, yes. Wren did. She went out to find some wild mushrooms for the spaghetti sauce. She warn't gone for over fifteen minutes."

"Okay. Did you go out of the kitchen while she was gone? Maybe into the pantry or to the bathroom or something?"

"No, Mrs. Sadie. I was making the rolls, so I was right here the whole time."

Sadie moved around the room, thinking. "Go on, Louisa. What happened next?"

Louisa walked to the counter where she had prepared the rolls. "Let's see. I finished the rolls and set 'em up to rise a bit. Then I brewed some tea and got out the big pot to start the water boilin' for the pasta."

Sadie stood beside her. "Then?"

Louisa looked around. "Wren came back in with a basket full of mushrooms. I asked her where she found 'em, and she said under the trees at the water's edge. I never picked any there before." She whirled around and ran to a large sink where a few mushrooms still lay. She picked up one at a time to look them over. Then she picked up the basket and peered inside. She gasped, and her face paled as she reached inside the basket. "Here's the problem, Mrs. Sadie. Wren knows which mushrooms are good to eat, but she must have got ahold of a bad one." She held up a piece of a small, red mushroom. She sat down, covered her face, and bawled.

Sadie grabbed the mushroom from her and ran out the door. Tashina would know how to treat the clients when she learned the source of the problem.

Tashina took the mushroom from Sadie and looked it over. She ran to her office and pulled down a book from the top of a shelf. Inside, she found a section about mushrooms, read it, then closed the book.

"I'm afraid there's nothing we can do but wait this thing out," she said. She glanced at her watch. "According to the book, we should have about another hour for the hallucinations to stop."

She was right. In another hour, most of the clients returned to normal. The children lay down and went to sleep. The women complained of headaches and laughed at those who still swatted at invisible bugs. Wren vowed never again to pick wild mushrooms.

"Anytime you want mushrooms," David said, "We'll order them from the grocery. No more wild mushrooms around here."

Meanwhile:

An old johnboat drifted up at the island's bank under a grove of willow trees in the early morning. The banks were slick and muddy from the rain that had continued the day before, and all night. Water dripped from the branches of the willow trees onto a dismal figure that lay inside the boat. The figure—a woman—rose and looked at her surroundings, then dropped back down. The boat bobbed on the water, moving out until the waves carried it back to the shore.

An island fisherman returning with his morning catch saw the boat and went to check it out. He drew in his breath when he saw the black-clothed figure inside. He pulled the boat onto the sand and leaned over the body.

"Are you okay?" he asked. The figure moved and moaned. The man reached in and pulled the shoulder, causing the person to roll over. A woman turned a swollen, bruised face to look at the man. "Oh, my," the man said. "What happened to you?"

The woman moaned again and lay back.

"Here, let me help you up. We gotta get you to a doctor. Who did this to you?" The fisherman helped the woman out of the boat and led her to a log to sit. He persisted. "Miss, what happened? Who did this to you?"

Bruises covered her face and arms. Blood oozed from cuts on her forehead, cheeks, and neck. Both eyes were black. She shook her head. "I'll be all right," she murmured.

"Miss, you're not all right. Did someone beat you up? Did you come here on your own? Where did you come from?" Dark eyes stared at him.

"Oh, I'm sorry," he said. "Too many questions. Let me slow down." He sat beside her. "Can you tell me how you got here?" He jumped up. "Oh, what am I thinkin'? I need to get you to a doctor."

He looked around. "We can get into your boat to take you to the hospital."

"Please, I don't wanna go back. He'll hurt me. Take me to the shelter."

"Oh, you mean Willow Grove Shelter?"

She nodded.

"Sure, I can do that. We'll still need to take the boat. The shelter is too far for you to walk."

He helped her back into the boat, and soon they drifted into the Willow Grove dock. He led her to the shelter and knocked on the door.

SEVENTEEN

David, Sadie, and Sophia boated over to visit Mason, a man who ran a similar shelter in a suburb of Memphis. David had called him, and he agreed to offer advice and relay what he had learned to help them. The shelter therapist sat in on the meeting to offer her expertise.

Mason told them a little about the history of the shelter he ran as they sat in his office. "We opened this place twenty years ago," he said. "We've learned a lot of things the hard way, you know, trial and error. If I can help you, maybe you won't make as many mistakes as we made."

"We sure have a lot to learn," Sadie said. She opened a legal pad and readied her pen.

"Yes, and we appreciate your help." David sat forward in his chair. "Anything you can tell us to make life easier for us and the clients."

Mason explained the procedures used by the shelter and the importance of daily routines and responsibilities. He advised them to be ready for unexpected conflict and spoke about new client intakes and transitions into the system. "One thing we learned the hard way," he said, "is maintaining privacy for your shelter and clients. Be cautious about telling anyone much about the shelter. Curious people often want to know the details, but it's best to tell as little as possible about how the system works."

The therapist, a young woman named Kyla, laughed. "Mason is right when he said we learned some things the hard way. A woman approached me one day and started to ask questions about how I deal with clients. She was nice and seemed concerned. Being young and trusting, I answered her questions and gave her some information about dealing with an addict, using examples from my experiences. A week or two later, an article appeared in the newspaper about our program with details that I should never have revealed. I was so ashamed and embarrassed, and the clients felt violated. Some left, and some never trusted me again with their feelings or needs. That was a hard lesson."

"Another thing to be careful of is allowing someone not involved in the shelter to go inside and look around," said Mason. "That is a breach of the client's privacy. We also learned that the hard way. When we opened with only two clients, a guy asked to look around. We were so proud of the place we allowed him in. Later, we found out he was looking for someone related to him who had been taken to a shelter. It wasn't ours, but it could have been."

Kade strode into David's office and plopped down in a chair. "Man, I've been thinking about your situation here, and I think I have a brilliant idea."

"Well, hello to you, too! I'm so glad you've decided to honor us with your splendor. We need a brilliant idea or two. Whatcha got?"

Kade grinned and put his foot on the desk. David knocked it down. "These women need to know how to defend themselves so no one can beat them up again. Right?"

David turned away from his computer and nodded. "I hadn't thought of that, but you're right. Got an idea how we can make that happen?"

"I sure do. I know a guy who teaches self-defense to women. He's good, too."

David's eyes narrowed. "How much will he charge?"

"Man, that's part of the beauty of it. For the shelter, he will do it for nothing. He says his sister was a victim of abuse, and her husband killed her. He'll do it in honor of her."

"That sounds great. When can he start?"

"I'll find out." Kade jumped up. "Is Sadie here? I'd like to see her and my nephew."

David rose. "She isn't here right now. She and Benji are home. I'm sure they'd love to see you. Tell you what, I'll walk over to the house with you, and she can fix us lunch."

"David, that government woman called again." Sophia stepped into David's office. "She says she's sending someone out in a few days for a visit. I told her we aren't a government-run office, but she says it doesn't matter."

David scrunched up his face. "I wish she'd just leave us alone." He stood and massaged the back of his neck. "Wonder what she wants now."

Sophia went to the coffee pot and poured herself a cup. "She asked what we are doing about our children's education. I guess that is a problem."

"You know, I thought about that the other day. We do need to be providing them with an education. Since all of you ladies passed the self-defense classes, I haven't considered what the children need. I guess we've let down on that."

Sophia tapped her forefinger on her chin. "I don't know why—I guess we haven't thought everything through very well, but we don't know much about any of our clients. We've been so busy trying to save them that we've neglected getting to know them."

David sat back down at his desk. "Mason told me that they work closely with the local schools when they deal with their clients."

"But we don't have a local school," Sophia said. "You were raised on this island. Where did you go to school?"

"I went to a school in a small town just across the chute," David said. "It was called Tomato."

Sophia laughed. "Did they have fields of tomatoes?"

"No. Just a small town in Arkansas," David said. "I could have gone to a Tennessee school—even one in Memphis. But I preferred a small school, and this one was closer. My parents knew someone there, so they boated me across the chute every day until I was big enough to boat myself. It was a good little school."

"My school in Australia was huge. I didn't even know all my classmates. I'll bet you knew yours."

"Oh, yes. I can still name them." David laughed. "I knew where they lived and what they ate for dinner."

Sadie popped her head around the door. "Sounds like you're having fun without me, and that isn't right," she said.

David motioned for her to join them. He explained the situation.

"Wait! Juliet said something about becoming an elementary teacher," Sadie said. "Most of our children are elementary."

"Wonderful!" Sophia and David did a high five.

"Think she's ready to step back into that role?" David asked.

"She's doing well," Sadie said. "I think she could do it if she's willing. And come to think of it, Loreen said something about working at a school. Let me go to my office and check her file."

David and Sophia chatted until she returned. "Yes. She's a certified teacher. She can teach the older students and Juliet the younger ones. We'll have to set up a classroom."

"If she's willing," David said. "Sadie, you talk to Juliet, and I'll talk to Loreen. Do you happen to know where these ladies are?"

He found Loreen in the lounge. "Loreen, I hear you're a certified teacher." When she nodded, he sat beside her. "Would you be willing to teach these children if we can set up a class for you?"

Her eyebrows arched. "You mean the shelter kids?" She looked at the ones playing a game just outside the window. "Those kids?"

David nodded. "Well, of course, you'll have help. We're checking on another possibility." He watched her face. "Where did you teach? And what levels have you taught?"

Her wide eyes jerked back to his face. "Uh, I taught in Memphis. I taught middle grade but am certified to teach middle through high school levels." She shrugged. "I am certified to teach math, but I have a master's in special education, so I can teach pretty much anything."

David jumped up. "Perfect! You're exactly what we need." Then he sat back down. "Would you be willing to be our teacher if we set up a place for you? A classroom?"

Her head nodded slowly. "I guess I can." Her eyes widened again. "You said you have someone to help me? It's been a while."

"That's possible." David stood. "We're checking it out. Of course, we can always get someone to work as an aide, and all of us will be around."

Loreen's face lit up. "You know, I heard Juliet mention something about attending college before she married."

David snapped his fingers. "Wonderful! We'll check out her credentials. Maybe she'll be willing to help."

"I think I might like to be in a classroom again," Loreen said.

"We'd pay you," David said. "It might not be as much as a public teacher, but we'll put our heads together and work something out." He hurried out of the room, singing, "It's a good day after all."

Two days later, they equipped a room with desks, books, and a blackboard, and school was in session. The government agent, this time a Mr. Fields, showed up to find students working quietly at their desks, the older ones on one side of a room divider with Loreen while Juliet worked on the other side with the little ones. Working as an aide, Caroline sat at a table in the back with some middle graders, helping them with a math lesson.

Mr. Fields stood by the door a while, then moved about the room for a closer inspection. David watched from the doorway, pleased with the results of the hard work of the staff.

"Looks like you are doing fine with these children," Mr. Fields said. "You said this teacher is certified?"

David nodded. "Mrs. Loreen is certified to teach all grades. Another client will soon complete her degree for a teaching certificate." He led Mr. Fields out the door and down the stairs. "We love our children and want the best for them," he said. "They've had a rough time, but we intend to offer them the guidance they need to have a successful life. We have a licensed therapist and a licensed nurse practitioner on staff."

Mr. Fields smiled as he shuffled down the hall. "Thank you, Mr. Kingston. I'm convinced that you are handling things here just fine." He scribbled on the pad he carried. "You sure have a beautiful place here." He waved as he walked to the dock to board the waiting boat.

David returned to his office, where Sophia and Sadie waited.

"Well?" Sadie put up her hands, palms up. "What happened? Are we in trouble?"

David sat in his desk chair and leaned back. "It went well," he said. "Mr. Fields is satisfied with what we've done. He said we have a beautiful place."

Sophia signed. "I'm glad, although I don't know why it matters to him. I guess it's important that we follow the rules and educate our children."

"Yes, that's true." David glanced out the window, then jumped up. "Who was that?" He leaned over to look across the lawn.

"Who was what? Is someone out there?" Sadie joined him at the window, followed by Sophia.

"Someone just ran behind the building," David said. "I know I wasn't imagining things." He ran to look out the back door but returned, shaking his head. "I couldn't see anyone, but I'm sure I saw a man."

"Probably just one of our clients running loose." Sophia sat back down.

Sadie peeked out the door. "A man? None of our clients are men. He has to be one of the staff. Or an islander. Everyone should be doing chores or in school at this time of day." She shrugged. "Who knows what's going on out there."

Meanwhile:

On the west side of the island where most of the islanders lived, a young island woman threw herself over a small casket, weeping inconsolably. Her distraught husband attempted to pull her away.

"Rebecca, it's time to go. Come on, honey."

"I can't. Larry, we can't leave our baby here alone." Her mumbled words turned into a wailing sound that ripped the hearts of those standing nearby.

The minister's grip tightened on his Bible. He had tried to console the couple, but nothing he could say helped. How could this happen to such dear people? They were good parents with a positive outlook on life and a great future in sight. As a result of the child's infirmity, the couple lost their home on the mainland and moved to the island to stay with Larry's parents.

The young couple's child was born with a deformed heart and lived only for a year. They had spent time going back and forth to the hospital and had astronomical doctor and hospital bills. The islanders did what they could to help with the finances, but none had much to give beyond their own needs. Regardless, nothing could replace the hole in the hearts of the parents who had buried their precious baby.

EIGHTEEN

A scream pierced the night, shattering the quiet like splintering glass, scaring the swans that swam at the edge of the river into immediate flight. Another scream followed, and then another.

Tashina jumped out of bed and grabbed a robe as she ran out her bedroom door. She ran into the hallway, meeting several clients and staff members who ran toward the torturous sound coming from an upstairs bedroom. Marleigh leaned against the railing, fists clenched, making the dreadful sound.

Tashina bounded up the stairs to her. "Marleigh! What is wrong?"

"Oh, Ms. Tashina, he's gone! My baby is gone." Tears streamed down her white face. Tashina ran into Marleigh's room while Juliet and Caroline ran to comfort the hysterical woman.

"What happened to little Aiden?" asked Caroline. "Where has he gone?"

"I jus' don't know." Marleigh sobbed. "I put him to bed las' night, and I woke up, and his crib is empty. He's gone. Gone."

Tashina came out of the room holding a blue crocheted blanket. Marleigh grabbed the blanket and buried her face in its softness.

"What time did you put him to bed?" Tashina asked.

Marleigh sobbed harder, emitting the soulful sound that had awakened the entire building. Tashina gently shook her shoulders. "Marleigh, what time did you put him to bed?"

"It—it—it was about nine, I think. He wakes me up about midnight for a bottle, but he didn't cry for me. I woke up, and he's gone. Gone!"

"Did you leave your window open?" Tashina asked. She turned and spoke softly to Wren, who was patting Marleigh's hand. "Go to her room and check. I think it's open now."

Marleigh drew in a sharp breath. "I may have. I opened it to look out when I heard an owl screech." She fell against the banister. "Oh, no! It's all my fault." The wailing started over until Tashina shook her again.

"Marleigh, we're going to call David. We'll find little Aiden." She spoke to Juliet. "Take her to the lounge and calm her. Get her some hot coffee. You ladies all help her." All the clients surrounded the sobbing woman and led her down the stairs and into the lounge.

Tashina grabbed her phone and called David. Soon he and Sadie hurried into the building along with several island guards. Wren reported that the window was open and said there was a streak of mud on the window seal and footprints leading to the elevator. David and a couple of the guards went to inspect the room. Their hushed voices and solemn faces told a grim story when they returned. Someone appeared to have climbed up to the balcony and entered the open window to take baby Aiden.

David called law enforcement from the mainland and soon had an army of people surround the island, hoping the culprit hadn't had time to leave. Islanders appeared from everywhere to help with the search, and flashlights flared through the darkness as searchers scoured the wooded areas, around buildings, and along the banks on each side of the island.

"Don't allow anyone to leave the island," David ordered the guards. "We've got to find that child."

The night dragged on as the determined searchers combed the area. The three-mile by five-mile island was soon covered with no results. The light of dawn revealed the sad faces of a defeated group of men, women, and children who gathered behind the shelter.

One man approached David and Jerome as they stood looking up and down the river. "I heard a motorboat last night. It sounded close. I didn't think much of it because boats always go up and down this river, but for some reason, I noticed it."

"Josiah, you live just downriver a piece, don't you?" David asked.

Josiah nodded. "Yeah, not far. I live west on the chute side, but jus' happens I was pullin' in a line on the river side 'bout midnight. Weren't long after that I noticed it."

Another man joined the men. "I noticed it too," he said. "And I saw it. It was a long johnboat chugging along slow like. It banked a ways from here, just out of reach of the shelter lights. I'd say about thirty minutes later, it started up again and sped up when it got further downriver."

Jerome spoke to the man. "Hank, you didn't happen to see who was in that boat, did you? Or what kind of boat it was?"

Hank looked at the ground, thinking. "You know, I believe there were two guys in it or at least two persons. In the moonlight, it looked like an older rig. Of course, I couldn't tell much about it in the dark." He thought some more, then jerked up his head. "There was one thing, though. The motor sputtered real bad. Like it was going to die. Then it roared and lit out."

"I'll talk to Kade. Likely some of his guys might have an idea. They're always on the river, so they may know of a boat that fits that description."

Hank shook his head. "I'm sorry, Kingston. It ain't much to go on, but it's all I got. Wish I had more to tell ya."

David nodded. "Hey, it's better than nothing. We'll have to trust God that what happened in the darkness will be brought to light."

He raised his voice to be heard by the crowd. "Everyone, keep your eyes and ears open. Something will happen soon that will help us solve this mystery and find the little guy. In the meantime, keep praying."

The crowd dispersed, and David entered the shelter to comfort the distraught mother.

Sophia had called the city for help, and a couple of detectives were questioning Marleigh and the other clients and staff. Two more were investigating the area outside between the building and the river. When David told them about Josiah's and Hank's stories, they called aside the two men and questioned them further.

One of the detectives—a guy called Boozer—pulled Jerome aside. "The lady says she's hiding from an abusive husband. Do you think maybe he found out where she is?"

"I guess it's possible," Jerome said. "Would be worth finding him. We always hope that doesn't happen."

Boozer took out a pen and pad. "Do you know where the guy lives?"

Jerome shook his head. "No. I picked up Marleigh at the mission. You can ask her. Evidently, she had gone there to escape him, and they called me. That's the way it usually happens."

"I'll ask her," Boozer said. "Since she went to the mission, she might live in that area." He looked around. "Seems like you guys have a good thing here. Do you have many clients?"

"Several." Jerome counted on his fingers. "I'd say about fifteen or so. Women and children."

"All domestic abuse victims?"

"Most. Some abandoned kids and a few strung out on drugs. We help 'em detox and get their lives back on track."

"Do you find them, or do they find you?"

"Some find us, but mostly someone calls us. Those at the mission steer some here. City cops call us sometimes when someone shows up at their departments. We take those who need help. We will as long as we have room, and this place is pretty big."

"That's good," Boozer said. "I'll keep you in mind when our department finds a victim who needs help."

The two men shook hands, and Boozer went to talk to Marleigh before he joined his waiting partner. Jerome went into the shelter to find David.

"How's Marleigh?" Jerome asked.

"Not too good. Sadie and Wren are with her."

"How in the world are we gonna find that baby?" Jerome paced the floor.

"I don't know, but we've got to. There has to be a clue somewhere." David rubbed his neck. "I'm going back upstairs to look again."

Jerome followed him. They searched the room and inspected the mud on the windowsill and the footprints on the balcony.

David scratched his head. "These footprints are pretty small. Look." He measured with his hand. "It had to be a smaller person."

"How did he get up here?" Jerome asked. "That elevator is locked at night, isn't it?"

"It is," David said. They looked around the railing on the balcony.

"Look. Bet he climbed that tree and swung from it to the balcony."

"I don't know," David said. "That's too far to jump, don't you think?" He went down the elevator and inspected the ground below.

Jerome joined him. "This area has been searched already. I don't think we'll find anything else here," he said.

David saw something under a large clump of Hostas.

He pulled out a pair of muddy tennis shoes.

"Here's what made the tracks on the balcony," he said. "Now, to find the owner."

"Yeah," said Jerome, "and why the shoes are here. Why would the owner take them off here? Seems like they would keep them on if they were running away with a baby."

"That is a puzzle." David jumped up. "Maybe they weren't running away. Could it be a foil to get us off track? To make us think someone from outside did this?"

Jerome rubbed his chin. "Are you thinking someone inside the shelter took Aiden?"

"I don't know. Could be. But what did they do with him?"

"They would have to hide him somewhere. And we've searched the whole island."

David's jaw tightened. "Who would do such a thing? These women support and help each other." He pivoted and headed toward the shelter. "Come on. Let's go talk to some ladies."

"And kids," Jerome said.

Meanwhile:

"You mean you expect a fix when you haven't done anything yet?" Carp snapped his fingers in front of the young woman's face. "I can end everything for you just like that," he said. "I promised Cosmos you would take care of business, but you ain't done one thing I've asked you to do."

"I promise, I tried." She whimpered as her fingers twisted together. "Please give that to me." She motioned toward a bag Carp held. "I'll do it. I will."

"I'll give you one more chance, but I guarantee you, Madison, if you don't deliver, you'll pay." He handed her the bag, and she ran down the path to the shelter.

NINETEEN

Before David and Jerome could get to the lounge, Sadie met them in the hall and pulled them into her office.

"There's something you should know," she said. "The new girl brought in the other day is stirring up trouble among the clients. She's trying to convince them that we are making money off them."

"Where did she come from," David asked. "Who brought her here?"

Sadie shrugged. "A fisherman brought her in the other day. Said she was lying in a boat at the edge of the water. Tashina said someone beat her. He wanted to take her to the hospital, but she asked to come here."

"Did you get any background information from her? Like who she is and who beat her? Is she a druggie?"

"Her name is Madison Hershel, and she's from Memphis. Said her boyfriend beat her, but she refused to give his name. And yes, she's an addict. Tashina is dealing with her on that end."

A commotion outside drew their attention away from Sadie. Jerome went out the door to see what was happening. One of the islanders from the craft village confronted him.

"I'm here to see Kingston." The man puffed his chest out. "This has gone on long enough."

David walked up beside Jerome. "What's going on?" he asked.

"Ted is concerned about our situation here," Jerome said.

Ted stepped back. "Mr. Kingston, I heard you was havin' some trouble around here. I came to see what it's all about."

David stepped off the porch, forcing Ted to take another step back. "How are you, Ted? How's it going with your woodshop? Business good for you?"

Ted blushed. "Yeah, sure. We're doin' real good down at the shop." Then he ruffled. "So, what's this I hear about a young'un kidnapped? That true?"

"Yes, a baby has disappeared." David touched Ted's shoulder and walked him away from the shelter. "I don't suppose you'd know anything about that?"

Ted stuttered. "Why — why, no! Why would I?"

"I just thought you came here to help. Maybe you'd heard something on your side of the island."

"No. No, I ain't heard nothing about no baby. Exceptin' one's been missin'."

Sadie came running out the door, followed by Wren. "David! David," she called. "Wren found out something." She turned to Wren. "Tell him, Wren. Tell David what you told me."

Wren wrung her hands. "I left early this mornin' to go to my mama's house when I saw somethin' weird — looked like a guy carrying something. The thing wiggled, and he almost dropped it. Then it made a noise, and he started running fast. I followed him and saw him go into an old shed at the village."

She looked back and forth between David and Ted, still wringing her hands. "I think it was the baby."

Ted started. "Girl, what are you talking about? You sayin' one of the crafters took the baby?"

She shook her head. "No — well — I don't know. He went into a building is all I saw. I don't know who it was."

"Come on, Jerome," David said. "We'll go check it out." They headed for the village, Ted following.

When they arrived, the crafters were busy selling wares. They called out to David and Jerome to visit their shops. David went from shop to shop, asking if anyone had seen the baby. Heads shook, and smiling faces turned sad as he talked to the islanders. At last, one of the crafters nodded and pointed. "I heard something strange over that way," she said. "I haven't had time to go check it out."

David and Jerome ran to the shed pointed out by the lady crafter. Inside, they found the baby in a corner, wrapped in a large shawl, sound asleep. A bottle lay beside him.

David looked the little fellow over but could see nothing wrong. The baby woke and smiled at David and Jerome, showing two front teeth.

"Hello, Aiden," David cooed to the child as he picked him up. "You seem to be well cared for. Now if you could tell me who took you and why."

When the two men and the baby exited the shed, a crowd from the village watched. David looked over the group. "Did any of you see who put this baby in this shed?" he asked. Heads shook in response, and shopkeepers returned to their customers. One man stood to the side and waited for David.

"Jeb. How are you?" David shook the hand of the older man. He had great respect for the overseer of the craft village.

"David." Jeb's face was solemn. "Ifin' you're thinkin' it was one of the villagers that took the child, you're wrong. These people are honest and carin' for others. Nary a one would take someone else's child and especially would not put a baby in a place like that."

"I believe you, Jeb. But someone did. I need to figure out who and why."

Jeb nodded. "I understand that. Ifin' I hear of anything that will help you learn who did it, I'll let you know." He turned to go back to the village, and David carried the baby as he and Jerome returned to the shelter to take the child to his mother.

Joy filled the shelter when baby Aiden was in the arms of Marleigh once more. She vowed she would never let him out of her sight again. All the shelter mothers pulled their children close and agreed with her.

Juliet took the shawl when Marleigh unwrapped Aiden. She held it up. A frown creased her eyebrows. "Where'd this shawl come from?" she asked. No one answered.

David and Sadie met with the clients once a week to check their mental and emotional progress. Some situations arose when disputes developed over trivial matters, but life was smooth until — once more — rumors started about the shelter closing.

"Who is telling you that?" Sadie demanded when Juliet asked her about it.

Juliet threw up her hands. "I heard Marleigh and Loreen talking about it," she said.

Sadie went from person to person, but each attributed it to another until the circle returned to Juliet. No one could say who started the rumor.

"Well, I'm tired of hearing it," Sadie said, "and I want it stopped. Tell them to hush the next time someone says anything about this shelter closing. Only you can stop these rumors."

"I heard one of the crafters say something about it the last time I was there," Wren said. "Some of them don't like us. I heard Bob say once that he wished we would all leave."

"I know Bob has a problem with us," Sadie said, "but we can't listen or believe him."

"Yeah," said Wren. "We never did find out who took Aiden, did we?"

"We didn't, but it probably wasn't Bob."

"Sadie, where did this come from?" David held out a handwritten note.

"I don't know," she answered. "Where did you get it? What does it say?"

David turned the paper over and over. "It was on my desk." He held it up and read it. "It says, 'Check out Caroline's room for something interesting.' That's all."

"Wonder what that's about." Sadie took the note and examined it. "I don't recognize this handwriting. We'd better check it out."

"Maybe. It's almost time for supper. Could you do it while everyone is in the dining room?" He gestured. "Take Jason with you."

Sadie didn't have to look long until she found a bag of marijuana in Caroline's room. After supper, she asked Caroline to meet with her, David, and Jason in Sadie's office.

When Jason held out the bag of marijuana, Caroline looked at it, then at each of them. "What is it?" she asked. Her face was a picture of innocence.

"Don't you know?" asked David. "Have you seen this before?"

"I know it looks like pot, but I haven't seen it before. Where did it come from?"

"Someone found it in your room."

She jumped to her feet, her eyes wild. "No! I don't have pot in my room. How could someone find it there? It isn't mine." Tears filled her eyes. "Please, Mrs. Sadie. You know I don't do that stuff anymore. Don't you?" She grabbed Sadie's arm. "Don't you believe me? I would never go back to that. My life is good now."

Sadie patted her hand. "I want to believe you, Caroline. But how do you explain this? It was in your room."

Tears flowed down the girl's face. "I don't know. I just know that it isn't mine. You gotta believe me. Please."

David pulled the note from his pocket. "Do you know who wrote this?"

Caroline wiped her eyes and looked at the note. She shook her head. "I don't know. I haven't seen that writing before." Her face contorted. "Please, Mr. David. You have to believe me. This stuff isn't mine. I'm clean, and I intend to stay clean."

David and Sadie both nodded. "We're going to believe you, Caroline. But we've got to find out how this got into your room."

"Do you keep your room locked?" asked Jason.

She nodded. "Most of the time, except when I'm helping with the chores. We stripped beds this morning."

The adults looked at each other, and Jason nodded. "So, someone must have put it in your room."

"But who would do that?" Sadie asked. "Caroline, did you see anyone go into your room?"

"No. I stripped my bed and took the sheets to the laundry room. I'm on laundry duty this week and was there for a while. I didn't think about locking my room. I trust everyone here."

David smiled at the distraught girl. "Yes, we have trusted everyone. But it looks like there's someone we can no longer trust. We've got to figure out who that someone is."

Meanwhile:

A scraggly bearded man with brown teeth leaned over to talk to a young man sitting in a red speedboat. "Ifen you want, I can get you some kids from around here. They run loose up and down the river all the time. It wouldn't be hard to nab 'em."

"I don't know about that," the younger man said. "You'd have to be careful. Since what happened here a while back, Kingston would likely be on the lookout for anything suspicious."

"For the money, though, it might be worth takin' a chance. Some of these river rats don't seem to watch their young'uns very good. It'd be easy."

TWENTY

At the weekly meetings, David talked about the benefit of being honest and how the clients should be loyal to each other. They listened and nodded in agreement. Sadie discussed the dangers of drug use, and again, they agreed. She had the pastor of the Island Chapel come in and talk about how important it is to honor God. At the end of his talk, he invited them to enter a season of prayer, and they knelt to pray with tears flowing. Still, no one had admitted to putting the bag of marijuana in Caroline's room, so they were at a loss as to who the guilty party was.

They spent evenings discussing the events. Who would sneak into the shelter and steal a baby? Whoever it was fed him and changed his diaper, so they seemed to care about him even if they put him in an old shed. But why would they do it?

"It had to be one of the islanders," Kade said. "We thought someone from outside did it, but they would have taken him off the island."

"No, I don't think so. The islanders wouldn't have put the child in a shed like that." Sadie argued the point, and David agreed.

The shelter staff and clients also tried to solve the mystery as they gathered in the lounge and around the tables in the dining room.

"It must have been a fisherman," said Loreen. "He was probably planning to return for the baby when he started home with his catch."

"Yeah, I heard that one of the islanders recently lost a child," said Juliet. "Maybe she took baby Aiden to replace her child."

"Then why was he in a shed?" asked Marleigh.

"Maybe she saw someone and hid him," said Caroline. "Then she could return for him later."

"It had to be one of the crafters," said Wren. "They hate the shelter being here. I'll bet they did it to scare us away."

Louisa shook her head. "I can't see any of those people doing something like that. They're good folks."

David and Sadie squelched conversations about the drugs found in Caroline's room. "Until the guilty party comes forward," Sadie said, "we'll not discuss it. We'll pray and let God convict." They all agreed.

Then something else came up. David, Sadie, and Sophia took the staff and clients on an excursion along the island's edge for a day of fishing and picnicking on the chute side. The water was low but just right to pull in some nice bream and a catfish or two. They left early when the fishing would be good, and sure enough, they were catching several. Kade brought a small boat over and took the children on boat rides. After they ate a picnic lunch prepared by Wren and Louisa, they decided to walk over to the Island Craft Village and shop a little.

Sadie allotted each client some money and appointed the adults with no children a child to look after. Wren and Louisa helped keep watch on the young ones. It was a fun day for everyone.

Mid-morning the following day, Jeb from the craft village came to the shelter looking for David in the middle of the morning.

"He isn't here right now," Sadie said, "but I'll call him. He can be here in a few minutes."

When David came in, he could tell by the look on Jeb's face something was wrong.

"David, I hate to tell you this, but...." Jeb removed his hat and scratched his head. "It's been reported to me that some things are missing from a couple of the village shops."

David sucked in his breath. "Oh, no." He sat across from Jeb. "What exactly is missing?"

"Travis Shelton says he is missing a couple of leather jewelry pieces, and Miss Amy is missing a pair of sandals. Now David, you know I believe in you and what you're doing here, but we can't abide people stealing from us."

"Jeb, are you sure one of ours took the things? Surely we weren't the only customers you had all day."

Jeb rubbed his beard. "No, you weren't. And I'd gladly think it was someone from the resort or the city, but we got an anonymous tip that one of your bunch stole something from us."

"An anonymous tip, huh?" David lifted an eyebrow. "How did you get this tip?"

Jeb reached into a pocket, pulled out a piece of paper, and handed it to David. It was a note similar to the one David found on his desk when marijuana was found in Caroline's room.

"That's odd. May I keep this?" Jeb nodded, and David stuck the note into his pocket. "I'm really sorry about this. I guess we won't take the clients to the village again until this issue has been resolved."

Jeb shoved his hands deep into his overall pockets. "I hate for you to do that. Your business is important to us. And our crafters love it when y'all come. I sure wish there was another way,"

"We'll try to get to the bottom of this as soon as possible," David said. "Maybe it'll work out that it's all a mistake. I sure hope so."

The two men shook hands, and David entered his office where Sadie waited. He relayed the problem to her and paced as he tried to think of a solution.

Sadie watched him for a while, then stopped him long enough for a kiss. "You need to visit the grove," she said.

David walked to the willow grove and sat on his favorite log. The sky was low over the river, and rain clouds from the east threatened. He knew he couldn't stay long, but a little time at the grove was healing. He leaned back against a tree after he checked the limbs above to make sure they were clear of birds. He didn't need a face full of bird poop again.

What was he going to do about the things happening at the shelter? He closed his eyes and listened. The water gurgled at the bank, luring him into a peaceful stupor. Just what he needed. The stress had been interrupting his sleep lately. Images drifted through his mind like transparent butterflies, threatening to disturb his peaceful slumber. Sadie's concerned face after she'd counseled a distraught client. Benji's bubbling laugh when Gus licked him with sweet doggie sugars. Kade's hysterical laugh when a practical joke backfired. He smiled when he thought of Sophia's blazing eyes when a client's family threatened a lawsuit against the shelter. He shuddered at the thought of clients' faces when they first came, so frightened at the unknown facing them and the thought that an abuser might find them. He loved to see his and Sadie's parents' faces when they played with their grandchildren.

His life was good. It always had been. But lately, the stresses of the shelter seemed to be weighing on him. What would he do if he couldn't figure out who came into the shelter and took the baby? Who started the fire in the laundry room? Who planted drugs in a client's room? And now, who stole from a village shopkeeper? Who is the informant sending false information to the DHS? Is it a client or someone else?

He absently swatted at a fly that kept buzzing around his face. That's how these things felt—like a pesky fly that kept returning to annoy him. *Actually, annoyed isn't the right word. A much stronger word is needed. Vexation? Scandal?* It would become scandalous if he didn't get to the head of the problem.

"Father in Heaven," he prayed, "in all your mercy and grace, will you please help me—us—figure this thing out? Will you please bring to light the things that are hidden? I trust you to show me what to do and how to handle these problems. I know you have the answers. Thank you. In Jesus' name." He raised his head to see a man standing in front of him.

He drew in a sharp breath, then composed himself. "Hello."

The man stared at him, then smiled. "Hi. I'm sorry. I didn't mean to startle you."

David stood and extended his hand. "That's okay. I'm David. David Kingston."

The man shook his hand. "I know who you are. I'm Stewart Polk. I've been fishing, and I saw you lying here. Thought maybe you were hurt. But then I heard you praying. Sounds like something is bothering you."

David ran his fingers through his hair, making it stand on end. Then he self-consciously smoothed it. "Yeah, I guess. When I have problems, I come here to think and to pray." He hesitated as the man looked at him. "You a praying man?"

Stewart laughed. "Wouldn't be much if I weren't. You're the one who runs the shelter, right? I've heard of you. And it."

"Yes, that's me, and my wife, Sadie. It's really her baby. I help out when I can."

"I understand why you have to come here to pray," Stewart said. "Dealing with the problems of others is hard, especially when it's women and children."

"You sound like you've been there before."

"I have—more often than I'd like to admit." Stewart gestured toward the log. "Mind if I join you?"

The log was large enough for both, and David scooted over. "So, what's your story?" David asked. "You work for DHS or something?"

Stewart laughed. "No, nothing like that. As a minister, I deal with women and children a lot. I go to the inner-city streets and talk to the homeless, druggies, and people there. I hope to change their lives for the good."

"That's admirable work. We may have some of your people in the shelter."

"It's possible. Do you accept just anyone, or do you have criteria for one to get into your establishment?"

David shook his head. "We take anyone who comes to us needing help. Law enforcement sent most of those we have at the shelter. Some came on their own."

Stewart watched a blue jay that squawked in a tree nearby. "I may know some people who need help. Do you accept men?"

"No. Our primary purpose is to shelter women and children who have suffered domestic abuse."

"Do you take druggies?"

"We have a few who have come to us requesting help, but as I said, our primary purpose is to help women and children from domestic abuse situations. We want to keep it that way. We could easily fill the building with those who abuse drugs, and that would limit our ability to help people. It would spread us too thin."

Stewart pressed his lips together. "I see what you mean. I guess you can do a better job if you limit yourself to only certain needs. How many clients do you have?"

"At this point, we have nine women and ten children. Of course, that can change at any time."

"How about staff members? Do you have a staff, like a therapist, nurse — things like that?"

"Yes, Sadie is a therapist, and my sister-in-law is a lawyer. We do have a nurse practitioner. We have kitchen staff and housekeeping, and others who lend a hand when we need it. We've started a school for the kids and have a chapel nearby where clients can walk to attend services."

"Sounds like you have a good system. I've thought about opening something like that in the city. Think I could visit the shelter sometime, and you could show me around?"

David hesitated. Something kept nagging at him. This man was asking a lot of questions. Then he recalled the visit with Mason and Kyla. 'Be careful about sharing information with people.' Wasn't that what they said? But this man was a minister. Surely, he was trustworthy. Besides, he might open a similar shelter to help more people.

"We don't allow visitors at the shelter, but I can refer you to someone in the city who can give you information. He helped us when we first opened." He gave Stewart the name and location of Mason's shelter and bade him goodbye. The peace he had felt was gone as the nagging in his mind persisted. Did he tell too much about the shelter? Did he relay any information that would cause trouble later? As he walked home, he kicked at a root sticking up. His toe hung in a loop made by the root, and he fell forward, banging his head on the tree trunk.

"Ouch! That hurt." He dragged himself up, rubbed his head, and nursed his skinned knee. He hobbled a few feet down the path, then straightened himself. "God, if you're trying to tell me something, do you have to make it so rough?" He set off in a jog, taking the long way home. He didn't need to see his family until his mood improved.

Meanwhile:

A tiny cry startled a blue heron, causing it to drop the fish it had just caught and fly away. A young woman in a torn dress cradled the newborn a moment, tightening the blue blanket around it and adjusting the name label pinned to the blanket. Glancing toward a house built close to the water, she kissed the child.

"My sweet Elijah, you'll be better off here where someone good will find you," she whispered. She laid him on a bed of dried leaves close to the water next to a basket filled with diapers, a sleeper, and two bottles of milk. She had made the bed with clean leaves free of dirt and bugs. She dragged a small johnboat from under limbs that protruded over the water. After one last glance toward the baby who had stopped crying, she pushed the boat from the shore and crawled in. She started the motor and fled down the river without looking back.

TWENTY-ONE

The place was in an uproar. An excited Sadie waved papers at David, and Sophia shut her office door so she could get the paperwork finished. They had a forever home for five-year-old Lacy. Her mom signed papers giving up legal rights, and a family on the island who had recently lost a child wanted to adopt her. Lacy had spent some time visiting with Rebecca and Larry and loved them. Sadie and David had checked out the family and were satisfied that they would be perfect parents for the child. It was a happy time.

After all the celebrations and congratulations, Sadie collapsed in the dining room while the staff and clients cleaned the mess. She felt a small hand on her arm and turned to look into Randall's sad little face.

"What is it, child? Why are you so sad? Aren't you happy for Lacy?"

The little boy nodded and wiped a tear that slipped down his face. "Yes, I am happy for her. But…"

"But what? What is it, child? What's wrong?" She pulled him close, and he laid his head on her shoulder.

"My mama ain't comin' back, is she?"

"Oh, sweetie, I wish I could tell you something," she said. She tried to comfort him, but she understood her sympathy would do little to make him feel better. She pushed him back and lifted his chin to look into his face. "I have an idea. Mr.

David and I will look into trying to find her. How does that sound?"

One corner of his mouth turned up. "I'd like to have a forever home, too, with my mama."

Sadie squeezed him. "I know you would. We'll see what we can do, okay?"

He ran to Emmie and whispered into her ear. She looked at Sadie and grinned. Sadie would start looking for their mom as soon as possible.

And she did. With the help of Jerome and a downtown detective, after three days of searching, she and David found Emmie and Randall's mom, Tina. She was strung out on drugs and working as a call girl.

Someone pointed her out, and Sadie approached her while the others stayed in the vehicle.

"Tina?" Sadie smiled and held out her hand. Tina scoffed and turned her back to Sadie. Sadie moved around her, but Tina kept turning away from her. "Tina, I want to help you," Sadie said.

Tina turned around. "Are you a cop?" She looked her up and down. "You don't look like a cop."

"No, I'm not a cop," Sadie said. "I have some news for you about your kids."

"My kids? You know where my kids are?"

"Yes, and they are asking for their mama. I want to help you."

"Where are they? Did you take them? Are they okay? Just how do you plan to help me?" The questions came at Sadie like bullets.

"Slow down, please. Your children are fine, but they want their mama back. If you'll let me, I can help with that."

Tears filled Tina's eyes. "Are my kids okay?"

Sadie handed her a tissue. "Emmie and Randall are fine, but they miss their mama."

Tina lowered her head. "I don't deserve to be called their mama."

David and Jerome exited the car, and the minute Tina saw them, she ran. Sadie turned to the men. "You came too soon," she said. "You didn't give me enough time. It will be harder for me to get her to talk now."

The next day when Sadie finally found her, Tina ran. Sadie knew there was no need to try again. The next day, Sophia went. She wore jeans with holes and a short, tight tee shirt. Her long, blonde hair was in a ponytail, and she wore dark makeup.

When they found Tina, they parked around the corner, and Sophia shouldered a large bag and walked by her. Tina was laughing about something another girl said and paid no attention to Sophia. Sophia walked to the end of the street, then turned and walked back. She stopped a couple of times and spoke to other people she met. She laughed at something someone said and continued toward Tina. When she approached the two ladies, she smiled and talked to the other woman before looking at Tina.

"Hello," she said. "Business good today?"

The woman laughed. "It has been so far. But don't think you're gonna cut in on our territory."

"Oh," said Sophia, "I have no intention of doing that. I'm just passing through."

"So," said Tina, "where ya going?"

"It's my day off, so I'm making the best of this beautiful day just takin' a walk."

Tina frowned. "Well, you can continue your walk and git on outta here."

Sophia smiled at her. "Isn't your name Tina?"

"Yes. What of it? Do you know me?"

"Not really, but I know someone who does know you. Do you remember Emmie and Randall?"

Tina gasped. "How do you know Emmie and Randall? You got my kids?"

Sophia nodded. "They are quite wonderful kids, you know. They miss their mama."

"Yeah, well, if it wasn't for my nosey neighbor, they wouldn't miss their mama." She turned to leave, then stopped. "Wait. Who are you? How did you get my kids?"

"Please don't leave," Sophia said. "I'm only here to help you if you'll let me. Don't you want to see the kids? They sure want to see you."

"They do?" Tina teared up, then shook her head. "They deserve better than me." She looked Sophia up and down. "But you don't look much better than I do. Are you a cop?"

"No, I'm not a cop. I work for the shelter where your kids are. Wouldn't you like to see them?"

"Well, yes, but...."

"I can take you to them. I can help you escape this lifestyle if you want."

Tina scoffed. "What makes you think I want to escape this lifestyle? Are you delusional? This is my job. It's what I do. Someone like you may look down on us working ladies" — she made air quotations — " but it's our livelihood. And not a bad one, either." She flipped her hair and looked down her nose. "Probably better than you make at that shelter."

"Doesn't matter," Sophia replied. "I like my job. And your kids are great. Seems like you did a pretty good job raising them."

Tina shrugged. "I cain't take the credit for them being good. They had a good dad." She sniffed. "Then he was killed in an accident. It ain't his fault or theirs that I turned out this way. I guess I'm just like my mama. That's what my daddy always said."

Sophia laid a hand on her arm and gently led her away from the other woman. "Tina, your kids love you. Please go with me to the shelter where they are. We can help you find a better life and be a good mama to your kids again."

Tina looked around as Sophia led her to the vehicle where David and Sadie sat. "What is this? You are a cop!" She started to run, but Sophia held her arm.

"No, Tina, we're not cops. I told you we work at the shelter where your kids are staying. They asked us to find you. They want to see you."

Tina hesitated, and David and Sadie exited the vehicle. "Did you bring my kids?" she asked David. "I want to see them." Then she saw Sadie. "Wait. You're the one I saw the other day. Do you have my kids?"

"Yes," Sadie said, "we have your kids at our shelter. You abandoned them, so someone brought them to us."

Tina's face contorted. "I didn't abandon them," she said.

"Yes, you did. They were left alone for days." Sadie was firm. "And without anything to eat."

Tina broke down and cried. "My poor babies. I've been such an awful mother to them."

"That can change," said David. "If you want it bad enough."

Tina looked at him. "How?" She motioned toward her body with a skin-tight, revealing dress, spike heels, and thick makeup. "This is my life now. This is all I have. This is who I am."

Sadie peered into her face. "Tina, is this the life you want for yourself?"

"You can change your life if you want to," David added. "You do have a choice."

Tina looked from one to the other. "What do you mean? What choice? I don't know how to change."

"You can't change by yourself," Sadie said. "But there's someone who can help you change."

"Who, you?" She scoffed. "You think you can help me change? Believe me, others have tried, but nothing works. My nosey neighbor who took my kids tried to help me, but she couldn't."

David whispered a silent prayer and then touched her hand. "Tina, I'm talking about your Creator. The one who made you. Not your mama or your daddy, but the God who created all of us. He wants to help you, and He is able."

Tina's eyes rounded, and she straightened. "Are you for real? You think God wants to help me?" Again, she scoffed. "Why would He want to help me? I'm no good. I'm not like you. I've never been any good."

"That's how you see yourself, but He doesn't see you like that. He loves and wants to help you if you let Him."

"I don't believe you," she uttered. "No one loves me."

"Come with us," urged Sadie, "and you'll find out what we're telling you is true. Come with us to see your kids. We won't make you stay if you don't want to. Just give us a try."

Tina looked from one to the other and finally agreed to go to Willow Grove Shelter for rehabilitation. Soon, Emmie and Randall would have a mom again.

David cast his line into the river, hoping to catch some fish for supper. He and Kade had left early that morning for a day away from the office when their wives insisted that they take some time off. They had caught several, and Kade suggested they dock to eat the lunch the girls had packed for them.

"Ah, man! Sophia forgot to pack celery and peanut butter," Kade said. "Now I'll have to eat this sandwich without it."

David laughed. "You and your celery and peanut butter. Yuck!" He bit into a sandwich. "Say, this lunch meat is pretty good. What is it?"

"It's bologna, you stooge. I picked it up at the deli the other day. It's garlic bologna."

David stuffed in another bite and grabbed a handful of potato chips. "Good thing we're out here away from the girls. They wouldn't be happy with our garlic breath."

"That's true." Kade swigged from his bottle of Coke. "I heard you have a new client."

"Yes. We found Emmie and Randall's mom and brought her in to detox."

"Bet Emmie and Randall are happy. How's she doing?"

"Pretty good. It's been rough, but Caroline and Grace are helping her."

"They help a lot, don't they?"

David nodded. "We've assigned them as counselors and pay them a little for their work. They have a heart for doing that."

Kade slapped a mosquito on his arm. "Yuck. That sucker swigged my blood, and I splattered it all over." He wiped up the mess with a napkin and handed it to David.

David wrinkled his nose. "I don't want that nasty thing."

Kade pointed to an empty bag. "Put it there, please." He leaned back and rubbed his belly. "Have you come up with any more clues about the kidnapping? That was kinda weird."

"No, none. And now the marijuana situation. And the theft at the village. I can't imagine that any clients would do such a thing."

"Dang, man, I wish you could figure it all out. Sophia thinks someone outside took Aiden, but I don't know how they would have gotten into the shelter."

"I don't know either. We lock it up tight at night." David slapped at a fly. "On another subject, Sadie and Sophia have been saying maybe we need an office for adoption services here on the island."

Kade sat up. "Sophia mentioned that the other night. She told me about the baby an islander found. Are you having many requests for adoptions?"

"Not now, but we may in the future. Sophia handled Lacy's adoption well, but she's busy keeping things going at the shelter. We don't want to overload her."

"She said she can handle it if there aren't too many," Kade said. "It makes her happy to pair these kids with families who want them. Are you going to try to find parents for the baby?"

"Not yet. We're hoping his mama will come back looking for him. The ladies are ga-ga over the little fellow right now. We'll give it some time."

They picked up their lunch basket and jumped into the boat. "Tell you what," Kade said. "There is a room at the resort we can turn into an office for adoption needs. That is if you want it there instead of at the shelter."

"We'll talk to the girls about it," David said. "Let's get these fish home and cleaned."

As they entered the center of the river toward Crandall Island, a red speedboat barreled up beside them. "Watch out!" yelled David. "He's going to hit us."

The driver lifted a hand as the boat flew around them, snipping the side of their boat enough to push them crosswise. Kade slowed and righted the vessel.

"Pull over there." David pointed to a nearby dock. They checked the boat, but only a small dent was visible. It was a close call.

"Did you recognize that driver?" asked Kade. David shook his head, but something nagged at him. *Who was that?* He had seen that face somewhere.

Meanwhile:

Iris pulled Claire aside after lunch. "Who made you boss over the backyard playground?" she demanded. "Why did you tell Angie that Micah couldn't play on the swing?"

Claire's eyes bulged. "I didn't tell her that. I don't care if Micah plays on the swing."

"Randall says you did. And he said you didn't want Millie out there either."

"Iris, I don't know who's saying that, but it isn't me. I watched the kids play yesterday, but deciding who plays on what isn't my place. Of course, I want them all to be safe."

"Well, my daughter is my responsibility, and I will make sure she's safe. You need to worry about your own kid, not mine."

"When I went inside, Wren was out there with them," Claire said.

"Yes, Sadie appointed her to watch the children, so you needn't be bothered with them. Just keep an eye on your own from now on." Iris jerked Micah's hand and tugged her into the house.

TWENTY-TWO

Sadie answered a knock on the door in the middle of the morning, and there stood Ms. Woods, the DHS agent.

"May I help you?" asked Sadie. Ms. Woods looked like she was expecting someone to jump her any minute.

She fluttered a paper she held in her hand. "May I come in, please?"

Sadie let her in and then led her to the office. Ms. Woods sat on the edge of a chair while Sadie stood behind her desk. The woman's eyes darted around the room, and Sadie watched her.

She opened her briefcase and took out some papers. "I've been sent to investigate an adoption procedure that recently took place. Do you know anything about that?"

Sadie sat down. "Sure, I do. The question is, how do you know about it?"

Ms. Woods blinked several times. "Uh—someone reported that an illegal adoption took place here. Is that true?"

"Of course not. An adoption took place, but it was not illegal." Sadie picked up the phone. "Sophia, will you come in here, please?"

A moment later, Sophia entered. "Well, if it isn't Ms. Woods," she said. "How are you, Ms. Woods?"

"Uh—I'm fine, I guess."

Before she could say anything else, Sadie interrupted. "Sophia, you remember Ms. Woods. She is accusing us of an illegal adoption procedure."

"Really? That's interesting. Ms. Woods, I'm interested to know how you find out about what goes on in this institution."

"Uh—it was reported to our office."

"That's interesting." Sophia moved around to stand beside Sadie. "Ms. Woods, do you remember that I am a licensed attorney? What makes you think I would do anything illegal? I am an upstanding, law-abiding citizen. The directors of this establishment are law-abiding citizens. Before you believe everything you hear about us, you should consider that."

"Uh—I—"

Sadie cut her off. "Is there anything else, Ms. Woods?"

"No, I guess not."

"Then good day, ma'am." Sadie led her to the door and shut it behind her.

Sophia's eyes blazed. "Someone from here is reporting lies to the DHS. I wonder who would do that?"

"I don't know," said Sadie. "I just wish they would stop. We don't have time to deal with the aggravation. We have clients who need to heal and get on with their lives.

Jesse and Oliver plowed up a section of land behind the shelter and, with the help of Melody and Kathleen, planted a garden. It would help feed the clients and allow them to experience the joy of raising their own vegetables since most were from the city and had never done that. The clients learned to run the tiller that would keep the rows clean, and Jesse taught them how to use hoes and rakes to do the necessary work.

Mandy took charge of the work schedule, assigning older clients to take turns with the heavy duties and the younger ones to help with the lighter jobs. She posted the list in the dining room and insisted everyone do their part.

Mandy put the smaller kids to work removing cabbage worms from the cabbage, broccoli, cauliflower, and tobacco worms from the tomato plants. When the corn became high enough to hoe, Emmie and Randall were assigned the job of removing the grass. They worked hard, sweating and drinking water. When Mandy checked on them, she found they had chopped down the corn and left the grass.

She leaned over to inspect the cornrow. Her eyes widened as she picked up several corn stalks that lay wilting on the ground. "What have you done?" She shook the corn stalks in front of their faces. "This is corn. Why did you chop it down?"

Emmie looked up and down the rows. She extended her hands, palms up. "But there was more of that," she pointed to the grass, "so we thought that was the corn."

Mandy rolled her eyes. "Oh, good heavens! There's no corn left in this row. How do you expect us to have corn on the cob if you cut down all the corn? It's a good thing we have three rows left."

She sent the two kids to fill buckets and water the beans and asked Juliet and June to finish hoeing the corn. She made sure they knew which was the corn and which was the grass.

At first, the clients worked hard to maintain the garden. They discussed the dishes they would make using fresh vegetables—candied carrots, cabbage rolls, German green beans, garden salad with radish roses. The list was endless. They found recipes on David's computer and printed them to make a book. Evenings found the ladies with heads together, pouring over recipes and discussing sauces and spices they would need. They made a list for Mandy to pick up when she shopped for groceries in the city.

They harvested the early vegetables, replacing them with more plants and seeds. They planned to fill a large freezer and preserve what they could for winter.

But when the weather grew hot, the clients grumbled about working in the sweltering heat. Mandy fixed the schedule so they could work in the early morning and cooler late evenings. Some diligently attended to the assigned work, but a few refused to cooperate.

"Why do I have to pick these beans," complained Claire. "I don't even like green beans."

"Well," said Iris. "I don't like carrots, but I still have to pull the grass from the carrot row. That's a hard job because there's a lot of grass."

"Stop complaining," said Mandy. "You should all appreciate the food we can raise for ourselves."

"That's right." Juliet plopped down a bucket of new potatoes. "These will be wonderful with those green beans you're picking. Some of us didn't have it so good in our previous lives. Did we, Loreen?"

"Sure didn't," Loreen said. "I love that we can raise our own food."

"I didn't have a place to raise anything in the city," said June. "I had no money to buy seeds anyway. This garden may be a lot of work, but it's worth it. I'll gladly hoe out the weeds and dig taters and carrots. I'll pick beans and can them. Whatever it takes to have fresh food now and preserved food for winter. Yummie!"

"Hey there, little critter." Iris leaned over to speak to a black bug crawling on the ground. "Where're you going so fast, huh?"

Juliet laughed and spoke behind her hand to Loreen. "Iris is talking to the insects again."

"I know," said Loreen. "The other day, she was talking to a spider. I started to squash it, but she wouldn't let me."

"Oh, no, she doesn't want to see any insect killed. This morning, she picked up a wasp and took it outside. It didn't sting her, either."

The conversation was interrupted by a shrill scream from the other side of the garden where Marleigh ran the tiller. The cry startled the group, and heads jerked up from among the rows of plants.

"What was that?" Grace ran out from between the rows of beets and looked over the pole beans climbing up cane poles Mandy and Wren had put up. "Did someone scream?" Caroline threw down her hoe and ran toward Marleigh.

"Snake! Snake!" Brent and Jax were jumping up and down while Marleigh wielded a hoe, slamming it on the ground. A huge water moccasin coiled beside a potato vine, ready to strike.

"Stay back," Marleigh yelled when the women and children surrounded the viper. "He's a poisonous snake, and he will bite."

The snake started moving, and the women drew back to give him room. "We need to herd him back toward the river," said Loreen. They picked up sticks and tried to guide the snake, staying far enough back to be safe. Jax and Brent yelled, causing the creature to turn toward them.

"Get back, Brent," Loreen shouted. Brent ran toward the snake with his stick raised, and Loreen rushed to pull him back. The snake struck, but Loreen was between it and the boy. It bit her on the leg and then slithered toward the river. A group of screaming ladies and kids followed.

Loreen fell to the ground when the snake bit her, moaning and holding her leg.

"We have to get her to Ms. Tashina," said Marleigh. She motioned to Grace, and they helped her to Tashina's office.

Tashina treated the patient and moved her into a room next to her office to keep an eye on her. The other clients made her a special meal with fresh vegetables from the garden.

"I caused my mama to get bit by that mean old snake," Brent said. Angie and Lyric tried to comfort the boy, but he was inconsolable. He took her bouquets of black-eyed Susans and sat by her bed, holding her hand. Jax and Jamie tried to get him to play with them, but he refused to leave his mom. "She needs me," he said.

When Loreen recuperated, Brent still didn't want to be away from her. One day while Loreen was working in the laundry, Brent sat outside the door watching her.

"Brent," Sadie said, "will you come to help me with something, please?"

"But I have to stay with my mama," he replied.

"Go with Mrs. Sadie," Loreen said. "I'll be fine for a little while. She needs your help."

The boy looked from one to the other, then rose and followed Sadie. She took him to the patio, where she had started setting up a pup tent. He looked around and back at Sadie.

"What are you doing?" he asked. "Why are you putting up a tent?"

Sadie smiled. "Well, I thought maybe you, Jax, and Randall would like to sleep out here tonight. I asked Louisa and Wren to make some hotdogs, and Lyric will start a fire in the firepit so you can make smores. But I'm not sure I can put this tent up by myself. Would you help me, please?"

The boy's chest swelled, and he nodded. "I can do that. Me and my dad set up a tent once. Well, he wasn't really my dad, but he felt like it."

"Great," said Sadie. "Let's get it up." She held up a rod and looked at it. "Where does this go?"

Brent picked up the rest of the rods and then the tent. "These are tent poles. They hold the tent up." He put them in place and used a hammer to drive in the tent stakes. He brushed his hands together. "There it is—all done." He looked at Sadie. "Want me to bring some blankets?"

"I have some sleeping bags for you," she said. "You and the other boys can bring them out later tonight. Right now, let's go see if Ms. Louisa and Wren have the food ready."

Brent skipped around Sadie as they prepared a table for the food and carried out lanterns and flashlights. He chattered non-stop about his mom and his sister.

"Since she turned ten," he said, "Sage thinks she's all grown up. She tries to boss me around."

"Oh, my, she's quite a big girl now."

"But not that big. She just thinks she is." He wrestled with a tablecloth the wind tried to blow away. "I'm almost as big as she is."

"What was the name of your almost dad?" Sadie asked.

"His name is Kevin. I liked it when he took me fishing."

"Did he take you fishing a lot?"

"Not a lot, but sometimes when he had time. He worked all the time and came home tired. He yelled at Mama when she didn't clean the house or cook supper. That's why he left. 'Cause she didn't cook supper, and we were hungry."

"Oh," said Sadie. "Did he cook for you?"

"Sometimes he did. But he got tired. That's what he said. He was tired of doing everything himself. He was going to take Sage and me, but Mama wouldn't let him. She said he wasn't our daddy, and he didn't have a right. I don't know what that means."

"Sounds like he was a good man." Sadie handed him a bowl. "Here, we'll put the marshmallows in this." She set a platter beside a bag of chocolate bars. "This is for the graham crackers."

"Sage and me liked him. He told us we could live with him if Mama changed her mind. She didn't, though. Now we're here. I wonder what he's doing."

"I'll bet he still thinks about you. Maybe you'll see him again someday." Sadie hugged the boy and watched as he ran to tell Jax and Randall about the campout. She picked up a bag to put into the trash. *I wonder where this Kevin is now?*

Meanwhile:

A young woman read a story to the children and encouraged them to talk about it.

"The boy in the story didn't behave. He was supposed to listen, but he didn't." Sage pursed her lips. "Sometimes Brent and Randall don't listen to Mr. David and Mrs. Sadie like they're supposed to."

The reader raised her eyebrows. "Why do you think you have to listen to them? They aren't your bosses."

"But Mr. David and Mrs. Sadie are over us," Sage said. "Mom says they are the bosses here at the shelter."

"Well, yes, in a way, but the only ones in charge of you are your parents."

"I only have a mom to be in charge," said Randall. "I don't have a dad. I like for Mr. David to be my boss."

"All I'm saying is that if Mr. David and Mrs. Sadie tell you to do something, you don't have to unless your mom tells you. And if your mom isn't around, you don't have to do anything they say. They aren't your bosses."

Brent's head bobbed up and down. "Mr. David told me to stay out of the woods because I'd get ticks or maybe snake bit, so I don't have to listen to him? I can go into the woods whenever I want to?"

"Yes. As long as your mom doesn't tell you to stay out of the woods, you can go there to climb trees or hunt berries or whatever you like any time you want to."

TWENTY-THREE

In the middle of the night, someone beating on the door woke Tashina, and she looked through the peephole. At first, nothing was visible. Then, a blackened eye peeped back at her.

"Who is it?" Tashina called.

She could hear a mumble and called out again. "Who's there?"

"It's Nora. Please let me in, Ms. Tashina."

"Are you alone?" Nora stepped back so Tashina could see the expanse of the porch through the security camera.

"Yes, I'm alone. Please hurry."

Tashina opened the door a crack and peered out. Then she opened it further, and Nora squeezed in. She was bleeding, and her face was bruised and swollen.

"Will you help me, Ms. Tashina?"

Tashina took her by the shoulders and looked her over. Then, she led her into her office for an examination.

"What happened? Did your husband do this to you?"

Nora nodded. "He's been beating me ever since he got me back." She sniffed, then sobbed. "Mrs. Sadie told him someone would keep an eye on him. He wouldn't let me leave the house so no one would know. It never lets up. I can't stand it anymore, so I got him back."

"What do you mean, you got him back?"

"He drank a bottle of whisky like he does every night. He went to bed and passed out. I wrapped the sheet around him and tied it up. Then I beat him with a skillet 'till he quit moving."

"Did you kill him?"

"Probably not, but I don't care. He has killed me over and over since we married fifteen years ago. Now it's his turn."

Tashina cleaned her wounds and bandaged them. "You know, of course, that if you killed him, you could be charged with murder."

"I don't care about that either. Anything is better than the torment I've lived through these fifteen years. They can't do any more to me than he has already."

Tashina went to the other room and returned carrying a camera. "We'll take pictures of you and record the date and time. This is, without a doubt, a case of self-defense." She took pictures of Nora from all sides and wrote a report on a form she placed in Nora's case file. She pulled out other documents from the file and looked them over. She and Sadie had recorded the previous abuse Nora had endured. She wished she had taken pictures of her then.

Nora would stay in the room she'd had before, and Tashina helped her up the steps. Nora stopped about halfway up.

"Is Iris still here?" Nora asked.

"Yes. Why?"

"Just wondered." Nora took a few more steps. "How is she doing? I've been concerned about her."

Tashina frowned. "Why? Did you and she form a friendship while you were here before?"

"No. She's married to my husband's brother. He treats her just like his brother treats me. Maybe even worse."

"I didn't know that. Neither of you mentioned it before."

"No, because we were never close. We don't like each other."

"Why?"

"It's a long story. Bad history. I don't want to talk about it."

"Okay. That's fine." Tashina started back up the steps, holding Nora's arm. She talked to Sadie about the situation the next day after Sadie had counseled Nora.

The others welcomed Nora back, but Sadie noticed that Iris held back. She hadn't seen that before, probably because she hadn't paid attention. Later in the dining room, Nora seemed irritated by Iris's conversation with Juliet. Sadie had stepped out the door but was close enough to see and hear the argument.

"I heard you talking about our mother-in-law," Nora told Iris. "Just because Jill caters to you doesn't make you better than me."

Iris rolled her eyes. "Jill doesn't cater to me. Unlike you, I get along with her, that's all."

"Sure. Because you do whatever petty little thing she asks you to do."

"Nora," Iris said, "I try to get along with my mother-in-law. I know she can be a witch. She likes to dominate everything and everyone. I want to keep peace in my home, and you know how impossible that is living with her sons." She pointed to a scar on her cheek.

"I guess keeping peace means sleeping with my husband?"

Iris jumped up, her face beet red. "I've told you a thousand times I didn't sleep with your husband."

Nora pressed her lips together. "Then how do you explain how your youngest child looks like Griffith?"

Iris leaned over until her face was inches from Nora's. "Well, stupid, Griffith and Hudson are brothers. Duh." She whirled and started walking away, but Nora grabbed and spun her around. A slap reverberated around the room. Iris shook her head, rubbed her face, and rammed her shoulder into Nora. Nora slugged Iris in the stomach. Iris doubled over, and Nora shoved her backward. Then she dove on top of her. The two women writhed on the floor, slapping, hitting, and pulling hair.

Juliet tried unsuccessfully to separate the two until Sadie ran into the room and helped her pull them apart. Iris jumped to her feet. She piled into Nora, knocking Sadie down. While Juliet helped Sadie up, Iris grabbed Nora by the hair.

"Stop it!" Sadie yelled. "Stop it right now!"

They had only heard Sadie speak in soft tones. Surprised, they turned to look at her. Her hands were on her hips, and, like a sudden thunderstorm, she looked ready to strike lightning.

"Why are you fighting like animals? Didn't you come here to get away from such uncivilized behavior? How dare you fall back into that kind of boorish conduct."

Nora scowled at Iris and gritted her teeth. Iris hung her head.

"I'm sorry, Mrs. Sadie," Iris said.

Nora glanced at Iris, then lowered her eyes. "I'm sorry, too. When I think of my mother-in-law, I get so mad."

Sadie crossed her arms and glared at them. "The two of you need to make up and support each other instead of fighting."

Iris held out her hand, and Nora took it, then burst into tears. "Do you know that she laughed at me when you said you were pregnant with Micah?"

"Jill laughed at you? I didn't know that." Iris moved close to Nora. "Why did she laugh at you?"

Nora grimaced. "She said she was glad I couldn't have children because I would never be a fit mother." The tears flowed again.

"Oh, Nora. I'm so sorry. I didn't know that." She hugged Nora and comforted her until the tears stopped."

"I guess I've been angry at you for being able to have kids when I can't." Nora wiped her face with a tissue Sadie gave her.

"I'm sorry Jill treated you like that," Iris said. "You would be a perfect mother. I think Jill is jealous of us because her sons chose to marry us instead of staying home with Mommie."

"Well, she has them now. Since we left, they'll move back home because they can't care for themselves."

Iris grinned. "That's probably true," she said as they turned to leave the room.

Sadie watched them leave, then sat in a dining chair. She laid her head on the table and wept. She'd had such a good home with loving parents. *Why do some people have to endure such unspeakable behaviors from those who are supposed to love them?* Since the shelter opened, she had heard unbelievable things from the women and children who came for help. How could she possibly help these people? She had no experience in that area. Even when her dad turned into a crazed man and tried to destroy David, he never mistreated her, Kade, or their mom, and she knew he loved them.

And what about arguing and slacking off duties? Should the clients be responsible for the household chores? Mandy did most of the housework, but the clients were responsible for keeping their rooms clean and helping with general housekeeping. Maybe they should hire another person to do the laundry and housework like they did the kitchen work. But no, Mason had advised them to have the clients take care of the household chores. He said responsibilities give them purpose and make them feel like they belong. So why are they constantly fussing?

David may be right. I may need to be stern with them about their responsibilities. Maybe I should discipline them when they fuss and argue.

She raised her head and wiped her face with a napkin. "I'm not their mama," she stated aloud. "I'm their counselor. It's my job to counsel them, not discipline them."

She heard something behind her, and when she turned, there stood Louisa, smiling at her.

"Sugar babe," Louisa said. "You arguing with yerself? Sounds to me like maybe you gots a problem that needs worked out."

Sadie looked at Louisa with tearful eyes. "Oh, Louisa. I just don't know what to do. The ladies keep fussing, and sometimes they won't do their chores. They are grown women, for heaven's sake!"

Louisa pulled out a chair and sat down. "These ladies have been through a lot," she said, "but they gotta get their lives back to normal. Those who have been abused have been made to feel like they have no value. I know. I've been there. And those addicted have thought of nothing else but the next fix for a long time. They need to relearn the basic things about responsibilities."

"I haven't been there," Sadie said, "but I understand that. I mean, I learned about that when I was taking classes."

"It's one thing to learn from a book, but quite another to learn it by experience." Louisa laid a hand on Sadie's arm. "Girlie, you are these ladies' counselor, but you may have to take another role. You may have to be sorta a mama to them, too."

"Really? You think so?" Sadie wrinkled her nose. "Some of them are older than me."

"Age has got nothing to do with it, Sadie. With what these people have been through, they ain't the same. Their sense of value needs to be restored. And their sense of responsibility."

"How can I do that?"

"I believe one thing is to hold them accountable for their behaviors. When one client puts down another, that reinforces the feeling of worthlessness. They cain't get by with that. They have to honor and uphold each other." Louisa fiddled with a napkin. "At least, that's what I think."

"Louisa, I value your opinions. You make a better counselor than I do by far." Sadie smiled at the older woman. "I'm glad you came by and even happier you stopped to talk to me."

Meanwhile:

"You all right?" Madison sidled up to Tina during the afternoon personal time. "You look terrible."

Tina rubbed her nose and leaned against the wall. "Yeah, I'm okay."

Madison looked around. Then seeing they were alone, she lowered her voice. "If you need one, I can get you a fix."

Tina's face lit up. "Really? How?" Then she shook her head. "No, I'd better not. I gotta consider my kids."

Madison snickered. "How does it benefit your kids when you need a fix so bad you can barely function? Tell me that."

Tina slumped. "Ms. Tashina told me she would help me. She says it takes time."

"Yeah, right." Madison snickered again. "Forget that. I can fix you up so's you can feel better right away. You just say the word."

Tina's face contorted, and she twisted a lock of hair while Madison waited. After a while, Madison turned away. "When you can't stand the pain, holler. I'll be around."

"Wait." Tina moved toward her. "What do you want me to do? I need a fix bad."

Madison grinned. "Oh, I think I can make a deal you can afford."

TWENTY-FOUR

Sadie took Louisa's advice and started a program to teach the clients to encourage and promote one another. She set up a reward system for those who gave compliments and praise. Things went well until Sadie realized the compliments were dished out like pecan pie, too sweet and too often to be healthy. She stopped the rewards and brought in a speaker who talked to them about building up the self-worth of others.

The improvement was noticeable, and the clients seemed to offer sincere compliments to one another. When Sadie counseled individuals, she could see positive results from the effort.

She also tightened the reins with discipline for those who neglected their duties, making them do their chores during their free time. She found it harder for the ones who were addicts than the ones who were in the shelter because of abuse. Those who were there because of abuse quickly learned to help those who struggled with addictions as they faced the temptation to regress.

David completed his coursework, earning a degree in Social Work. He enjoyed taking over therapy with the male clients, who were all kids. He and Sadie swapped stories every night about the clients.

"I can't seem to get through to Madison," Sadie said. "She resists everything I suggest to her. She doesn't seem interested in being rehabilitated."

"Have you found out her background?" David asked.

"A little. As much as she will reveal. She's so secretive. She says her parents divorced when she was little, and her dad was never involved in her life."

"What about her mom?"

Sadie grimaced. "She won't say much about her. Only that she drinks a lot. I get the feeling her mom never paid much attention to her."

"That's too bad. Sometimes, parents are unaware of what they do to their kids. Or else they don't care."

"I think they care," Sadie said. "They're just so broken and trapped by their own bondages, they can't see how it affects their families."

"If we can provide mental help to these we have, maybe they will make good parents for future generations."

"Yes, for sure." Sadie stretched and yawned. "By the way, did Claire tell you she wants to return to the city and get a job? It seems someone she knows works at a bank and has offered her a position."

"Really? That's great. Do you think she's ready?"

"Yes, I do. She's strong now, and she's good with numbers. The person who notified her said she has room for them until Claire gets on her feet. I think it will be good for her."

"Well, then, we'll help her out."

"Also, June is asking about the cost of attending nursing classes. I told her I would find some information for her."

"That's great. I'm sure you can find something to help her." David reached out his hand to pull her up. "I'm glad to see our clients return to normal lives and make it on their own."

As Sadie started to go into the bedroom, she pulled up short. "I almost forgot to tell you. Some money is missing—again. Not a lot, but enough to cause concern."

"Really? You looked everywhere?"

She rolled her eyes. "Yes, I looked everywhere. So did Sophia. It's missing, David. Not lost—missing. Someone around here has sticky fingers."

"That's crazy. How can anyone get into the safe?"

"It wasn't in the safe. I took out the bank bag to give to Sophia. She was leaving to go into the city, and I wanted her to deposit it. I laid it on my desk and turned to get my purse and jacket. I thought it was different when I picked it up like it wasn't where I thought I put it. But I shrugged it off and took it to Sophia. When she opened the bag, two twenties and a ten were missing. I know I counted it right. I wrote the amount on a sticky note and put it with the adding machine receipt. We can't figure it out."

"We'll have to watch for anyone with unexplained money or purchases. That's all I know to do. I don't want to search the client's rooms. That would be an invasion of their privacy."

Mandy came into the dining room at the end of lunch. "Has anyone seen Tina?" she asked. "She didn't bring out her sheets for the laundry."

Heads shook as the clients looked at one another. "I saw her last night," said Grace. "She said she wasn't feeling good and went to bed early."

"I'll go check on her," said Angie. Soon, she ran back into the room. "Something's wrong with her. She's in her room, but she isn't acting right."

Tashina ran to Tina's room, followed by Grace and Caroline. Caroline picked up a small bottle from the nightstand. White powder with a few small crystals fell into her hand when she shook it.

"Tina, what have you done?" asked Tashina.

"Oh, Ms. Tashina, my head hurts something fierce." Tina held her head in both hands and groaned.

Caroline held up the bottle. "Where did you get this? What is it?"

Tina looked at the bottle through squinted eyes and waved her hand. "Oh, that. It's nothing." She giggled and jumped up. "Give it to me, Caroline." She grabbed her head and moaned.

Tashina pushed her down onto the bed. "Let me look at you," she said. She listened to her breathing and measured her pulse. She took the bottle from Caroline and looked at the contents.

"Where did you get these drugs?"

Tina laughed. "It doesn't matter, now does it, Ms. Tashina? As long as I'm happy. Right, Caroline?"

"Sit down in this chair," Tashina said. "We've got to get your heart rate down and your breathing regulated. We'll talk later about where this stuff came from." She sent Caroline downstairs to get a glass of water.

"Tina, you were doing so good with your rehab. What happened?"

"Ah, Ms. Tashina, I needed a fix so bad, and someone gave it to me. Is that so wrong?"

"Yes, it is. Very wrong. You'll have to start all over. You don't want that, do you?"

Tina's head rolled back. "But it feels so good! Way better than needing a fix so bad I can't stand it. Better than feeling tired all the time."

Tashina put a hand on Tina's brow. "Better than getting well so you can be a mother to Emmie and Randall? They need you, Tina."

Sadie came rushing through the door. "Tina, Caroline says you got some drugs from somewhere."

"She did," Tashina said. "But she's going to try harder and get better. Aren't you, Tina?"

"Oh, Tina." Sadie sat on the bed beside her. "I know it must be hard, but don't you think it will be worth it to be drug-free? Don't you think you deserve that? Don't you think Emmie and Randall deserve that?"

"I don't know about me, but my kids deserve it," Tina said.

"If you want it bad enough, you can do it," Tashina said. "We'll help get you through it. Caroline and Grace will also be there for you. They know what you're going through, and they'll help you."

"Will you do it, Tina? Will you agree to go through the program to be better?"

Tina nodded. "I'll do it for my kids," she said. "And for myself."

David and Sadie were taking a break on the patio one afternoon when they heard a commotion.

"Look what we found!" Randall, Brent, and Jax came running to the back of the shelter, dragging a toe-sack.

Lyric and Angie ran to look. "What is it?" Lyric asked.

Angie peered in when Brent opened the top of the sack. "It's a turtle. What are you gonna do with it?"

"Yeah, a big one!" Jax yelled. "We caught it down by the river."

"Mr. Jeb says turtles make good soup, so we're gonna take it to Louisa so she can make turtle soup," said Randall. "Man, I bet she'll make it good. She's a good cook."

David and Sadie looked at each other. "I've got to see this," said David.

"Me too," Sadie said. They jumped up and followed the kids to the kitchen door at the back of the shelter.

"Ms. Louisa!" yelled Randall. "We have something for you."

"What in the world?" Louisa ran to the door and peeped into the sack they held open. Her eyes grew round, and she put a hand over her mouth. "Why, it's a turtle! Now, what would I want with a turtle?"

"For turtle soup," Jax said.

"Yeah." Brent's head bobbed up and down. "You can make turtle soup. I bet you make the best turtle soup on the island."

Lyric looked into the sack. "It's a big ol' snapper. You let him get a hold on you, he won't let go until it thunders."

Louisa's boisterous laugh made her belly shake. "I don't know iffen it's true, but I always heard that. I sho' don't want 'im gettin' a hold on me."

David winked at Sadie. "Louisa, are you going to make turtle soup?" he asked.

"Well," she drawled, "I guess it depends. I need someone to clean 'im. I ain't gonna cook 'im 'til he's dressed and ready. You gonna do that fer me?"

David's eyes widened. "Are you serious? You'll really cook him and make turtle soup? Have you made turtle soup before?"

Louisa nodded. "Shore have. It's good, too."

David scratched his head while Sadie laughed at him. "I've cleaned and dressed venison, rabbit, squirrel, and fish, but I've never cleaned a turtle," he said. "I think I'll see if Jerome will do it."

Lyric and the little boys ran to find Jerome, who laughed and agreed to do the job. The next day, they would have turtle soup for supper.

Some ladies hesitated to try the soup, and some outright refused, but most agreed it was delicious. The boys were delighted, declaring Louisa their hero.

"We're gonna catch more turtles so you can make turtle soup every day," declared Jax.

Juliet rubbed his head. "Son," she said, "Ms. Louisa doesn't want to make turtle soup every day. Maybe wait a while before you catch another one."

Meanwhile:

"Come on, Millie." June hurried the little girl as they ran toward the dock. "We've got to get off this island before the storm gets here."

Millie clung to her mother with one hand and wiped her tears with the other. "Why can't we stay at the shelter with the others? I'm scared."

"Because it ain't safe on this island no matter where we are. If the tornado hits this place, there'll be nothing left. We need to get to the mainland."

They reached the dock, and June untied a small motorboat. She lifted Millie into the boat and started the motor. She steered the boat around the port into the river and then headed around the end of the island toward the chute. The wind picked up as she entered the chute, pushing her against the island bank.

"Hold on, Millie," she shouted. She wrestled with the tiller, trying to steer the boat to the other side. She was determined to reach the mainland.

As she reached the deeper water, angry waves lapped over the side of the rocking boat. Blackness descended, and the thick air felt stifling. Lightning flashed across the sky, and the vessel drifted back toward the island. Millie cried out, and when June turned to her, the tiller jerked out of her hand, and the boat spun. June fought to regain control, but the wind whipped the boat crossways, tipping it over.

TWENTY-FIVE

"Everyone get into the safe room," David shouted as the clients and employees left the dining room after lunch. "A tornado has been sighted heading this way."

As they herded everyone into the room that had previously served as the vault, David remarked to Sadie. "Thank God we had the foresight to turn this into a safe room."

"Yes. It's a little small, but everyone will be safe here." Before David shut the door, Sadie counted heads. "Someone is missing," she said. She turned to the ashen faces looking at her. "Who's missing? We're short two people."

Marleigh spoke up. "Ms. Sadie, June said she's scared to be here with a storm coming. She said she and Millie are getting off the island. She headed for the dock."

"Yeah, Mr. David," Loreen said. "Why can't we leave the island? It isn't safe here."

"For one thing," David said, "it's too late. We don't want to get caught on the river in the middle of the storm. But I've lived on this island most of my life, and it's been through many storms. A tornado has never hit here before."

"But there's a first time for everything," Iris said. The others nodded, their eyes wide.

"And that's why we're sheltering in this safe room. So, we'll be safe whatever happens." David pulled the heavy door shut. The lights went out, and the generator took over to provide light and air.

"What about June and Millie?" Sadie whispered. "They're out there. You know they're in danger."

David called Jerome and Officer Jason, then reassured Sadie. "They will find her."

Mamas comforted their frightened children, and Sadie tried to lighten the mood by starting a familiar song. "Come on, everyone, sing along!"

A few joined in, and soon, everyone sang and made motions to children's songs. Sadie moved to stand close to Juliet when she heard Jamie crying.

"Mama," Jamie said, "what will happen to Millie?"

"Officer Jason and Mr. Jerome will find her," Juliet said. "She'll be all right."

But she wasn't.

The storm ended quickly, leaving uprooted trees and some structural damage. Thankfully, the levees built by Oliver in the past couple of years held the water back, so minor water damage occurred.

June and little Millie were missing, along with a boat from the dock. A search party spent the rest of the day looking for them. Islanders came to help.

"Jason, over here," an islander yelled. Jason and Jerome ran to see what was going on. There, against an uprooted willow tree, a johnboat lay upside down.

Jerome turned the boat over. "Yes," he said, "this is our boat." He looked at David, who joined the two men. "It doesn't look good," he said.

Other members of the search team walked up. "At least it's on the chute side," one said. "If it were on the riverside, there'd be little hope to find them."

The rescue team searched the island through the night, then started working along the chute the next morning. When they found nothing, they started dragging the river. The river was at an average low for summer, so the work went quickly. The rescue team in a boat working on the mainland side of the chute yelled.

"We got something," a member yelled. All the boats pulled to the bank, and the teams crowded around to see. A woman's body lay crumpled against the roots of a tree, and a child's body lay half-buried in mud and leaf mold several feet away.

Sadness consumed the shelter. Clients wandered around aimlessly or slumped in chairs for days. Food was left uneaten, and daily routines abandoned.

"Mama, where is Millie?" little Jamie asked for the hundredth time. "When will she be back to play with me?"

Juliet tried to explain every time the child asked her mama the question. "Jamie, Millie is in heaven with Jesus." She didn't know how to comfort the child over losing her best friend. She needed comfort herself. Willow Grove clients had become a close-knit family; losing one was hard, but Juliet had felt a closeness with June.

They held a funeral in the island chapel and transported the bodies to June's hometown for a service with her family. Sadie met with each client to help them deal with their feelings. Willow Grove would never be the same.

Soon after that, Mr. Fields from DHS visited the shelter.

"We've received a report that someone has died here due to an unsafe environment," he said.

David fumed. "Sir, I think the best thing for you to do is to leave now. We lost a client because she tried to leave the island during a major storm. Everyone who stayed here was safe. It was a bad decision for her, and we would have stopped her had we known. Now we are mourning the loss of someone close to us, so goodbye." David slammed the door in the man's face.

Meanwhile:

"You'll do what I say!" The man slapped the young woman hard, and she fell beside a young girl. "Now, get up and make yourself presentable. Both of you," He kicked the woman in the side. She cowered, pulling the adolescent female close to her. The man slammed the door and locked it behind him.

"Mama, what are we gonna do?" The child whimpered, and the woman pushed the girl's dark hair out of her face. "I don't know," she said. "We have to find a way out of here."

She rose and pulled the girl to her feet. She rummaged in a trunk and found a floral dress and a matching shawl for herself and a red dress for the girl. They dressed themselves and combed their hair. The woman wiped the girl's face and then her own. Soon, the door opened, and the man jerked them out into a hallway. A man waited there, grinning at them.

"This is Roy," he said. "Do what he asks you to do." The man shoved them toward Roy. They followed Roy into a room, and he closed the door.

The woman pushed the girl behind her as she approached Roy. "What a handsome man you are." Her soft voice wavered as she touched his cheek. His eyes sparkled, and he put his arm around her. He moved her aside so he could see the girl. "I'm looking forward to you," he told the girl.

The woman wrapped the shawl around the man's neck while rubbing her thin body against him. He reached for the girl, and she jerked the cloth tight, pulling him back. He grappled, but she used all her strength to strangle him. He fell to the floor, and she gave one last jerk, grabbed the girl's hand, and fled.

TWENTY-SIX

A fter the storm, Willow Grove clients and employees worked together with island families picking up debris, and men used chainsaws to remove fallen trees from yards and roadways. New friendships formed as the islanders became acquainted with the shelter clients.

"I thought y'all were dumb crackheads," one man told Juliet. "Actually, y'all are all pretty nice."

"I've never been on any kind of drug," Juliet replied.

"Isn't the shelter for druggies?"

Juliet smiled at the man. "Not really. There are a few here who were addicted to drugs, but others of us are here because of domestic abuse. And some fell into hard luck and became homeless."

The man gaped at Juliet. "Domestic abuse? Why, I thought—"

"We're just people, Mr. Walters, who need some help. The Kingstons have offered us a hand-up so we can have normal, successful lives."

Iris had an idea to sow wild-flower seeds in the bare spots where trees had fallen. Lyric wanted to plant trees, and Angie suggested they grow fruit and nut trees. David found a company in the city that donated tree seedlings and a seed company that donated flower seeds for the project. The clients and islanders discussed what to plant where and shared their anticipation for the beauty of the island the following year.

While they were working to restore and add to the beauty of Crandall Island, a tall, thin, white-haired man appeared and began working alongside them. At first, no one noticed him. Without a word, he picked up a shovel and dug a hole for a tree Marleigh was holding. As she planted the sapling, he moved to stand by Loreen.

"Is this where you want to plant it?" he asked.

"Yes, I think this is the perfect spot." She planted the young tree and picked up another one.

When the man put his foot on the shovel to dig a hole, his ankle twisted, and he fell to the ground.

"Oh, are you alright?" Marleigh looked at his ankle, which was starting to swell. She yelled for help, and David ran to investigate the trouble.

"We'll have to get him into the clinic," he said. They helped him onto the Ranger and took him to see Tashina.

"Who is that guy?" David asked Sadie. "I don't remember ever seeing him before."

"I don't know," Sadie said. "I've never seen him before today. He was helping Loreen earlier. Maybe she knows who he is."

"I haven't seen him before today," Loreen said. "I thought he was one of the islanders."

"I'd better go find out who he is," David said. He arrived at the clinic just as the man was hobbling out on a pair of crutches. He approached the man and introduced himself.

The man smiled, moved the crutches to one side, and bowed. "Name's Cox. Charlie Cox. I'm glad to know you, David." He looked down at his bandaged ankle. Ms. Tashina fixed me up with a comfrey poultice. She says if I leave it on all night, I'll be fine in a day or two."

"Tashina knows what she's doing," David said. "I know for a fact that comfrey works wonders."

Charlie adjusted his crutches. "Tashina was telling me about the work you're doing here. It's good for you to help those who've suffered so much at the hands of others. God bless you for doing that."

"Thank you," David said. "Are you from here, Mr. Cox? I was raised on this island, so I thought I knew about everyone."

"Well, I guess you might say I'm from here," he said. "Your dad, Jesse—a fine man—was raised on this island, right? And Oliver Crandall was, too. Isn't that so?"

David cocked his head. "Yes. You know my parents and Mr. Crandall?"

"Well, yes, you might say that. You know, this island has seen a lot through the years." He laughed. "If only it could talk, right?" Another gentle, infectious laugh.

David agreed. "Do you need a ride somewhere? Do you live nearby?"

Charlie glanced around and shook his head. "Oh, no. I'm okay. If I could just sit here a while, that would help. These old bones aren't as pliable as they used to be."

David helped him to a chair and sat across from him. "I'm just curious," he said, "about how you ended up here helping us today."

Charlie laughed. "That's a story. I was on my way to the craft village to pick up some of those fine jellies and jams they sell over there. Have you had any of those? They are the best I've had, and I've tasted a lot."

"Yes, they are very good," David said. "They don't last long around here."

"Well, anyway, I decided to take the path around the island. It's such a beautiful day, and I always enjoy a good walk. You walk, don't you? I think I've seen you and your pretty wife walking a few times."

"Yes, we like to walk, and we do quite often." David scratched his head. Why had he never seen this man before?

Charlie smiled and continued. "When I came to this end of the island, I saw people all over the place working. I started to go in a different direction. I'm a little shy about being around a lot of people, you know. It's an impediment I need to overcome, I guess. I like people, but...." He thought for a moment. "You know, I had a feeling I needed to help. That I should help. Something inside me wouldn't allow me to leave."

"Maybe that small, still voice that often guides us to do things we don't want to do, huh?" A small voice inside David encouraged him to befriend this stranger.

"Yes!" Charlie blinked and nodded. That's it. I guess God wanted me to meet you for some reason." He gazed toward the ceiling. "I wonder why?" The question seemed to be directed more at himself than at David.

"Who can tell the mind of God?" David said. "Guess He directed you here for some reason."

"God has a way of putting us with those we need and those who need us. Guess He figured I need y'all. I've been feeling lonely for the past year." Charlie looked at the floor. "I don't like to admit it, but I guess I've needed someone."

David put a hand on his shoulder. "I have a feeling that's why you're here. Say, have you had supper? Would you join us? Our Louisa is the best cook around."

"Why, thank you so much," Mr. Cox said. "I'd like nothing better. A little work stirs a man's appetite, wouldn't you say?" He hobbled inside, and David introduced him to everyone. He bowed at each person when they were introduced.

The conversation was pleasant, and whenever anyone broached the subject of Mr. Cox's past, he changed to a different topic. His stories kept them laughing, so it wasn't hard to forget that he was a stranger. In fact, he knew so much about the island, the shelter, and the Kingstons that they felt they had known him forever.

"You've done a good job turning the casino into this shelter," Charlie said to David and Sadie as they sat on the patio overlooking the beautiful backyard. "Oliver had a great idea designing this building in the colonial style. It's almost like he had a premonition that this wouldn't always be a casino. It's perfect for the role it plays now."

"That's true," said David. "Sadie and I love the design. It gives class to the island, we think. And the layout is perfect for our needs."

"Have you seen Kade's resort?" asked Sadie. "It's really nice."

"Oh, yes," Cox replied. "The hotel Oliver built. I think it makes a better resort than just a hotel. Kade did a great job with it."

David frowned. "Have you met Kade?"

"Oh, well, I've seen him and heard good things about him. He's a great guy. And his beautiful wife, Sophia. That boy of theirs is a dandy, too. Such a wonderful family." Charlie motioned toward the river. "You know, this big ol' river has quite a past. It's seen a lot of traffic. That sure was something when it ran backward back in 1812 during that big earthquake. That was a hard time for a lot of people." He looked back at David. "You know, that was before your ancestors purchased this island." He grinned. "Buying this property while it was cheap was a genius move on the part of your great, great grandfather."

David didn't know how to answer. *Who is this man? How does he know these things?*

Charlie rose "Guess I'd better be going. Don't want to overstay and make myself a nuisance."

"Let me bring around the Ranger, and I'll take you home," David said.

"You can drive me a ways. My house is kind of secluded, so I'll have to walk to it. I don't mind, though. It's a beautiful day and I have these things to help me." He hit one crutch against the other and laughed.

A few days later, David ran into Jeb at the craft village and asked about Mr. Cox.

"I don't know 'im," Jeb said. "I know pretty much everyone around here. We all thought he was one of your bunch."

"Help! Somebody!" Jax ran through the kitchen door of the shelter. "Ms. Louisa, Brent is hurt."

Louisa ran to the boy. "What happened? Where is he?"

Jax sat down to catch his breath. "Oh, Ms. Louisa, Brent fell out of a tree. He's hurt bad." He started to cry.

Louisa ran into the hall. "Mr. Kingston!" she yelled. David came out of his office to see what was going on.

Jax wiped his sweaty face. "Brent climbed a tree and fell out, Mr. David." He gasped for air again. "He's hurt." He jumped up and ran out the door with David close behind. They ran through the brush until they came to where Brent lay with Randall kneeling beside him. Randall jumped up.

"Mr. David, he fell from there." He pointed to a limb several feet from the ground.

"What in the world are you boys doing out here climbing trees?" David yelled. "Haven't I told you to stay out of the woods? Now look what has happened."

He leaned over the hurt boy and examined him to ensure he was conscious. Then he checked to see if any bones were broken. "Go get Ms. Tashina and Jerome," he ordered Randall. "And tell Jerome to bring the Ranger as far as he can. And bring a stretcher. We don't know what damage has occurred.

Brent moved to show David he could sit up, but yelped and lay back. "I'm sorry, Mr. David. I wanted to look at that nest up there."

"Yeah," said Randall. "Jax said he saw a squirrel go in it, and Brent wanted to see if there were baby squirrels."

David looked up into the tree branches. "It's too late for baby squirrels, guys. They are too fast for you to catch. Even if you did catch one, the squirrel would bite you."

"But Mr. Jeb told us he had a pet squirrel once. Said he caught it when it was a baby and raised it."

"Well, you can't catch a squirrel. If you want a pet, we'll find you a cat or something."

Brent winced when Randall jumped up. "I want a pet skunk," Randall said.

"No pet skunks. No wild animals for pets." David rose when the sound of the Ranger reached him. He was relieved Jerome was able to drive it through the bushes.

Tashina checked Brent over before they put him on the stretcher and loaded him on the back of the Ranger. David and Randall held on to him as they rocked back and forth over the rough terrain. She diagnosed him as bruised when they carried him into Tashina's clinic.

"He'll have to stay in bed for a couple of days to heal," she said. "He'll soon be as good as new."

The boys' mamas put them in a soapy bath to remove ticks, chiggers, and dirt. Something fell onto the floor when Iris picked up the boys' dirty clothes for the laundry. When she searched the jeans pockets, she found several old coins. As she threw the jeans into the washer, she laid the coins in a dish on a shelf and forgot them until supper when the boys talked about finding them.

"Jax, what did you do with those old coins we found?" asked Randall. While Jax thought about it, Randall continued. "There was a big ol' tree almost rotted down," he said, "and it had a hole at the bottom."

"Yeah," Jax said. "We followed a rabbit, and he went into the hole. We tried to get him out with a stick, but an old box fell out. It had coins inside."

The adults in the room looked wide-eyed at each other. "An old box?" Wren asked. "Where is it now?"

"We left it there," Randall said. "It's too old to bother with. All rusty."

"What was inside it?" asked Madison. "Did you say you brought some home?"

Iris jumped up and retrieved the coins from the laundry room. She spread them out on the table, and everyone gathered to look at them.

"David, these may be worth something," said Sadie.

He looked closely at one. "I guess so! This is gold!" Hands reached out to grab the coins, but David stopped them. "Whoa," he said. "We need to have these evaluated to see what they're worth. Sadie, put them in a container. I'll take them in the next few days."

After supper, he asked Randall and Jax where they found the metal box. David followed the boys through the woods. He wondered if they were taking him across the island as they made their way through vines, bushes, and trees. He did a doubletake when he saw someone running through the trees.

"Who was that?" Randall yelled. The person disappeared through the brush.

Finally, they came to a log over a crevice in the ground. "There it is," shouted Jax. "It's that big tree over there."

Sure enough, the rusty metal box lay beside a large oak tree. A large hole in the bottom of the tree stared back at them like a one-eyed forest gnome. David picked up the box and looked inside. It was empty. He used a stick to poke around the inside of the hole. Something was there. He reached inside and pulled out another box. When he opened it, he gasped.

Meanwhile:

"Franny, I've found out where the kids are. You know that island across from Ashport? That's where they are."

"On an island? Are you sure? How'd you find out?" Franny hadn't seen her grandchildren since her daughter-in-law left and took the twins.

"Yeah, I'm sure. Some woman told Dover about a shelter they have over there, and I checked it out. She's there, all right. Her and the kids. No wonder we haven't been able to find them. I don't know why in the world she would take them to a place like that."

"Now, Ralph, you know how mean Rafe was to her. I guess she finally got tired of it. Anyway, how are we gonna see those kids? I sure am missin' 'em."

"I'm gonna borrow a boat from Dover and go get 'em, that's how. We are those young'uns grandparents, and we got a right to see them."

"We sure do. You bring 'em back here, and we'll take care of 'em. If Juliet wants to come, bring her, too. Rafe'll be outta jail in a month or so, and he'll be glad to have her back."

TWENTY-SEVEN

"Mom! Help!" Loreen ran into Brent's room in the middle of the night.

"What is it, son? What's wrong?" Brent was squirming in his bed, scratching all over.

"Mom, I itch all over."

Loreen pushed back the covers and pulled the lamp close. Red whelps covered Brent's stomach, underarms, and private parts. "I'll go get Ms. Tashina."

Tashina looked closely at the boy and sighed. "It's chiggers. See those tiny red dots? That's chiggers. I'll get something for him."

While she went to the clinic, Randall stumbled down the hall, followed by Jax and Juliet. Both boys were scratching and groaning.

Ms. Tashina returned with ointment to kill the chiggers and vinegar to stop the itching. "Now, don't scratch," she ordered. She gave them a bottle of vinegar and some cotton balls. "Use these when you itch," she said. "It will help. But the more you scratch, the more you'll itch, so don't scratch."

Brent started to scratch, but his mom slapped his hand. Juliet did the same when Jax's hand reached for his belly.

The following day, three red-faced boys hobbled to breakfast. They would start to scratch, then fling their hands and grimace.

"What's wrong with the boys?" asked Mandy.

David looked at them, and then recognition dawned on

his face. "Chiggers, right?" He laughed. "I'm sorry, but I had a couple of those. You know why I didn't get more like you guys? I put a little bleach in my bath water. Yep. Washes those tiny red monsters right down the drain."

Juliet glared at him. "Why didn't you tell us? We could have saved the boys from the torment caused by those creatures."

"I'm sorry. I should have thought of that." David patted the boys' heads. "Sorry, guys. And sorry, moms.

Another visit from DHS, this time a Mr. Green.

"Someone reported that you are providing clients with drugs," he said to David. "And--" he looked over his horn-rim glasses. "That children here are being abused. Did one of your child clients recently suffer from a broken arm and bruises? And is it true that you did not take him to the hospital for care?"

David stared at the man, then excused himself. "Give me a minute," he said. "I'll be right back." In a few minutes, he returned with Brent and Tashina.

"Brent, will you tell Mr. Green what happened to you?"

Brent looked from David to Mr. Green. "I got chiggers all over and thought I'd itch to death," he said.

David blinked. "That's true, but I meant how you got hurt."

"Oh," Brent said. He turned to Mr. Green. "I fell out of a tree. I wanted to catch a baby squirrel. I wanted one for a pet."

Mr. Green sneered and leaned down to look into the boy's eyes. "Did someone tell you to say that?"

Brent shook his head. "No. I still have some red spots. You want to see?" He pulled his shirt up.

Mr. Green stepped back. "No, I don't want to see your spots."

Brent lowered his shirt. "Well, that's what happened.

Don't you believe me?"

Tashina stepped forward and put her hand on Brent's shoulder. "The boy is telling the truth, Mr. Green. There are no broken bones, only bruises. I am an APRN. If you don't know what that is, it means Advanced Practice Registered Nurse. I am well qualified to care for my patients, sir."

"Well, what about providing your clients with drugs?" Mr. Green pressed his lips together. "Huh? What about that?"

Tashina's eyes flashed. "Mr. Green, the only drugs provided to our clients are those necessary for relief from pain and necessary for healing. There are no other drugs here."

"Someone told us that you gave a client marijuana."

"No, sir, no marijuana was given by us to a client. Our clients may obtain drugs from another source, but that is not our doing. We don't have absolute control over everyone here. We do our best to monitor what comes in, but we are not omnipotent, sir. Are you?"

Mr. Green backed toward the door. "I guess I'm through here," he said. He made a mark on the paper he held. "I'm sorry to have bothered you."

"There's just one thing I'd like to know," said David. "Who is making these allegations? Who is your informer?"

Mr. Green blushed. "I'm not at liberty to say." He turned to leave, then turned back. "To tell you the truth, Mr. Kingston, I don't know who sends these reports. We have the job of investigating these matters. I'll tell my boss there's nothing improper going on here."

"Mrs. Sadie?" Sadie turned to see Nora in the doorway.

"Yes, Nora. Do you need me?" Sadie smiled at the woman. "Come in. Sit down. How can I help you?"

"Have you found the baby's mama yet? I mean, baby Eli?"

"No, we haven't yet. We've asked around on the island and notified the authorities on the mainland. They have requested we keep him here since they are short on foster care facilities."

"Do you think I could have him? I don't have children, and I think I'd make a good mom. Do you think I would?"

"Why, yes, Nora, I do. Are you asking to adopt him?"

Nora nodded. "May I? I mean, we all share him right now. But wouldn't it be nice for him to have a real mom? I know I don't have a husband, so he wouldn't have a daddy, but at least he would have one parent."

"I tell you what. I'll talk to David and Tashina and see what we can do. How about that?"

Nora jumped up and threw her arms around Sadie. "Oh, yes. Then you'll let me know?"

"Yes, we'll let you know. I'll talk to them right away."

"I've covered all the channels to try to find the mom," Sophia said when they discussed Nora adopting little Eli. There's one thing we need to consider, and that's getting Nora out on her own."

"I agree," said David. If she is to do this, she needs a home for herself and the child. She has a paying job, so maybe we can find her a place she can afford."

Sadie agreed. "We'll have to speak to her about what she wants. Of course, she can stay here until she's ready for her own place."

They met with Nora, and she admitted that she did want a home. Excitement once again filled the shelter as the occupants celebrated an adoption, and Nora prepared to move into a small house not far from the shelter. Clients helped her collect furniture and household goods from what little they had, and islanders contributed to the cause. It was a happy occasion for the shelter.

A few days later, an islander came to see David, requesting to speak privately. David led the man to his office.

"What can I do for you?" David asked.

The man rubbed his head, making his thin hair stand on end. "I understand you help women and kids who are in trouble," he said. "Is that right?"

"Yes," said David. "We help those without homes or who need to escape an abuser. Do you know someone who needs our help?"

He twisted his hands together and glanced around the room. "A woman and her young daughter are hiding in a shed behind my house," he said. "I found them the other day. I gave them some food but didn't know what to do about them. They cain't stay there forever."

David sat on the edge of his desk, watching the man's face. "Do you know where they came from? Do you know why they are hiding?"

The man shook his head. "I've tried to talk to them, but they won't say much. I can tell they're scared. I guess they don't know who they can trust."

"Will you bring them here, or do we need to come for them?"

"I don't know if they will come with me. Maybe you and Mrs. Sadie can come to get them."

The man led David and Sadie to his house and pointed to the shed. There they found a disheveled woman and girl who looked about ten crouching in a corner behind an old mattress.

Sadie approached them, explaining who she was and urging them to come out. They hesitated but finally exited the shed. The young girl clutched the floral dress her mama wore and hid behind her when Sadie came close.

"Please don't be frightened," Sadie said. David stayed back with the man, allowing Sadie to offer help.

"I am from Willow Grove Shelter on the other side of the island. Have you heard of Willow Grove?"

The woman nodded. "Yes, I've heard of it. I've never been there, though."

"We'd love to take you there and help you. Will you let us do that?"

"I think so. I don't want anyone to know where we are, though. Will you protect us?"

"We will. Who are you hiding from, so we'll know who to protect you from?"

The woman glanced at David. "I messed up." Her face contorted, and tears flowed from her eyes.

"I understand," said Sadie. "We all mess up sometimes." She gave the woman time to compose herself. "Can you tell me your name?"

"My name is Nancy. I came here with him because I thought he loved me, but he didn't. He just wanted us to earn money for him." She cried harder, her words punctuated with sobs. "He—kept—us—in a building—over that—way." She pointed. "I don't—know if it's—his name, but—I heard him—called—Drax. I just know he's—mean."

"You mean he lives here on the island?"

"Yes. He ordered us to—you know—go with a man who came for us. Ruby and I ran when I choked the man with my scarf." Her pleading eyes searched Sadie's. "Will I get into trouble for that?"

"You're not to worry about that, lovie." Sadie led them toward the Ranger. "Right now, let's get you to the shelter. You can talk later about what happened. Okay?"

When Sadie situated them in a room after they bathed and ate, she found they were victims of sex trafficking. Officer Jason notified the authorities, and soon three men were arrested and charged with sex-trafficking crimes.

Officer Jason and David discussed the matter later. "I hope that's all on this island," said Officer Jason, "but I'm afraid there's more."

David massaged the back of his neck. "I thought we were through with that. I'd hoped this island would be a safe haven. Now I don't know. We need to talk to Jeb and the others to keep a lookout. You'd think it wouldn't be hard to keep such a small place as this free from those kinds of people."

Meanwhile:

A woman with a tooth missing in front and others black with decay pulled on the young woman's arm. "I need you, Caroline," she said. Her voice sounded low and gravelly, like someone who had smoked for years. "Your dad left while I was in jail, and now I have no one. Please come back home."

"Mom, I don't want to move in with you," Caroline said. "I like where I am. Mr. Kingston has hired me at the shelter, and I'm working as a client counselor."

The woman snorted. "Yeah, I'll bet he don't pay you much. You could get a better-paying job in the city. Then you'd be able to help your mother for once."

"Sure, I don't make that much. But it's enough. I have a room and food. All I need. And I love it."

"Don't you even care about me? I have nothing."

"Mom, you have nothing because of your lifestyle. And you chose that, not me. Not only did you take drugs, but you got me hooked, too. Now, I'm clean and getting my life straightened up. You can choose that, too.

The woman grimaced, and her lower lip trembled. "I cain't, Caroline. I just cain't do it."

"Mom, if you go with me to the shelter, people there will help you. You won't have to do it alone. I'll help you. Together, we can get you clean."

"Nah, I'm all right. Thanks for nothin'." The woman turned and trudged off down the narrow road to the island's west side.

TWENTY-EIGHT

One day after breakfast, David had all the clients meet in the shady backyard of the shelter. Sadie had prepared games and activities for the kids and adults while Louisa and Wren worked on a big picnic lunch with fried chicken, potato salad, and corn on the cob. They had been working so hard harvesting and preserving food from their garden and cleaning up after the storm that David and Sadie felt they needed a fun break.

Sack races followed by horseshoes and croquet put them in a competitive spirit, and limbo kept them laughing. By lunch, they were starving. After stuffing themselves on BBQ and corn-on-the-cob, they played corn hole and giant backyard tic-tac-toe. The day would end with a scavenger hunt, then an outdoor sing-along with David and some islander musicians and singers.

"Look over there." Marleigh pointed to a tall plant to help Sage find a particular leaf. The adults ran around the yard and into the edge of the woods to help the kids fill their bags with leaves and bugs for the scavenger hunt. Juliet remembered seeing a pawpaw nearby, so she took Jax and Jamie down the path by the river. They squealed when they saw the tree and picked some sweet fruit and leaves. They were sure to win the scavenger hunt.

Juliet noticed someone watching them from a boat that floated a short way out in the water. She started walking closer to the shoreline to look, but the twins called for her to hurry. They were ready to return to the shelter. Sadie would check their bags to see who found the most things on the list she had given them.

Later after enjoying Louisa and Wren's sandwiches, islanders joined clients, employees, and staff on the grounds to listen to the music. Guitars, fiddles, banjoes, and other instruments accompanied the sweet voices of the singers. David, Sadie, Kade, and Sophia joined other couples dancing under the large oak and maple trees. The children moved to the outer circle of the audience and danced to the fast tunes. When the adults started waltzing, the bored children chased fireflies and played tag

Iris was patting her foot in time with the music when she heard something. She strained to listen, but the music filled the air. Then she heard it again.

She turned to Caroline, who sat next to her. "Did you hear someone yell?"

Caroline listened. "Yes. Sounds like someone screaming down by the river." As they jumped up and ran toward the river, they saw the children running toward them, yelling something.

Caroline reached them first. "What is it? What is wrong?"

Elfi pointed. "Some strangers. They took Jax and Jamie."

Juliet reached them in time to hear. She sat out on a dead run in the direction Elfi pointed. Others followed when they realized something was going on. Juliet reached the shoreline in time to see two men forcing Jax and Jamie into a boat. It was the same boat she had seen earlier.

"No!" she screamed. "Jax! Jamie! Those are my children. Leave them alone." Rage contorted her face as she waded into the water to stop them, but the boat was out of her reach. The motor started, and the vessel headed downriver. She could hear Jax and Jamie screaming and crying.

Jerome reached Juliet and pulled her back to the bank. He pointed to the boat and shouted. "Two men in that boat have Jax and Jamie." Pulling Juliet along, he ran to the dock. "I'm going after them," he said to David.

He piled into his boat, followed by David and Officer Jason. When Juliet tried to board, David shook his head, but Jerome pulled her up. "We may need her," he said.

They sped down the river after the johnboat that carried away Juliet's children. They watched, but they didn't see the boat. It had to be around somewhere. Jerome's speedboat made waves as they canvassed both sides of the river.

"There it is!" Juliet pointed. Sure enough, they saw the johnboat partially hidden under some tree branches. Jerome steered the boat to the shore on the mainland, and they jumped out. "We'll split up," said Officer Jason. "They can't be far."

They combed the wooded area along the bank and went to a nearby house. After a while, a man came out to rescue them from several barking dogs.

"We're looking for a couple of men and kids," Jason explained. "Have you seen anyone in the last few minutes?"

The man pulled his hat off and rubbed his head. "I haven't, but I just now got home. Why are you looking for them?" he asked. "Have they committed a crime or something?"

"Something like that," Jason said. "The two men grabbed the kids from the island. We need to find them fast."

"Are they armed?" the man wanted to know.

"We don't know. We have to be cautious. We don't know who they are or why they took the kids."

The man looked at Juliet, whose face was ashen. "Ma'am, are they your young'uns?" She could only nod.

The man gestured toward some outbuildings. "You're welcome to look around."

Jason instructed them to surround the buildings. He cautioned them to be careful while opening the first shed door. Tools lay scattered about, but the men weren't there. The door flew open as he approached a second building, and a man ran out. He slammed himself into Officer Jason, knocking him to the ground. David punched the man, who came up swinging. David ducked, then landed a blow on the man's chin. Then another. The man fell and held up his hands to shield his face.

Jason pointed his gun at the man. Jerome turned to open the door to the building. Inside, a second man held onto the kids.

"Jerome!" yelled Jax. "I knew you'd come for us."

The man turned them loose and put up his hands. "I'm not armed," he said. He got to his feet and went past Jerome to join his buddy.

Juliet wept as she embraced her children and looked at the second man. "Ralph! I shoulda known you'd be behind this!"

Ralph's face grew red. "Look, Juliet, me and Franny just want to see our grandkids. You had no right to take them from us."

Juliet glowered at the man. "Right? You talk to me about rights? How dare you. Did you try to stop your son from beating me and my kids? No. You made excuses for him. You blamed me. 'You shouldn't make him so mad,' you said. 'You should be a better wife to him,' you said." Rage covered her face as she held her children close. "The last time I let my kids go to your house, you let that devil hurt them. Don't you ever mention seeing my kids. If I let them near you, the first thing you'd do is hand them over to that mean…." She spun around and pulled the twins back toward the river.

Officer Jason cuffed the men and made a call. "You all take them back to Willow Grove," he said to David and Jerome. "I'll have to take these two in. Then someone will bring me over after I've filed a report."

A woman stumbled to the door of the shelter and knocked. When David opened the door, she fell. "Quick,

Angie, get Tashina."

They helped the woman into the clinic. After a while, Tashina called for Sadie. "She says she is Caroline's mom," Tashina said. "She's so strung out she can't function. She barely knows her name."

Sadie picked up some forms from her desk and went to fill out the paperwork. In soft tones, she interviewed the woman for the usual required information. "My name is Evelyn," the woman said. "Is Caroline here? She said this is her home now. I asked her to come live with me, but she wouldn't. Of course, I cain't blame her. I never treated her right."

Sadie nodded and continued to fill out the papers. "Her daddy was no good either. We weren't no good for our little girl. She was such a pretty little thing. Those big blue eyes and that silky blonde hair."

"She is a pretty young woman," Sadie said.

Her daddy used to laugh when he'd give her a drink of his liquor, and she'd get so drunk. That weren't no good for her, was it?"

Sadie shivered. "No, it wasn't."

Evelyn continued like she couldn't stop. "I was so proud when she got her first boyfriend. She was eleven. Her body matured early. Isn't that early for a girl? She was always so pretty, and the boys flocked around her. I tried to warn her to be careful, but it made me proud to see how the boys all liked her. I was like that when I was her age. I married when I was fifteen. I married again when I was eighteen, Then again when I was twenty. I don't know why I couldn't seem to keep a husband. I was twenty-three when I married her daddy. You know, it don't matter anymore whether you get married or not. Marriage is too much trouble."

Sadie completed the paperwork and took Evelyn to a room. She hoped the woman would sleep the rest of the day. Then tomorrow, maybe the drugs would wear off enough for her to be in her right mind. At least, she hoped her mental condition was because of the drugs, not her normal personality.

Meanwhile:

"Who's there?" A man leaned over to peer under the side of a building where several steep steps led to a hole in a wall. Once, a wooden door covered the hole. But now the door hung on one attached hinge. Darkness almost enveloped the narrow alley.

A pair of thin legs sticking out from under the steps pulled in until only a pair of ragged tennis shoes showed.

Once again, the man demanded an answer. "I say, who's there? Come out so I can see you."

A shaky voice answered. "It's nobody. Only me, sir." A thin torso topped by a large head with stringy dark hair appeared. Brown eyes peered from dark recesses in a thin face. Arms and legs not much larger than the baton the man carried swung loosely from the torso. Dirty rags barely covered what the man guessed to be a girl.

The man watched as the figure almost fell when it tried to stand. He reached to help, but it drew back.

He held up his hands. "Okay, I won't touch you. But please don't fall." He gestured toward a bucket nearby. "Why don't you sit here?" he said. "Then maybe we can talk. Don't worry. I won't hurt you."

"Are you the police?"

"I am. Haven't you heard that policemen are nice guys?"

The big head shook. "I don't want you to arrest me."

"I promise I won't arrest you. I want to help you. Looks like maybe you could use some help, right?"

"I guess."

He pulled a package of peanut butter crackers from his pocket and handed it to her. He assumed it was a girl. She ripped the package open and scarfed the crackers. She sat looking at him, licking her lips.

"I'm sorry I don't have a drink to offer you." She watched him. "What's your name?" he asked.

"Arena."

"Are you from around here, Arena?"

"No."

"Where is your family?"

"I don't have one."

"What happened to them?"

"They died."

"You don't have any relatives you could stay with?"

She shook her head. "I have no one."

"How old are you?"

"Sixteen."

"How long have you been out here alone?"

She shrugged. "I don't know. A long time, I guess."

"If you let me, I can take you to some people who will feed and care for you."

Sad eyes filled with tears. "Are you talking about jail? I don't want to go to jail."

"Oh, no. I would not take you to jail. I'm talking about a place where they help people who need someone. These people are friends of mine, and they are good people." He watched her process this information. "Will you go with me?"

The deep eyes were sad as the big head nodded.

TWENTY-NINE

Sometime later, Sadie went to pick a fresh bouquet of wildflowers. She walked through the backyard where the little girls played in the new playhouse one of the islanders had built for them. It had a furnished kitchen and living room with cute little windows—a perfect place for them to use their active imaginations.

The smaller girls pretended to feed their babies while the older ones stirred pretend food on their play stove. Four-year-old Micah sang to her baby doll as she rocked.

Sage and Ruby, both ten, told the smaller girls what to do. "Wash those dishes," ordered Sage. "Sweep the floor," demanded Ruby.

Eight-year-old Elfi put her hands on her hips and pursed her lips. "I don't care to do the housework," she said, "but I won't do it all by myself."

Five-year-old Susan mimicked Elfi. "We won't do it all," she said.

Ruby stood beside Sage. "You have to do what we tell you 'cause we're oldest, and we get to be the boss."

"I'm 'most old as you," said Elfi, "and just as smart."

"And I'm right under Elfi." Jamie stood beside Elfi. "Look. I'm as tall as her."

"No." Ruby wrinkled her nose. "We're older, and we tell you what to do. That's the end."

Elfi's lips fluttered, and she picked up a pot. Ruby's face blanched. She covered her head and dropped to the floor.

190

Elfi ran to her. "Oh, Ruby, I'm sorry. I wasn't going to hit you." She hugged Ruby. "I would never hit you. I was just gonna wash this pot."

Sadness drifted across Sadie's face. She would have to work with Ruby to help her overcome her fear. As she watched the girls, she realized she needed to work with all of them. She started thinking about activities she could do.

She walked on the path beside the river, picking wildflowers and enjoying the birds singing. About a mile away from the shelter, she looked at the time and decided she should start back.

"Hello, there." A man pulled his boat to the shoreline beside the levee and threw his tackle onto the sandy beach. "Pretty bunch of wildflowers you have. I'll bet they'll look fabulous on your dining table."

Sadie looked past her bouquet to the stranger. She glanced around in case she needed a safe place. *Nowadays, one must be careful, even here.*

"Hello," she answered. "I'm sure they will. They would look pretty anywhere." She sauntered further up the path toward home. "Caught many fish?" She said as she continued to walk.

"A few. Say, aren't you Mrs. Kingston? David Kingston's wife?"

She hesitated. "Yes. You know David?"

The man climbed out of the boat. "I met him a while back. He was telling me about the shelter y'all have. Sounds impressive. I'm thinking of opening one in the city."

"Polk? Stewart Polk? David spoke of you."

"Yes, ma'am. That's me. He agreed to give me a tour of the shelter the next time I came over. Think today would be a good day for a visit?"

Sadie caught her breath. She knew David had told him they didn't allow anyone to tour the shelter. The man was lying.

"I'm sorry, Mr. Polk. Today is not a good day for a tour. You'll have to talk to David."

"I just want to look around a little," he said. "Nothing wrong with that, is there?" He started walking toward her, so she walked faster. "David is not around today, is he? You could let me look around a little bit."

How could he know David had gone to the city for some business? He would be gone all day. She walked faster. He started jogging toward her. She was a good bit ahead, and she began to run. It would not be good to be caught out here alone with someone who had ill purposes. Maybe she could defend herself with self-defense training, but she did not know his abilities. She knew she could run a mile, but not at a fast pace. *Could he?* Maybe at a sprint, she could leave him behind. As she came to a curve in the path, she sped up until she was running at top speed. She ran a distance, then glanced backward. He was nowhere in sight.

When David arrived home at supper, she told him what happened. "The man lied," she said. "I don't think he is a minister. And I doubt he is planning to start a shelter. There's a different reason he's here. I can't understand how he knew you were gone."

David agreed. "We'd better keep an eye out for him. I'll give Jerome and Jason a head's up."

A few days later, Shelton appeared again. This time, he approached the shelter after David and Sadie had gone home. Jerome saw him walking from the river up the sidewalk to the shelter.

"Sir! Sir, is there something I can do for you?" he asked the man.

"Oh, no. I'm going to see Tashina. I'm a friend of hers."

"Oh, really? I'll take you to meet her, then." Jerome walked beside the man.

"You don't have to," Shelton said. "She's expecting me."

Jerome smiled and continued to walk beside him. When they got near the porch, Shelton stopped. He looked at his watch. "Uh," he said, "I think I have the wrong day. I'll come back another time." He fled down the walk to the river, boarded his boat, and left.

Jerome asked Tashina, but she didn't know who he was talking about. "I don't know any Shelton," she said. "No one said anything to me about a visit. Sounds like maybe he's trying to get in here for some reason."

"Maybe," Jerome said. "I'll ask Officer Jason to check him out."

The next day, Tina and Nancy were working in the garden when a man appeared from around the corner of the shelter. They didn't notice him until he was right beside Tina.

"You sure have a beautiful garden," he said. "Those beans look like they're about ready to pick."

The ladies looked up, then at one another. "Do we know you, sir?" asked Tina.

"I'm Shelton," he said. "I'm looking for a friend of mine. You aren't the only ones here, are you?"

Tina edged away from him while Nancy set her basket down. She was ready to fight if the need arose.

"Sir, you aren't supposed to be here," Tina said. "You need to leave at once."

Shelton pulled a bean off the bush and opened it. "These are some healthy-looking beans," he said. "What are you gonna do with them? Freeze them? Or eat them? That'd be a lot of eatin' unless there are more here than just you two. How many live here?"

Tina looked toward the back door. "Sir, please leave. If you want some beans, we'll give you some. Here. Take these I picked. You can have hers, too. Just take them and leave."

Nancy had eased further toward the back door. When the man leaned over to pick another bean, she ran. She almost ran into Louisa, who was coming out. "What's goin' on out here?" Louisa asked. "Who is that man? What does he want?"

"We don't know," Nancy said. "Says his name is Shelton, but he won't say what he wants. He keeps asking questions."

Louisa picked up a hoe from a nearby shed and approached the man. "Sir," she said, "you'd best be gittin' on your way."

Shelton backed up, his eyes huge. Louisa continued toward him until he turned and ran back toward the river.

Officer Jason talked to David and Jerome the following day. "Is this the man who keeps coming around?" He showed them a photo. They agreed it was him and showed Sadie the picture. It was the same man.

"He is Marleigh's husband," Jason said. "His name is Elliot Hobbs. He's trying to find her. Says he wants baby Aiden. Says he has a right to his son."

"I guess we need to tell Marleigh," David said. "I hate to. I'm concerned she'll be scared, knowing he found her."

Jason grimaced. "He thinks she's here, but does he know it for sure?"

"That's right," said David. "He never actually saw her, so he's guessing she's here."

Sadie pursed her lips. "Only one thing concerns me. How did he know you weren't here the other day, David? And he must have known we were both gone yesterday. How could he know that?"

"Yes," said Jerome. "And how did he find out she may be here? How does he know about this place?"

"Seems to me someone is giving out information." Jason studied the ground. "How else does he know? Someone stole and hid baby Aiden. Who did that?"

"Yes, and someone stole merchandise from the village." David started pacing. "And someone planted drugs in Caroline's room." He stopped. "Who is doing these things? Is it the same person? Is it different people?"

"That isn't all," said Sadie. "Who keeps reporting things to the DHS? Someone is."

Jerome pulled the topic back to Elliot. "So, how are we going to prevent him from finding Marleigh? He may hurt someone if he wants that baby bad enough."

"Jason, we'll have to get a restraining order to keep him off the island," Jerome said. "Will you work on that?"

"Sure. I'll get Sophia to help me with it." Jason turned and walked toward the shelter while David and Sadie strolled along the riverbank. Jerome went to the dock to work on his boat.

"I guess I do need to warn Marleigh," said Sadie. "She's pretty stable. Maybe she won't freak out."

Marleigh didn't freak out. She boiled with rage. "How dare he even think he can get Aiden," she shouted. "I'll break him in two if he gets near that baby."

The other women agreed. "We'll keep a watch," said Caroline, "and if he comes near any of us, we'll make him wish he hadn't."

Juliet's eyes sparked as she remembered the trouble with her kids. "He'd better not come back over here," she said. "I'll hurt him myself."

"You won't have to," Iris said. "The bunch of us will be on him like a duck on a June bug. We'll teach him he can't mess with any of us."

They gathered around Marleigh and hugged Aiden until he protested with a shriek.

"I'm sure glad they're on my side," David told Sadie. "I really think they'd hurt someone who tried to get to any of them."

"They would," Sadie said. "Without a doubt. That man had better steer clear of this piece of land." She thought a moment. "Of course, he can ignore the restraining order. You think he might?"

Meanwhile:

Pushing back the curtain that separated her from the outside world, Katina adjusted the dirty blanket, which was her only bedding. Fleeting images of cold nights in the desert brought on a shiver as she wrapped the blanket around her thin shoulders. The cold hurt her knotted, curled fingers. Her stomach rumbled, and she dug deep into her black bag. Maybe she had somehow left a piece of a sandwich or half a candy bar that would give her some sustenance.

Finding nothing, she exited the small tent and shuffled through the alley to the sidewalk. People hurried by, busy with their lives. No one would notice her. They never did. Then, a woman strolled by, leading a child by the hand. The little boy smiled at her, then waved. He pulled his mama to a stop.

"Mama, wait." He walked over to Katina and looked her over. "What is that?" He pointed at the badge she wore on her camouflage jacket.

She smiled. "It's a badge," she said.

"What's it mean?" He leaned in to look more closely. "It has a dragon on it. It says, 'I've seen the Dragon'."

"Yes." Katina's finger moved to touch the patch. "It's for the time I spent in Vietnam."

The boy's mother moved closer. "You're a veteran?" she asked. "You served in Vietnam?"

Katina nodded and smiled at the little boy. The woman looked around. "Where are you staying?" she asked. "Please don't be offended. I'm not trying to be nosey."

Katina motioned to the alley, and the woman looked. "In that little tent?"

Katina nodded. The woman went to look inside the tent. "There's nothing here but a blanket," she said. "Is this all you have?" Katina nodded. "How long have you been out here?"

Katina frowned. "You sure do ask a lot of questions."

The woman backed up. "I know, and I'm sorry. It's just that-- well, my mother's brother served in Vietnam. He didn't make it home. My mother spent her life trying to help Vietnam veterans. I want to try to help you."

Katina stared at the woman, then slowly nodded. All the tiredness from days of living out here with nothing weighed her down. The cold. The hunger. The loneliness. Ever since she had returned to the States, she had suffered. She had no one to help her. No one to surround her with love. No one who was proud of her.

"May I help you?" the woman asked. "I have contact with someone who will give you a place to live. A family. A place with no judgment."

Katina looked around. There sat the only home she had known for the past several months. She hated it. She looked at the woman and nodded. The woman smiled and took her hand. The little boy grabbed the other hand. They walked slowly down the street together.

THIRTY

David heard a commotion outside one evening. He looked out and gasped. The women were in a circle, and it appeared they were hitting something. He ran out the door.

In the middle, a man lay in a fetal position while the women hit him with brooms, mops, and other weapons. He yelped and cried out, but they continued to beat him. "What's going on?" David demanded. The women turned to look at him. The man writhed on the ground.

"This man came here to stir up trouble," said Iris. "We're teaching him that he can't mess with us. We protect each other."

David leaned over the man, and when he uncovered his head, David blinked. It was Steward Polk.

"What are you doing here?"

"I...uh...I...I just wanted to see my wife," he said.

"Who?"

"Marleigh. She's my wife." Polk tried to get up, but Nora shook her broom at him. He withered and covered his head again.

"She doesn't want to see you," Juliet said. "Never again. Her words, not mine."

"Ladies, maybe you'd better let the man up. I'm sure he's ready to leave by now and will never return. Isn't that right, Mr. Polk?"

"Ye...ye...yes." He peeked out from between his elbows. "I promise I won't ever come back. Please, I'm ready to leave now."

The women backed off, and David helped him up. He hobbled toward his boat tied close to the dock. The women marched behind him, holding their weapons high.

"We have a new client," Sadie said to David. "A homeless girl found not far from here. Jerome brought her last night. Sixteen-year-old named Arena. Near starvation. Tashina has put her on a special diet until she can digest regular meals."

David set the table for supper. "Family?"

"She insists she has none. She says her parents died a year ago, and she has no other family to help her. So, she has been on the street all this time."

"How's she doing? Are the others helping her? Does she fit in okay?"

"Yes, yes, and yes. The ladies have surrounded her with love, feeding her all they are permitted and fixing up clothes she can wear. Tina fixed her hair. She gave her the cutest haircut. You know, she's good with hair and makeup."

David poured glasses of iced tea. "Has she said anything about becoming a cosmetologist? Maybe that would be a good career for her if she's interested."

"I don't know. I'll talk to her about it. When her treatment period has ended, perhaps we can get her into a hair and beauty school. I'm sure we can find a good one for her."

Sadie did talk to Tina, and they arranged for her to attend beauty school in a few months when her treatment plan allowed it.

That same day, Sadie answered a call from a friend in the city. "I have a favor to ask of you," the friend said. "I have an elderly woman here who needs a home. She's a Vietnam veteran. Think you'd have room for her?"

"Of course," said Sadie. "Does she have health or mental issues?"

"She has been living on the street for a few months and is malnourished. I'm not sure about her mental health. Nothing is visible if she has issues. I've had her for a few days, and she seems stable." She laughed. "Trent loves her. He wants her to stay with us. I had to tell him that was impossible since we travel so much. He's trying to understand."

"Is it okay if Jerome picks her up in the boat?" Sadie asked.

"Oh, sure. She'd probably love that. Maybe he could take her for an extra ride if he has time. You know, show her some sights. I think it would do her some good."

Jerome enjoyed driving Katina up and down the river. When they arrived at the shelter, her eyes were bright, and a huge smile covered her face. The clients met her at the dock and escorted her to the shelter, thanking her profusely for her service. They served her a special meal of grilled pork chops with cornbread dressing, mashed potatoes, and vegetables from the garden. Her face glowed as they supplied her with clothes and toiletries and designated her a room on the bottom floor next to the patio.

Mr. Cox appeared at the shelter again one day. Just dropped by, he said. No reason. After he greeted everyone with his unusual bow, he squeezed out from under the children who clung to him and sat down to have lunch with them.

"Kudos to the chef," he said. "These vegetables are wonderful. And this stir-fried rice is delicious. I haven't had such good dining in a long time. It reminds me of my trip to China several years ago."

Louisa stood in the doorway, blushing. She giggled and fanned herself. "Aww, Mr. Cox, you say such nice things."

He went to her, bowed, and kissed her hand, bringing on another fit of giggling. "I'm telling the truth," he said. "Your cooking is sensational, at the least. And healthy, too." Her blush deepened, and she ran into the kitchen to send out more food with Wren.

"You mean you went to China?" asked Lyric. "What was it like?"

"Are you Chinese?" asked Brent. "You don't look Chinese."

Mr. Cox laughed. "No, I'm not Chinese," he said to Brent. "China is a great country," he said to Lyric. "The people are so friendly, and the land is beautiful. I was there only a short time, but I loved it."

He told interesting stories about his visit there and then directed the conversation back to the island. "Of course," he said, "you have a beautiful piece of land here, even if it is tiny. And oh, the history of this little island."

"Tell us," begged Caroline. "I was born here, but I don't know much of the history of this place."

"Do you know that a tribe of Chickasaw Indians inhabited this island once?" The children pulled their chairs close to Mr. Cox and watched him with wide eyes. "Yes, three or four Indian families moved onto the island and lived here until the white people started populating the land around them. They finally moved further west to be with the rest of their tribe."

"What did they do here?" asked Randall.

"They used some of the timber to build huts and raised pheasants here. That's right, pheasants."

"You mean they raised poor people?" Angie was astonished.

Mr. Cox laughed. "No, not people — birds,"

"You know," Elfi said, "the birds with long tails. Pheasant birds. Some people eat them."

"Ewww!" Sage stuck her tongue out. "I wouldn't want to eat a bird. They're too pretty to eat."

"And too little," said Randall.

Elfi shook her head. "Not pheasants. They're almost as big as a turkey."

"What'd they do with the pheasants they raised?" asked Juliet. "They're such a pretty bird."

"They used them for game birds. People like to hunt them for sport. Others used them for pets. They were quite popular around here for a while."

"How come we don't have any pheasants here now?" asked Ruby. "I haven't seen any. Have you?"

"No. I guess the people took them when they left," Mr. Cox said. "Or maybe they all flew away. I've never seen one around here."

"What else happened on this island?" Mandy was interested in history, and since she was born and raised on the island, she wanted to know more about it.

"During the Civil War, a group of soldiers hid on the island for a few days until someone saw their smoke and routed them off." As Mr. Cox talked, David watched him. *How does he know these things? How old is he, anyway?* He would ask him later.

"Back before the Civil War, an outlaw named James Copeland and his gang camped nearby. Some say he had barrels of gold he stole from the mainland. No one knows what happened to it."

Thoughtful expressions covered the faces around the table.

"Do you think the gold found by the boys could be the gold that outlaw had?" Caroline asked.

Mr. Cox nodded. "I think it very well may be.

That brought the conversation to the gold found by the boys.

"Mr. David kept our gold." Jax puckered up his face.

"No, Jax, I didn't keep it. I talked to the authorities and learned that it belongs to the ones who found it. I put it up for safekeeping at the request of your mothers. The gold is yours, but your mamas want it kept safe until you're grown. Is that okay?"

Smiles broke out on the boys' faces. "Wow," Brent said. "We are rich!" The boys high-fived each other, then David.

"There's a lot of it," said Sadie, "so Mr. David and I discussed how much your mamas could benefit from some of it. Don't you think that's a good idea?"

Little heads nodded, and eyes sparkled. The mamas had already agreed to take advantage of the riches when they were ready to make homes for themselves. But not until then.

At the end of the meal, Mr. Cox rose to leave. He looked at each one in the room, then raised a finger. "Why don't we drop the mister? Just call me Charlie. That's who I am." He turned and disappeared in a northwest direction.

One evening not long after that, Randall, Brent, and Jax didn't show up for supper.

"Do you know where the boys went?" David asked Sage.

"Yes, they went to the woods," she said.

David growled. "I told them to stay out of those woods. Why won't they listen to me?"

"I heard them talking," said Ruby. "Brent said someone told them you aren't their dad, so they don't have to do what you say. And Randall says the last time they went into the woods, they got rich."

David organized a search party made up of the ladies and a few islanders, and within an hour, David's phone rang.

"We've found them," Marleigh said. "You need to bring a gun or something. A bunch of wild hogs have them up a tree."

Jason and Jerome ran to help David rescue the boys. They made so much noise the hogs fled, and they helped the scared little guys down the tree.

"I thought I told you boys to stay out of the woods." David set the boys on a log and scolded them. "I guess you know now why. There are dangerous things out here. Besides wild hogs, there are poisonous snakes. These creatures can kill you."

"We're sorry, Mr. David." Brent sniffed, and the other boys wiped their eyes. "We won't never go out here by ourselves again."

"Yeah," said Randall. "I never saw hogs like that. They're mean. One bit me on the leg." He pulled up his pant leg to show a bloody tear.

Tina ran to him. "Oh, son, that looks bad. We need to get you to Nurse Tashina fast."

The mamas looked over the boys and found ticks and chiggers covered them. Jax also had minor scrapes and marks on his legs from the hogs. They hurried them back to the shelter, where Tashina doctored their cuts and scrapes and treated them for tick and chigger bites.

Meanwhile:

"Get your fat self away from me. I can't stand to look at you."
The man adjusted his tie and looked in the mirror, turning one way
and another. He smiled as he buttoned his sports jacket over the
crisp light blue shirt and black, creased trousers. All new. He would
take the business world by storm. It was his first job with his own
office, a dream come true. If only he didn't have to look at her
every morning and every night. He glanced at her as she waddled
to a chair and lowered herself to sit. Why did she have to get
pregnant now? Just when things were going great.

The baby was due any day. The baby he never wanted. What
did he ever see in her in the first place? When they married, they
had agreed she would work to put him through college. When he
got a job, he would work to put her through. Then they would have
it made. They could afford a nice home in a good neighborhood.
Or a high-rise condominium.

They both came from low-income families and agreed they
would never live poor. They would not have children. Then they
could live high, travel, and be a part of society neither had
experienced. But then Bella got pregnant. That ruined all their
plans.

"Don't call me fat, Jackson." Sadness twisted her face as she
began to cry. "I'm not fat. I'm pregnant."

Disdain seeped from his words and covered his face. He
snickered as he glanced once more into the mirror. "Oh, darling,
you're fat. Come to think of it, you were fat when I married you. I
don't know what I ever saw in you."

"You once loved me," she said. "I guess now your new
secretary will have all your attention."

He grinned. "Miss West is quite attractive, and I will never have
to worry about her getting pregnant." As he passed her to leave
the room, he smacked her on the head. At least he didn't knock her

out of the chair as he had several times before.

When he was gone, she picked up a bag and walked to the door. She glanced around the room. Most of the memories here were good ones. They had purchased the antique lamp in the corner soon after they married. An elderly man sold it to them. He told the story of how he and his beloved wife were married fifty years, and when she passed away one night in her sleep a few years ago, he had to sell his home and move to an apartment without room for most of his treasures. Jackson and Bella had vowed to stay together forever like the man and his beloved wife.

A huge sigh escaped her lips as she closed the door. She had no place to go. No family who could support her and her child. She had no idea where to go, but she could not stay here with a man who detested her and her baby.

THIRTY-ONE

David and Sadie approached the Craft Village a little later than usual on their jog around the island. Jeb was opening his shop when David yelled a greeting to him. Jeb turned and waved, then gestured for David and Sadie. They laughed and joked for a moment, then he sobered.

"I've been thinking about the situation with the merchandise that disappeared a while back," he said. "I wonder if one of your clients did take the items. I talked with the shop owners, Amy and Travis, and they say the only ones who shopped with them that day were a couple of ladies and Sophia. They said the ladies were with Sophia the whole time, and neither looked at the items which disappeared. Oddly, whoever left the note left it by the register in my shop. A few younger women were in my shop that day, but I don't remember which ones. I think the Yarrow girl and maybe Mandy and one more. I know Mandy. She wouldn't do anything like that. I don't know much about the Yarrow girl or the other one."

David bounced on his toes as he thought about what Jeb said. "We questioned the ladies," he said, "but we have not yet found out who did it. We keep hoping and praying the guilty party will confess, but that hasn't happened yet."

"We are missing having y'all visit our village to shop. Our merchants have complained about it."

"What are you suggesting, Jeb? Are you saying you want us to shop there now?"

Jeb nodded. "Yes, we do. A couple of items missing are not worth us losing some of our best customers. Please bring the ladies and young'uns back to the shops."

David and Sadie both agreed they would do that soon.

They did return to the Craft Village for another shopping spree. As usual, they divided into groups. They decided to have lunch in a village café instead of having a picnic in the grove as usual. The young ones were excited. Most of them had never eaten in a restaurant, so the day before the excursion, Sadie and the mamas attempted to teach them restaurant etiquette.

"It's important we show good manners," said Sadie. "We want people to see how civilized we are at the shelter. We don't want anyone to think we're sloppy pigs, do we?"

That set off the little boys. They snorted and rooted each other, squealed, and rolled on the floor until their laughing mamas made them stop.

Sadie and Sophia instructed them to chew with their mouths closed, to say please and thank you, and not to talk with their mouths full. They taught them how to use their napkins and to keep their elbows off the table. They practiced at the evening meal and breakfast before they started for the village.

Emmie had taken charge of Arena to show her the ropes and help her get acquainted with the people and the area. Arm in arm, they giggled as they skipped down the path toward the village.

"Just wait until you see all the shops," said Emmie. "They have great clothes and makeup. Purses, jewelry — you name it. The crafters make unique items you won't find in the city."

The village crafters were delighted to see Willow Grove folks return to their shops. They ushered them from one shop to another, urging them to look at their wares. "Look at my new items," one shopkeeper said. "I just created these purses last week. You won't find any like them anywhere." Another announced a sale on her shoes, and a boutique ran deals on jeans and tops.

The clients met for lunch at the Village eatery. The kids were so excited the ladies had to remind them to use the manners they had been taught. The ladies chatted non-stop about their purchases, and the younger females compared the perfumes and makeup they found. At one point, Emmie and Arena whispered in a booth until they realized the boys were eavesdropping.

Randall and Brent made kissing noises as they left the restaurant. "Oh, I hope he kisses me," Brent mocked.

"I think I'll just die if he does." Randall held his hand against his forehead and pretended to swoon.

The red-faced girls slapped at the laughing boys, threatening to hurt them if they didn't stop. Sadie had to intervene before a fight ensued.

A few clients wanted to return to pick up some last-minute items before returning to the shelter. When they met to head back, Arena was missing. Sadie and Sophia questioned the group, but no one knew her whereabouts.

Sadie pulled Emmie aside while the others waited at the village fountain. "I noticed you and Arena whispering during lunch. Did she say anything about going somewhere? Anything?"

Emmie's face grew red, and she hung her head but remained silent.

"Emmie, if you know something, you need to tell me," Sadie said. "You know Arena could be in danger. Please. What do you know?"

Emmie looked up with tear-filled eyes. "Mrs. Sadie, she's been meeting a boy who lives on the island. He asked her to meet him behind Mr. Jeb's shop."

Sadie gasped. "How long have they been meeting? How does she know him?"

"He came one day to deliver some supplies to Mrs. Louisa. Wren knows him. She introduced him to Arena. He talked to her, and they've seen each other ever since. They meet down by the dock sometimes at night." Emmie lowered her head again. "She says they're in love."

"In love? She's sixteen!"

"She says they're gonna get married, Mrs. Sadie. Maybe tonight or tomorrow."

Sadie threw up her hands and groaned. She walked back and forth, rubbing her hands together. "Do you know where they were going?" she asked.

Emmie hesitated until Sadie leaned over to peer into her face. "She said they might go to the mainland," she said, "to a small town close to the river. Says she knows a preacher there."

Sadie took Emmie's hand, and they joined the rest of the group. "I've got to get David," Sadie said. "We'll have to go after her."

When they arrived at the shelter, Sadie found David at the dock talking to Jerome. She told him the situation, and they agreed they needed to go after the girl. After all, she was their responsibility.

Since Jerome knew most of the islanders, he drove them in the Ranger. They went from house to house along the chute side, then along the river. No one had heard about the girl.

"Guess they did go to the mainland like she told Emmie," said Sadie. "Now, what do we do?"

David called Jason, and Jason called law enforcement on both sides of the river. The search continued all night and into the next day. Radio and television stations broadcast the story with a picture of the girl. In the middle of the afternoon, someone called. They found her.

David and Sadie boated to the small town where an officer said they were staying. They found Arena and Tyrell at the home of Tyrell's friend.

They confronted the young people. "Why didn't you tell

us you were seeing this young man?" David asked.

Arena took Tyrell's hand. "I—I—I don't know. I guess I thought you would disapprove."

"How could you know that unless you gave us a chance? We know you're old enough to have a boyfriend."

"Yes," said Sadie. "Arena, we want to protect you, not imprison you. We care about you. How long have you known this young man?"

Arena looked from David to Sadie. "Well—not very long. But I know I love him."

"Would you consider staying at the shelter and dating him until you know him better?" David asked.

Tyrell and Arena looked at one another. "Sir, there's something else," Tyrell said.

"What else? What are you talking about?" asked David.

Arena blushed. "I'm pregnant."

David and Sadie spoke at the same time. "What?"

"Are you sure?" Sadie asked.

"I think so," said Arena. "I've been sick in the mornings."

"Okay." Sadie thought a moment. "Will you return with us and let Tashina examine you to make sure?"

Arena looked at Tyrell. He nodded. "That might be a good idea," he said. "You need to be sure. I'll go with you."

She agreed, and when Tashina examined her, she was pregnant.

David, Sadie, and Tashina met with the couple to help them make plans. They learned Tyrell was seventeen, still in school, and had no job.

Tyrell's parents agreed to come to the shelter to meet with David and their son. "What are your plans?" David asked Tyrell.

"I guess I'll quit school and get a job. My uncle works for a construction company on the mainland, and he can help me get a job there."

"Before you met Arena, what were your plans?" asked David.

Tyrell popped his knuckles. "Well, I had planned to go to a technical school to be an electrician. Guess it's too late for that, huh?"

His dad grunted. "I guess so," he said.

"How long does it take to complete that program?" David asked.

"A year of study, then some apprenticeship."

"How would you feel if we could make that happen? You and Arena can get married—if that's what you want—and you can complete the course."

"But I'm still in school."

"We'll help you study to pass a GED," David said. "You and Arena are too young to start acting as adults, but you've chosen that role by becoming sexually involved. Now, you'll be forced to live like adults. You'll have to work extra hard and miss the fun your teenage buddies are having. Can you live with that?"

Tyrell twisted his shirt tail. "Yes, I think so,"

"You can't 'think so'," his dad said. "You have to know so. Marriage is a lifetime commitment. Having a child is a lifetime commitment. You have a responsibility to someone besides yourself now. You have a responsibility to this child and Arena. There's no going back at this point."

Tyrell stood and straightened his back. "I love Arena, and I'll love this child. I will not shirk my duties to either of them."

His mom nodded. "I'm glad to hear you say that, son."

"Yes," his dad agreed. "I taught you always to do right no matter how much it costs."

"And I will," Tyrell said. "You'll see."

David grinned. "That's what I like to hear. Come on, Let's go tell Arena."

They entered Sadie's office, where Sadie and Arena had had a similar discussion. Tyrell put his arm around Arena. "We will do this," he said. She nodded.

David told Arena what he and Tyrell had discussed. Sadie told Tyrell that they offered Arena a chance to attend the college of her choice during her pregnancy and after if needed. She wanted to attend a cosmetology school and eventually have her own beauty salon. They would look for a place for them to live on the island.

"If they need to," said Tyrell's dad, "they can live with us for a while."

Tyrell's mom smiled at Arena. "They can stay in Tyrell's room. We don't have much but will help all we can."

A movement in the hall drew David's attention toward the partly opened door. Tapping footsteps rushing down the hall faded when David looked out.

Meanwhile:

The back door of the shelter opened, and in hushed tones, a young woman greeted a clean-cut man who appeared to be in his early twenties.

"Be quiet," she hissed. "We don't want to wake anyone. Let's get this over with so I can get back to bed.

He handed her a bag, and she gave him an envelope. "Now, don't forget—put it where no one can see it," he said. "We don't want any mishaps."

"Don't worry. I know what to do."

THIRTY-TWO

Katina talked Jerome into giving her a ride in his speedboat. Ever since the first ride when he brought her to the island, she wanted another one.

"Jerome, if you take me for another ride down the river," she said, "I'll tell you some of my favorite stories."

A wide grin spread across his face. "Now, Miss Katina, how could I refuse such a great proposition? Of course, I'll take you. Just give me a few minutes to gas up my boat."

Soon, they were skimming along the surface of the wide river. He slowed when they passed by old plantations with houses that resembled the shelter. They went along one side, and then he turned to show her the scenery on the other side. When they passed the dock at a small town, he pulled over.

"Miss Katina, are you hungry? This little town has a restaurant that serves the best hamburger you'll ever eat."

"Sure," she said. "I am a little hungry. Do they have good strawberry shakes?"

He laughed. "The best." He helped her out of the boat, and they walked the short distance to the little town. She told him stories as they ate their food, and when she slurped the last of her shake, he paid the bill and guided her back to the boat. Just as Jerome started the motor, someone yelled. A man and woman hurried toward him.

"Jerome! Wait." An officer stood beside a pregnant woman holding a small bag. "I'm so glad you happened by. I was about to call you. This is Bella. I found her wandering the streets, needing a place to stay. You guys have room at Willow Grove?"

Jerome smiled at the woman. "Sure do," he said. He and the officer helped her into the boat.

"Oh, my," said Katina. "When is the baby due?"

Bella smiled at the white-haired woman. "Any time," she said.

"Do you know if it's a boy or girl?"

"It's a girl. I'm naming her Beula Jane."

"I love that," said Katina. "I'm so glad many older names are coming back in style. I had an aunt named Beula. She always acted so prim and proper. She kept an immaculate house. My mom used to tell a story about when they were young. They lived in a small town, and one night, they were going home after a movie, walking through a narrow alley. They met a large dog running toward them, and Beula ended up straddling the dog, riding it backward through the alley. When my mom told us that story, she laughed so hard she cried."

Bella wiped laughter tears from her eyes. "Oh, that is the best story. I'll remember to tell my girl when she is old enough to understand. Thank you, Katina, for sharing it with me."

In a short while, they pulled up at Willow Grove dock. Jerome and Katina led Bella up to the shelter. Tashina examined her, filled out the paperwork, and soon had her settled into a room. The next day, the clients welcomed Bella and gave her a tour of the shelter.

Bella gazed around as they took her outside to the patio. "This is such a nice place," she said. "I love this backyard. It's so shady and pretty. I've always lived in the city and wished for a backyard like this. I'll want to draw it."

"Are you an artist?" Juliet asked.

Bella blushed. "Yes. I do charcoal drawings and paintings. I was taking classes until...." She turned her face away. "Oh, look at that little squirrel. He's so cute."

"Oh, my goodness," said Iris. "Maybe you can draw my

little girl, Micah."

Bella looked around at the faces. "Well, I'd gladly do some drawings if I have enough supplies. I brought some with me, but not many."

Grace turned to Sadie, who had just walked up. "Mrs. Sadie, can we get her some art supplies so she can draw us? I mean, our children? Please?"

Sadie laughed. "If she wants to do that, David and I will see what we can do," she said. "Right now, why don't you ladies take our new friend to the dining room for lunch before it gets cold?"

Randall ran to pull out a chair for the new client, bringing a smile to her face. Jax and Brent stood nearby, and all three boys bowed low. Since Charlie had been visiting often, the boys had taken up his habit of bowing to people. The mamas agreed it was better than acting like hogs.

After they offered grace for the food, Bella looked in awe at the grilled pork chops, vegetables, and rolls. "This looks and smells so good," she said. "But I'd better not eat too much. I need to lose some of this fat."

"Fat? You're not fat," Katina said. The others joined her in assuring Bella she wasn't fat.

"You have to eat for that baby," Marleigh said. "After she's born, you can see if you need to lose any. Right now, you're fine."

"I knew a young woman once who was pregnant," Katina said, "and she wanted her baby to be healthy, so she ate only spinach and carrots. I swear, she was orange by the time her baby was born."

"Was the baby orange?" asked Angie.

"No, I don't think so. But it's a wonder it wasn't."

"I like carrots," said Bella, "but I don't want to turn orange."

Brent twisted around in his chair. "That'd be great if it was Halloween," he said, "then you could be a pumpkin."

"I was a headless man once," said Katina. "And my friend

was a two-headed man."

"Cool!" Brent almost fell out of his chair.

A yell came from the hall beside the kitchen. "Help! Someone come quick!" Mandy was standing in the laundry room doorway.

Everyone in the dining room ran into a flooded hall. Water was pouring from the ceiling.

"Someone run upstairs," yelled David. "One of the bathrooms must be flooding."

Lyric and Angie ran up the steps, then yelled back down. "It's three of the bathrooms," Lyric said. "Looks like someone stuffed rags or something in the sinks and left the water running."

Everyone grabbed towels and mops, and soon, they had the mess cleaned up, but the ceilings were badly damaged.

"Everyone, meet back in the dining room," Sadie said. "We have to get to the bottom of this trouble."

David and Sadie stalked around the room while the clients sat wide-eyed. David slapped his hand on a table. "Someone is responsible for this," he yelled. "This was intentional. Who in this building wants to destroy this shelter?"

He stood in front of each person and peered into their eyes. Some trembled, and some turned their faces away. Not one accepted responsibility.

"But Mr. David," Wren said, "we were all in the dining room eating lunch. How could any of us be guilty?"

"That's right," said Caroline. "Besides, we love this place. Why would we want to do damage to it?"

Others nodded in agreement.

"All I know is someone stuffed those towels in the sinks and left the water running. That was intentional. Someone is responsible. Who else is here but all of you in this room?"

The clients looked at each other. It was like an air of suspicion filled the room, stifling them. Memories of past incidents floated before their minds' eyes. Who caused the fire in the laundry room? Who kidnapped little Aiden? Who put marijuana in Caroline's room? David and Sadie were now aware that everyone knew about that. Opinions differed on whether Caroline was guilty or not. There were other events for which there were no answers.

Wren raised her hand halfway. "I saw someone in the hall while we were eating," she said. "I think it was Louisa."

Mandy whirled around. "Don't you dare blame Louisa for that mess. She was in the kitchen working on supper while you all enjoyed lunch. She does that every day. Besides, she would never do anything so mean."

Wren wilted and remained silent.

"If any of you think of anything that might help us solve this mystery, please come see me in my office. I should be there all afternoon," David said. He dismissed them and left the room.

A handyman replaced the damaged ceilings, and the ladies painted them. Sadie enjoyed their chatter, which lifted the spirits of the place. About the time they finished the work, Lyric ran shouting into the backyard.

"The boys are in trouble," he yelled. "They're over on the chute."

David ran from his office. "What kind of trouble?"

Lyric bent over to catch his breath. "They're in the river on some boards."

"Call Jerome," David said. "Tell him to take his boat." He ran out the back door, followed by Sadie, Loreen, Juliet, and Tina.

When they arrived at the chute that widened out to meet the river, they could see the boys holding onto a contraption that looked like boards nailed together. They were floating toward the opposite bank. They kept looking back toward the island.

Loreen started wading into the water, yelling. "Brent, you come back here." And "Hold on, son." Sadie grabbed her arm and pulled her back.

"The men will get them," Juliet assured her. They watched as Jerome pulled his boat near them, and Lyric reached out and pulled each of them into the vessel. When they brought them to shore beside their mamas, Juliet and Loreen first hugged and then scolded the soaked, scared boys.

"What in the world were you doing?" Loreen asked.

"We wanted to build a raft like Mr. David said he did when he was a kid," Brent said. "We thought that'd be cool. It wasn't. It was scary."

"I guess we aren't very good at building things," Randall said.

Jax trembled as he held on to his mom. "I was scared," he kept saying.

Sadie punched David's arm. "Guess you'll be careful what stories you tell these kids next time."

"I sure will," he said. "I never would have thought they'd do something like this."

Meanwhile:

"Hey, Grandpa. I know where to get you some vegetables for your farmers' market booth." A young man sat on the rickety porch talking to an older man.

"That'd be just dandy," the old man said. "My garden ain't done very well this year. I sure need some things to sell. I ain't got much money to pay for them, though."

"Ah, don't worry, Gramps. I'll take care of it. Anything for you."

As he drifted by Willow Grove Shelter in his johnboat, he had witnessed some women carrying buckets of vegetables from the garden in the back. It would be easy to grab a bucket while they weren't looking. A bunch of women like them probably wouldn't miss one bucket. Or two.

THIRTY-THREE

David and Sadie relaxed in their lawn chairs as they watched Benji and his dog, Gus, romping around in the backyard. "I can't believe our boy is getting so big," Sadie said. "He loved going to the zoo yesterday with our parents. He keeps talking about the 'orsies. That's what he calls the zebras."

David laughed. "Oh. That's what he's talking about. I wondered when the zoo started keeping horses."

"I can't wait until little Jon starts talking more. Then, the two of them can hold conversations. I have a feeling that will be hilarious."

"Speaking of conversations—I overheard one yesterday that piqued my interest."

"Oh, really? What was it?"

"Caroline was talking to Madison, trying to convince her to let you put her in rehabilitation. At first, Madison was adamant that she didn't need it, but Caroline told her how she was before and after rehab. How much happier she is, and how much better she feels."

Sadie signaled with a thumbs-up. "Great. Good for Caroline."

"There's something else. Caroline told Madison she knows how she feels, but I finally realized she wasn't just talking about addiction. She was talking about doing jobs for a dealer named Carp who works for Cosmos."

Sadie jumped to her feet. "What? Cosmos? You're

kidding! What did you do?"

"I kept listening. I wanted to know the whole story. It seems that Cosmos had an operative who used these girls to sabotage the shelter. Evidently, Caroline was working for the same man who planted Madison when she came here."

"You have to be kidding!" Sadie bit her thumbnail, then snapped her fingers. "Yes, I remember. When I found her by the river, she was waiting for someone. She told me she was in bad need of a fix. I convinced her to return to the shelter, and we would help her. Remember?"

"I do. That's why I thought Caroline could do more for Madison than we could. And I was right. Madison agreed to submit to rehabilitation. Caroline told her she would stay with her tonight, and they would talk to you in the morning."

Tears ran down Sadie's face. "Oh, thank you, Jesus!" she said. "I'm so glad to hear that. Now I can't wait until morning to hear her myself and get her started." She sat back down in her lawn chair. "I just can't believe Cosmos is reaching his evil fingers from prison to cause trouble here. Why would he do that?"

"I guess for payback. We ruined his crime organization, remember?"

"Maybe we didn't. Maybe we just slowed it down. I'll bet he is mad at us."

"Yeah, some folks don't take responsibility for their own messes. It's always someone else's fault."

Sadie waved a hand. "Own up or pay up."

"He's paying up, but he'd like to see us pay instead. We'll have to be more careful of new clients and anyone coming around. We'll notify Jerome and Jason."

The following day, Sadie officially admitted Madison into the rehabilitation program. Caroline and Grace would see her through the process while the other clients prayed for her.

Cries in the middle of the night awoke everyone in the shelter. Loreen came to the head of the stairs. "Ms. Tashina! Hurry! The baby is coming."

Tashina donned a robe and ran upstairs. She pushed her way through the clients hovering around Bella's door. Grace was at Bella's bedside, instructing her to breathe.

"Oh, Ms. Tashina," Bella said. "It hurts so much. Can't you stop the pain?"

Tashina busied herself preparing for the delivery. She nodded to Grace to continue what she was doing. "You have to relax and breathe," she said. "Just like Grace is telling you."

Tashina's face turned ashen when the baby came out. It was not breathing. She worked with it, keeping herself between the baby and Bella. It was no use. Just as she turned away to give Bella the news, the baby made a noise. She whirled around and picked it up, rubbing its back. It gasped, then cried. Tashina smiled and handed the little girl to Bella. The new mother was overjoyed.

"Oh, my little Beula Jane." Bella cried and cuddled the tiny infant. Grace ran out to tell everyone and a cheer floated through the building. Then, the clients returned to bed so Bella and little Beula Jane could rest.

Tashina kept a close eye on the infant to ensure it was healthy. To be safe, she and Jerome boated Bella and the baby to a doctor on the mainland to check it out. Tashina was relieved when he pronounced her healthy.

The clients almost fought over who could hold Beula Jane in the following weeks. Determined not to let the baby become spoiled, Bella made some rigid rules. She soon realized it was useless and allowed them to hold her, rock her, carry her, whatever they were prone to do. When the baby was hungry, Mama took her into her room to nurse and spend alone time with her. She cherished those moments.

Most evenings passed with everyone gathered on the patio. Some played in the pool, and others swapped stories. Other times, they gathered in the lounge. They loved hearing Katina's stories about her life before the war, and, once in a while, convinced her to talk about her war experiences.

"I once had an uncle," she began one evening, "who didn't have toenails."

Instantly, the boys were all ears. "Why didn't he have toenails?" Jax asked.

"Well, because he pulled them all off."

"Ouch!" Several of the ladies visibly winced.

"Why in the world would he do that?" asked Elfi.

"You're joking," said Sage. "No one would pull off their toenails. That would hurt too much."

Katina pursed her lips. "But he surely did. He said he had an ingrown toenail when he was about the age of Brent here. His parents took him to the doctor, and the doctor had to cut it out. It hurt so much that he decided he never wanted another sore toe, so he crawled up in the middle of his bed with a pair of pliers and pulled the rest off."

"Ewwww!" Madison rubbed her arms and shivered. "That had to hurt. I think I'd rather deal with one sore toe than ten sore toes."

They all agreed.

Remembering another incident due to a story, David admonished the fellows. "Now, boys," he said, "I don't want any of you trying to pull off your toenails." He turned to Sadie. "Maybe we'd better hide the pliers for a few days."

Katina talked about her experience in the military. "Once, a man who somehow got in the women's bunk attacked me," she said. "By the time we females were through with him, he looked pretty bad. Then we learned he was drunk and accidentally got in our bunk. He never did that again."

One evening, she talked about the war. "We had this man who loved children." Her eyes had a distant look, and her voice was soft. "He came from a large family and had nieces and nephews. He missed them. He saved whatever candy he found to give the Vietnamese children when they came around the camp. They called him Chú, which means uncle in their language." Her smile disappeared, and her eyes misted. "One day, he saw a little boy standing at the edge of the camp. He called out, but the boy stood still. He ran to where the boy stood and, too late, realized the boy was booby-trapped. The North Vietnamese did that, you know. They'd booby trap women and children and send them into the American camps to kill our soldiers."

She sat looking out the window. Juliet spoke. "I read that the North and South Vietnamese looked the same."

Katina nodded. "They did. We couldn't tell them apart. We didn't know which ones were our friends or our enemies."

"What happened to Chú?" Lyric asked.

Katina looked at him, rose, and left the room. They all sat in silence until someone mentioned that it was bedtime. They went to their rooms without speaking.

The women often gave one another manicures and pedicures and tried various hairstyles on each other. Evelyn was quite the seamstress and fashioned clothing for the others. When Bella returned to normal activities, she started drawing charcoal images of the children. Mamas were so excited that they soon had paintings hung everywhere. With the help of Lyric, David built frames in his woodshop. Bella also did illustrations of the woodland creatures that often came out of the woods to visit the shelter's backyard, flowers that grew in abundance beside the river, and various birds on the island.

"You need to take some of your paintings and drawings to the craft village," David said. "They are unlike anything the crafters there have. They might want to sell them for you for a small commission."

One of the shop owners agreed to display Bella's artwork, and visitors from the mainland raved over them. Soon, Bella couldn't paint them fast enough. She made appointments and set up a studio in the village to do charcoal drawings of customers and their children. Her artwork drew customers from surrounding towns on the mainland, and the word spread. In time, an art center in the city invited her to exhibit her work.

"You're getting famous," Angie said to Bella one day. "Soon, you'll forget that you knew us."

Bella hugged the girl. "Never. Y'all have saved me, and I won't forget. Besides, I'm hardly famous." She giggled. "Maybe one day."

Sadie knew their artist would want to move into her own place soon. They would have to let her and baby Beula go. That's what she wanted for all the clients as they became self-sufficient.

Meanwhile:

Jackson slammed his fist on the steering wheel of his new silver Land Rover. What just happened? How could his boss fire him? He was trying to save money for the company, wasn't he? How did he know a senior agent had negotiated the deal with the boss?

Since Bella left, things had gone downhill. The affair with the company secretary had gone flat. His boss told him he was worthless to the company. He needed to get a job flipping burgers or something requiring less intelligence. Some senior agents told him he needed to listen and learn instead of talking so much. They laughed at him when he tried to comment in the meetings. Even his parents were angry with him for running Bella off. He tried to convince them he didn't run her off. That was her own decision. But they weren't convinced. They said he robbed them of their first grandchild and needed to do whatever it took to get her back.

He had an upcoming interview with a smaller company, which hurt his pride. Oh well, he'd try his hardest to get the job. Hopefully, soon, he could earn a promotion if he kept his ego in check. When he started drawing a decent paycheck, he might find Bella and get her back. By then, the baby would be born, and she would be desperate to return to him. He knew she wouldn't go to her parents. They were destitute and couldn't feed two more, especially a baby. If he couldn't learn to be a good dad, at least his parents would be happy to have a grandchild.

THIRTY-FOUR

Katina proved to be a wonder in the garden. She knew all kinds of ways to make things easier and to encourage the vegetables to grow.

"Put some Epsom salts in that water to fertilize those tomatoes and peppers," she said. "It will make them sweeter and stop those tomatoes from having bottom rot."

She helped the kids make a little garden, showing them how to plant the tomatoes deep and stake them up.

"Here, plant these marigolds with the tomatoes to help keep the bugs out," she said. She showed them how to put slivers of bath soap in the corn and beans to keep the deer away.

"How did deer get over here on the island?" Randall asked.

"Duh. They swammed," said Jax. "Deers can swim, you know. I seen 'em once."

"Brent, get some fertilizer for the squash," said Elfi. "I love squash and want them to make a bunch."

Brent left and returned with a box of salt. He poured it all around the squash, and Sage used a hoe to work it into the soil. Ruby watered the plants with a garden hose.

A few days later, the squash wilted. Elfi ran to Katina.

"Something's the matter with the squash," she said. "I think they're dying."

Katina followed her to the little garden to look at the plants. She inspected the stalk, but it looked fine. She could see no reason for the plants to be dying.

"We fertilized it good," Elfi said.

"What fertilizer did you use?" asked Katina.

"We used salt just like you said, and we put a bunch," said Sage. "Didn't we, Brent?"

Brent puffed up his chest. "We sure did. Elfi likes squash, so we want a lot." He ran to the kitchen and returned with a box of salt. "This is what we used."

Katina drew in her breath. "Oh, dear, young'uns. That's the wrong kind of salt. You have to use Epsom salts, not table salt."

The children's eyes widened. "You mean we killed the squash?" asked Sage. "Oh, Elfi, we're sorry."

Brent lowered his head. "I'm sorry, Elfi."

Katina looked at the sad children. "Hey, guys, it isn't too late to plant more. We'll plant some in a different place. We'll have plenty of squash to eat."

The next day, the ladies picked several buckets of vegetables to preserve. They put them on a table behind the shelter and went to eat lunch. When they returned, something was different.

"I thought these buckets were full," Loreen said.

"They were." Marleigh counted. "And one is missing."

"What's going on around here?" asked Juliet. "Seems like things come up missing all the time."

Evelyn picked up a large zucchini. "I think I'm gonna make zucchini bread from this one." She looked at Juliet. "I wasn't gonna say anything, but something of mine is missing. I had a necklace with a small diamond, and I haven't found it anywhere."

Iris came through the door carrying a wasp to release. "Go find your family," she said to the insect. "You're free now." She saw the concerned look on the faces of the others. "What's going on?"

"Stuff is missing," said Tina, "and we can't figure out what's happening to it." They told her about the bucket of vegetables and Evelyn's necklace.

"That's funny," Iris said. "A wallet I purchased at the Village is missing. I know I put it on my dresser, but it isn't there. It had a little money in it, too."

Soon, a group of women gathered around the buckets of vegetables. They reported other things missing. A bag, a trinket, a ring, a sack of new makeup. The ladies marched to David's office to report the missing items.

David looked at each face. He believed these women to be honest. They would not purposely hurt anyone. They worked together to keep things at the shelter running smoothly.

"Ladies, we do have a problem. We'll have to find out who is taking your things." He scratched his head. "I just have to figure out how."

"Sadie, we have a situation." Sophia ran into Sadie's office. "Someone has tampered with the safe. I don't know how they did it, but they broke in and stole some money. Some of the gold is gone, too."

Sadie called David, and the three discussed the solution to a growing problem. Sadie twirled a lock of hair around her finger. "Who could be doing this? I can't imagine anyone here being a thief."

"I can't either," said Sophia. "These people are hardworking, good folks. I can't see any one of them doing something like this."

"But the truth is," said David, "someone is. Someone has us all fooled. We've got to figure out who that someone is. I'm not sure how." He turned to Sophia. "Can you and Kade come to the house tonight for supper? We can try to come up with a solution while we eat."

Sophia nudged Sadie. "What are we having to eat?" She winked. "Kade will want to know."

"I think I have the stuff to make chicken alfredo. How does that sound?"

Sophia rubbed her stomach. "Sounds great. It makes me

hungry now. I'll call Kade and tell him to get Jon ready."

"Benji will be so excited," said David. "He'll want to show Jon his new tractor and trailer."

Later, after they ate, they relaxed in the shady backyard to discuss the situation. "I don't like the idea of searching them or their rooms," David said. "I just don't know what else to do."

Kade wasn't so concerned about their privacy. "I say we have a shakedown. Line them up in the halls and search them and their rooms. We have to get to the bottom of this one way or another."

"No." David rose and looked out over the backyard. "Most of the ladies were in my office reporting that they had items taken. So we know it isn't them."

Kade rubbed his beard and frowned. Then he grabbed a pad and pencil. "Tell me who all were in your office."

"Let's see…" David named the women. "Loreen, Juliet, Evelyn, Tina, Marleigh, and Iris.

Sadie counted off the names as he wrote them. "You didn't count Caroline, Wren, Grace, Madison, Nancy, Bella, Katina… and of course the help, Angie, Mandy, and Louisa,"

"I guess no one can be left out until we settle this matter," said Sophia. Her eyes brightened. "Maybe it's the kids. Have you all thought of that?"

"The kids?" Sadie protested. "No, it couldn't be any of the kids. Could it?"

Kade stuck up his index finger. "We must consider that it could be one of the ladies in your office. Maybe one of them just went along with the rest to make herself look innocent."

David turned. "That's possible. Then how in the world are we going to find the culprit?"

They were silent as they thought about the problem. Then Kade had an idea. "A surprise shakedown? Line them up in the dining room and search them, then search their rooms."

Sadie shook her head. "That's a major invasion of privacy. We could do it, but it could bite us in the butt."

"Sadie's right," said Sophia. "We need a substantial reason to search them and their rooms. Besides, we don't want innocent ones offended."

They prayed together for wisdom and agreed to keep an eye out for the next few days. Surely, something would come up.

The next day, David and Sadie started their evening walk from the back door and through the patio. The little girls were playing as usual in their playhouse in the corner of the yard under a lilac bush. They had tied a rope from a nearby tree to the bush where they played, making a little area where they parked their baby strollers.

David walked over for a look at the rope. Sage was busy making an imaginary meal on the little play stove. "Where did this rope come from?" he asked her.

She glanced up at him and continued to cook her food. "I don't know. Ruby had it."

"Ruby, where did this rope come from?" he asked the girl.

"Uh, I found it," she said.

"Where did you find it?"

"In a room upstairs."

"What else did you find in that room?"

"This." Ruby pulled an envelope from her pocket and handed it to David.

He opened the envelope, and his head jerked up. He handed it to Sadie, who had the same reaction. "Is that all you found in that room?" he asked Ruby.

"No. There was some of the gold the boys found."

Sadie kneeled in front of the little girl. "Ruby, will you show us the room where you found these things?"

"Sure." Ruby walked in front of them, up the stairs, and down the hall. She pushed open the door to a room no one was using. "In here," she said.

"Okay, sweetie," Sadie said. "You can go back to your playhouse." Ruby ran down the stairs, and David and Sadie looked around. The room had a bed, dresser, desk, and desk chair. An armchair was in one corner, and a bookshelf was beside it.

It didn't take long for them to find a few of the things reported missing by the clients. "Let's leave everything as it is," David said. "I'll ask Jason if he will set up a camera here."

He met with Jason and Jerome to discuss his idea. "Sure, it will work," said Jason. "Since that room is unassigned, there should be no problem. You take the clients on another excursion somewhere, and I'll do it while they're all gone."

"Are the ladies selling some of the produce from the garden?" Jerome asked.

"Not as far as I know," said David. "Why?"

"The other evening, I saw a guy carrying a bucket of veggies down to the river and loading them into a boat. I don't know where he could have gotten them except from here."

"What'd he look like?" asked David.

"Young man, slight build. Bigger than Lyric and probably older. Wearing a cap."

"Guess that explains the produce the ladies are missing," said David. "They're upset about it."

"I don't blame them," said Jerome. "They work hard to raise and harvest the produce. I'd be mad, too, if someone stole what I'd worked hard for."

David scratched his head. "Yeah, but I don't know what to do about it. We can't keep an eye on everything all the time."

"Think we need to install an outside camera?" Jerome asked.

"I don't think so. I'd hate to do that. Those women don't need to be spied on all the time. Maybe it won't happen again."

Meanwhile:

Just before dark, a young woman met a slightly built young man at the edge of the river a distance from the shelter. "I'm just waiting for a chance to grab the baby." She whispered to him as she handed him a box in return for a small package, which he slipped into her hand.

He peeked inside and whistled. "This will be worth some dough."

"Yeah, I know. Now, what's your plan?"

"Something will come up. These people like to have events and soon they'll plan something. When they do, I can get Jase and Sully to cause a distraction so you can get her. Just don't get caught. I'll be nearby to take her from you."

He grabbed her and pulled her close. She lifted her face, and their lips met before she shoved him away.

"What's the matter with you? You always push me away." He reached for her again, but she turned aside. "Don't you love me anymore?"

"Of course I do. It's just that—I'm on edge until this is all over. It's taking too long."

"Just be patient, sweetheart. When the man is here, things will move quickly. You'll see. Then payday will come."

THIRTY-FIVE

"Let's take all the clients and staff to the Memphis Zoo," Sadie suggested when David told her about the plan to set up a camera. "That would be so much fun and could take all day."

They discussed it with Kade and Sophia and set a time. Early on the appointed day, they all walked to the Craft Village, where they would board the ferry for the trip. They had strollers for Aiden and Beula, and Louisa and Wren packed lunch with plenty of drinks. The adults were excited, and the children even more so. It would be a great day for everyone. David did a headcount, and Kade loaded the lunch and drinks in a wagon they had brought. He and Sophia would lead while David and Sadie brought up the rear. Again, the adults watched the children. Louisa and Mandy would also help. They wanted no unhappy incidents to take place on this special day. A brief thought flitted through David's mind. Is it safe to take these people to a big city like Memphis now with everything happening? He shrugged it off and laughed at the jokes Kade told the children.

"Mama, look at that elephant!" Jax pulled Juliet's hand on one side, and Jamie pulled the other.

"Look, Mama," said Jamie. "Look at the big bird. Look at his big tail. Isn't it pretty?" Angie took Jax's hand and led him closer to the elephants. "Can I ride it?" he asked.

Susan and Micah loved to watch the sea lions. Sage and Ruby gravitated toward the monkeys while Randall and Brent ran to see the big cats. A white peacock in all her splendor strutted before them, showing off her lacey white feathers. Bella took out a sketch pad and sketched her while the others moved on. Caroline and Madison took turns pushing baby Beula around in her stroller.

They found tables for their picnic lunch and later enjoyed ice cream cones and flavored shaved ice.

"I wanna see the hippos," said Randall.

"Yeah, and the rhinos," added Brent.

"We want to visit the bird cage." Ruby and Sage held hands as they jumped up and down.

"Why don't you leave the babies here with Madison and me?" asked Wren, "We'll watch them nap in the shade. It's cool here." Madison nodded her agreement.

The mamas kissed their babies and hurried away behind the excited children. When they were out of sight, Madison leaned over to touch the soft baby face of Beula.

"I look forward to getting married and having a baby one day," she said. "They are just so sweet and innocent."

Wren dug in her bag and stuck a piece of candy into her mouth. "If I ever have a baby, I'll take care of it myself. I'll have to marry a rich man who can care for me and the child 'cause I don't want to work. I want to be a stay-at-home mom."

Madison adjusted the strap that held the baby in the stroller. "Yeah, me too. I'd like to stay home to keep house and raise a family."

Wren uttered a low chuckle. "Listen to us talk about having babies. Like it will ever happen."

"Why can't it happen?" Madison said. "I won't stay in the shelter forever. When I'm through the rehab program, I intend to find a job and get my own place."

"I'm not in the rehab program, so I guess I could leave any time. I like working in the shelter but only make a little money there. I've been thinking about going to the mainland to look for a job."

"Really? I thought you were here for rehab like me." Madison tilted her head. "Are you here because of domestic abuse?"

Wren shook her head.

"Then, if you don't mind my asking, why?'

Wren checked on Aiden, who was starting to wiggle. "I went to the shelter when it opened, and they offered me a job. I took it." She stood and gestured toward the gift shop. "How about a Coke?"

"Sounds good." Madison dug in her purse. "Oh, I don't have enough money. I only have a dollar."

"Here, I have some. Tell you what. I'll buy it if you'll go get it."

"Sure. I can do that." Madison took the bills and went to the gift shop.

While she was waiting on the soda, she noticed that two monkeys were going in the direction of Wren. A man in a uniform ran behind them, calling to them. "Here's your binky, Rosco. Come here, Rosie. Get your butts back here before I …."

Soon, a crowd gathered, watching and laughing at the man trying to capture the little creatures. They ignored him, laughed at him, and created a show with their antics. They swung from tree to tree, back and forth, over the heads of the people. They chattered as one sat on a man's shoulder and laughed when he tried to grab them.

"Be careful," the zookeeper said. "The little creatures may be cute, but they can be mean. Sometimes, they bite and scratch. "

Several people tried to help the officer catch the monkeys, but they teased and frolicked until they grew tired of the game. Then they went to the man, climbed onto his shoulders, and patted him on the head. The crowd laughed and applauded as the zookeeper returned his charges to their cages.

Madison picked up the order and returned to find Wren beside herself, running back and forth, looking everywhere. Baby Beula was gone. Her stroller was empty.

"How could that happen?" Wren cried. The distressed young women screamed out for help. Madison saw an officer looking toward them. "Please come help us, sir. Someone took our baby."

The officer ran to them. He looked at Aiden, at Madison, and then at Wren. As he gestured toward Aiden, he started to say something, but Wren stopped him.

"Not that one," she yelled. "It's our baby girl. She's gone."

"When did she disappear?" the officer asked.

Wren lowered her head. "I guess I was distracted by the monkeys. When I looked around, she was gone. Our little Beula was gone." Tears streamed down her face as she covered it with her hands. Madison put her arms around Wren, and they sobbed together.

"Ladies, I have to have information to fill out this report," the officer said. That's when David and Sadie came running toward them.

"What happened?" David asked. He looked at the two women and Aiden. "Where's the baby? Where's baby Beula?"

Wren and Madison turned to them. "Oh, Mr. David," said Madison. "Mrs. Sadie. We're so sorry. Someone took baby Beulah." Tears flowed down her cheeks.

"The monkeys were here," Wren said, "and people were all around. Someone took her while we weren't looking."

David pointed toward some people coming down the walkway. Kade led the group made up of clients and several others. Their voices raised as they strode toward the girls and the officer. As they drew nearer, Bella appeared to be carrying something, and Kade was half dragging two young men.

"It's baby Beulah!" Wren screamed and ran to meet them. She ran beside Bella, checking the baby over. "She seems to be all right," she said. "How'd you get her?"

They reached the police officer and Wren. Kade shoved the two guys toward the officer. "Here, officer, are the kidnappers. We caught them red-handed with our baby. They tried to run, but we surrounded them and brought them down."

The Willow Grove group nodded their heads and chattered about the capture. The kids were jumping up and down with excitement.

"When Ms. Bella saw them with the baby, she knew it was Beula right away," said Randall. "So Mr. Kade chased them down. Then we all jumped on them. "

"Yeah," said Brent. "When Ms. Bella saw strangers with her baby, she started screaming. I think she scared them."

"I thought Ms. Marleigh was gonna hurt them bad," said Elfi. "Ms. Juliet had to pull her off."

The officer cuffed the two men and, much to the children's delight, turned on his blue lights as he drove away.

David and Kade pulled Wren and Madison to one side while the ladies surrounded Bella and little Beula.

"Tell us step by step what happened," David said.

Madison said that she had gone to get a soda and saw the loose monkeys, and Wren explained how the crowd gathered to watch the zookeeper capture the creatures, and she was distracted by the show.

"When I turned around, Beula was gone." She wiped tears from her face.

All the way home, they chatted about the trip. The children talked about all the animals they saw until they boarded the ferry when the smaller ones fell asleep. The ladies guarded Bella and Beula and watched over Marleigh and Aiden until they were safe at home. Then, they all pitched in to help Louisa and Wren make a quick supper before they gathered in the lounge to wind down before bedtime.

A week went by with no results from the installed camera. The following week, Jason reported that someone had entered the room. They watched the video repeatedly, but the picture was blurry, and the person moved around so much they couldn't tell who it was. They could faintly hear a female voice, but not enough to identify it. Jason adjusted the camera, and a few days later, they had a clear video of a female in the room. They were shocked.

"I guess we've been taken," said David as he, Jason, and Jerome watched. "I would never have believed that Grace would be the culprit."

"Grace?" Sadie gasped when David showed her, Kade, and Sophia the video. "No, it can't be. There must be another reason she's in there. She would never do something like that."

"Do you think she's desperate for money?" Sadie asked. "There has to be a good explanation."

"I don't think there's ever a good reason for someone to steal from others," Sophia said.

David turned the video off. "We'll have to talk to her in private tomorrow. I sure hope this is all a mistake."

The next day, David and Sadie called Grace into Sadie's office. Her big eyes rested on their faces, waiting to see what they wanted from her.

Sadie started. "Grace, how are you and Elfi doing here at Willow Grove?"

"Oh, Ms. Sadie, we love it here. You saved our lives, and we are grateful." A smile spread across her face.

"Is there anything we can do to help you in any way?" David asked. "Do you feel at home here? Do you have everything you need?"

Her eyes flickered back and forth between their faces, and she picked at her fingernail. "We do feel at home here. We love it and everyone. There's nothing more we need. You all have been wonderful."

David looked at Sadie. Everything she was saying

pointed to her innocence. How could anyone believe she could have blackness in her heart? Maybe she had different personalities. But no, Sadie would have seen that already.

Sadie watched Grace's face for a sign of guilt. "We just want you and Elfi to know if you need anything, you can come to us."

Grace opened her mouth and closed it, then looked back from Sadie to David. "There is one thing I need to ask," she said. "I found an unused room upstairs, and I wondered — I guess I should have asked before — I wondered if you'd mind if I use it for something. I've been working on a gift for Elfi — her birthday is coming up soon — and I need a place to hide it. I put it in the room. I hope you don't care."

Relief flooded over both David and Sadie. Sadie jumped up. "Oh, Grace. We don't mind at all, do we, David?"

A smile spread across David's face. "We sure don't. But I might have a better place for you to hide it so no one will find it." He looked at Sadie, who nodded. "There's a room closer to you, and I'll give you a key. Then you can hide whatever you want in it. Come with me."

When they left her office, Sadie walked to the window and looked over the river — alive, moving, hiding, and sustaining God's creatures. Thousands of creatures. Willow Grove sustained a few, but those few were important. The smile on her face was still there when Sophia came in with a bottle of water for each of them. Sadie explained what had happened, and the two women clicked the bottles together in celebration. It was a good day, but they still had a culprit to catch.

Meanwhile:

"You say you know where my wife is?" The man in a business suit looked the young woman up and down. "How do you know my wife?"

The young woman smiled. "Just trust me. You're Jackson, right? And her name is Bella?"

"That's right. I'll ask again—how do you know my wife?"

She adjusted her tight skirt. "That isn't important. Do you want her back or not?"

"Did she have the baby yet? Is it healthy?"

"Yes, she had a little girl. She named her Beula."

His lips curled, and his nose wrinkled. "Beula! Why did she give our baby a name like Beula?"

"I don't know. Something about an aunt." She tapped one foot on the sidewalk. "Well, do you want her back or not?"

"Of course, I want her back. At least, my parents do. They want their grandchild. So, where is she?"

The young woman smiled. "You'll need a boat."

THIRTY-SIX

When David answered a knock at the door, a nice-looking, well-dressed man stood, shuffling from one foot to the other. Oh, no, not another DHS agent! But it was someone looking for Bella.

"Is Bella Portland here?" the man asked.

David looked him up and down. "Who wants to know?"

"I'm Jackson Portland, her husband."

David extended his hand. "Nice to meet you, Jackson. I'm David Kingston. Come in."

He seated Jackson in his office. "Can you verify that you are Bella's husband?"

Jackson pulled out his driver's license and handed it to David. David grunted and asked him to wait while he went to find Sadie. He found her in the kitchen chatting with Louisa and eating chips and dip.

"Sadie, I have a man in my office who claims to be Bella's husband."

"Did he show any verification?"

"Yes, a driver's license. You many want to meet him." He grabbed a chip and went back to his office.

Sadie followed him through the door. "Hello," she said. "I'm Mrs. Kingston. I'm the therapist here at Willow Grove. It's my job to lead my clients toward healing the wounds caused by those who have hurt them."

His nostrils flared, and he stood. "Bella is my wife. I have a right to see her."

Sadie raised a brow. "That, sir, is up to her. She's busy now, but I will let her know you are here." She breezed out of the room. He glowered at David.

"Mr. Kingston, I insist on seeing my wife now."

"Sit down, Mr. Portland. If she wants to see you, she will come." He sat at his desk and studied the man. "What are your intentions for Bella?" he asked.

Jackson's jaw tightened. "I consider that none of your business."

David leaned back in his chair with his hands behind his head. "Bella is a resident at Willow Grove, and I am the director here. So yes, it is my business what happens to our residents." He leaned forward. "So, Mr. Portland, what are your intentions for Ms. Bella, a resident of Willow Grove?"

Jackson's face reddened. "Uh, I want to talk to her. She walked out on me, and I want her to come back. I want my wife back."

"Do you think you have a right to ask her to return to you after the way you treated her? Have you changed your perception of how you should treat a wife?"

"I think I do have a right. I didn't treat her all that bad. She was just too picky and sensitive."

"Was she too sensitive for you to shove around? For you to denigrate?"

"Denigrate?"

"Belittle. Ridicule. Mock. Dismiss. Crush. Humiliate. Put down. Bad mouth."

"Oh. Well...."

"Did you consider how it hurt her when you shoved her down? Did it cross your mind that you might hurt her and the baby? Oh, that's right. You cared nothing for the baby. You didn't even want it."

Jackson's blush deepened. "Sir, I'm not the monster you make me out to be."

"I beg to differ. A husband who treats his wife — the one he vowed to love and honor — like you treated Bella is, in fact, a monster. I assume you made that vow to her. Most marriage vows do that. Or do you even remember those vows?"

Jackson fidgeted in his chair. "Uh, yes, I guess. Mr. Kingston, you're making me very uncomfortable."

"Do tell! Good. You need to be uncomfortable. It wouldn't be bad if you hurt a little bit to help you realize how you hurt her. I can arrange that, you know."

Jackson's eyes grew round, and he leaped to his feet.

"Oh, sit back down. I'm not going to hurt you. I'm just trying to make you look at things from Bella's perspective."

"Just forget it!" Jackson shouted. "I don't have to listen to this."

David jumped up. "You need to listen for once."

"I think I've heard enough." Jackson turned and fled. David watched him run to the river and pace along the shoreline. He started to get into a boat once but turned and paced some more. He jabbed his fist into the air, then stomped up and down the walkway to the shelter. Back and forth he went. Finally, David walked toward him. When he got close, he almost expected Jackson to hit him. But the face he saw when Jackson turned to look at him was half anger and half torture.

"You have no right to tell me what to do," he growled. "I'm a man, and I make my own decisions. Bella is my wife, and you don't have a right to keep her from me."

"I'm not keeping her from you," David said. "She knows it's her decision. What have you done to make her want to return to the life you gave her?"

"I graduated college and landed a good-paying job. But I guess that wasn't enough for her."

David sat down on a bench beside the dock. "Why do you think she left?"

"How should I know? She's selfish. She wants everything her way."

"What does she want her way? Give me an example."

Jackson stared at a boat going by. "Well, when I got some

new clothes for work, she demanded new clothes." He pursed his lips. "That's selfish. I had to have clothes for the office."

"Did that have anything to do with her being pregnant? When women get pregnant, their clothes no longer fit."

"Yeah, I guess so. I didn't think about that."

"Sounds to me like you only thought about yourself. When you're married, you have to think about your spouse as much or more than you think about yourself. Your wife has feelings, too, you know."

His eyelids drooped, and he pulled on his shirt collar. "I guess I never thought about how she felt. I guess I was too angry with her for ruining our plans when she got pregnant."

"She didn't get pregnant by herself, you know."

"Yeah, I know. It's just that..."

"All your well-laid plans were ruined, right?"

"Yeah...."

"And you blamed her, right?'

"Well...."

"You know, the blame game never works. It hurts the one who is blamed but doesn't solve anything."

"Yeah. I guess I can see that." He straightened. "But--she is blaming me for everything. Sounds like she already told you everything."

"She told her story, but she didn't blame you. She explained how she walked out to be homeless with nothing. But she said it was all her fault for getting pregnant when that wasn't what you wanted. That you had landed a good job and soon you'd be able to afford a nice house and everything you dreamed about together. Am I on the right track?"

"Yeah, but...."

"She came here seeing herself as fat and worthless. Where did she get that idea?"

"From me." His voice was a whisper.

"Did you think she was good enough for you when you married her? Evidently, you don't think she's good enough for you now."

"Of course, she's good enough for me. I just…"

"You sure have made her feel like she isn't good enough. How would you like it if someone made you feel like that?"

His head jerked up, and his mouth twitched. "Mr. Whitehead." His voice was low. "Mr. Whitehead made me feel that way. It was awful." He jumped up and looked toward the shelter. "Mr. Kingston, where is she? I must talk to her at once." He rubbed his eyes with the back of his hand. "I have to tell her what a monster I've been. I—I—I have to make her understand how sorry I am."

"She may not want to see you. Her wounds are deep, so it may take a while for you to convince her."

"I'll do whatever it takes. I'll give her as much time as she needs. Please, Mr. Kingston. I need to see her. I haven't realized in a long time how much I love her."

"You love who?" Bella came down the walkway toward them.

Jackson ran to her. "Bella, I do love you. I always have. I…"

She interrupted him. "You have a poor way to show that love, Jackson. Your kind of love isn't love at all. It's pure meanness, and it hurts."

He stepped back and bowed his head. "I know. I'm so sorry I've been so mean to you. Please forgive me."

"Are you saying you've changed?"

"Yes. I have changed."

"Humpf! Yeah, just like that, you've changed." Bella crossed her arms across her chest.

"I mean—well, I want to change. I want to be a good husband to you if you'll let me."

"How can I possibly know you mean it? How can I know you've really changed?" Bella reached the porch and opened the door. David invited them into his office.

"It will take time." Jackson and Bella turned to see who spoke. Sadie stood in the doorway. "She can't know if you've changed until you prove it, and that will take time."

"Then how can I show her? What can I do?'

Sadie lifted her hands, palms up. "Anyone can say they've changed. Anyone can put on a good front to look like they've changed. It's day-to-day living that shows they've changed. That takes time."

They stood in silence, Jackson with his head lowered. Sadie and David watched him, then looked at each other.

"Of course, it's Bella's choice to stay here or go with you," David said. "If she chooses to stay here, you are welcome to visit her on the weekends if she agrees."

Jackson looked at Bella. "What do you say?"

She nodded. "I can deal with that. We'll have to take it slow. Trust is hard to earn back once you've lost it."

"Why don't you two take a walk along the river," Sadie said. "You need to talk."

They agreed and headed for the river path. David and Sadie joined hands to pray for them.

Meanwhile:

The man behind the thick window grabbed the phone and held it to his ear. "Hey, Carp. Did you get it all set up?"

A tattooed, pierced man with a bulbous nose nodded. "Yeah, Cosmos. It's all done. Ready for you."

"Bout time. I've been waiting for this for a long time. There'd better not be a hitch anywhere, or somebody'll pay, and I mean big." A string of expletives followed as he swiped at spital coming from his sleazy mouth.

"Don't worry, Boss. We'll make it happen. Nothing can go wrong this time. We've worked hard to make sure of that."

"What about the law enforcement on the island?"

"We've fixed it so Jason will be gone. David and Jerome, too. An emergency will come up, so they'll have to leave."

Cosmos laughed. "How sad for them."

THIRTY-SEVEN

"Mr. Charlie! You came back." Elfi ran to meet the man they had all learned to love. He laughed as the children pulled and pushed him into the backyard, where the clients had gathered after supper.

David, Sadie, Kade, and Sophia had joined the clients for a weekly powwow, which proved to be instrumental in solving many problems in the shelter.

Kade jumped up and pulled up a lawn chair. "Come on over here and grab a chair, my friend."

Charlie bowed and accepted a glass of iced tea Louisa handed him. "Best tea around," he said. Louisa giggled and ran to cut a piece of pie for him.

They laughed and talked as they watched the sun lower over the river. Charlie was a true storyteller, and they loved to hear him. "One time," he began. They all leaned forward, and the children held their breaths. He continued. "One time, I was riding my mule, Rocket, through the desert in Arizona when a dust storm rose before me. I couldn't see anything, nor could Rocket."

"You named your mule Rocket?" Brent asked. He and Sage giggled behind their hands.

"Why?" Sage asked. "Is he fast or something?"

Charlie laughed. "Because when a big ol' horsefly bites him on the rear end, he shoots up like a rocket. And they seem to love to bite him on the butt." They all laughed at that.

"What happened in the dust storm?" Elfie asked.

"Well, we eased along, stumbling over rocks and cactus. If you've ever been to Arizona, you know there are lots of those. Then, all of a sudden, Rocket stopped. He refused to go any further. I could hear something but didn't know what it was."

Ruby's big brown eyes were round. "Was it a tiger?"

"Yes, it was. And a lion. And a camel."

"Seriously?" Randall scoffed. "You're joking, right?"

Charlie's audience elbowed each other and laughed. They all thought he was making a joke. When he looked back at them without laughing, they sobered.

"You mean all those wild animals were in the desert with you and Rocket?" Kade asked.

Charlie nodded. "Yep. Me and Rocket and all those creatures."

"What did you do?" asked Juliet.

"Well, they were right up on us when we saw them. I didn't know if they'd eat me or what. I knew I didn't want Rocket to take off and leave me afoot with them. So, I hung on for dear life when Rocket shot off like a rocket, right through the dust, kicking up rocks, cacti, and anything else that got in his way. The last time I saw those beasts, they stared at us like we were aliens or something. I guess they weren't hungry enough to try to catch us."

Once the laughter died down, David asked. "Why were those animals out there in the desert, anyway?"

"When we finally got out of the dust storm and to civilization, I learned there was a wildlife refuge nearby, and some animals escaped when the dust storm blew in. They were as confused as we were."

Charlie finished his pie and rose to leave. Kade and David walked with him to the edge of the path he always took to go to wherever he always went.

"Say," Kade said, "I'm going into the city tomorrow for errands. Why don't both of you go with me? It won't take me long to do my business. Then maybe we can catch a game."

David laughed. "After that story, it sounds like a good idea. I'm game. No pun intended." He chuckled. "How about you, Charlie?"

Charlie looked at the ground, then looked back up at them. "I guess I can go. I haven't been to the city in a long time. Maybe it's time I get away from here for a little while."

The next day after Kade finished his errands, they ate at a popular restaurant and then went to the stadium to cheer for the Redbirds. At first, they paid no attention to a man staring at Charlie, but when he moved to sit close to them, he was obviously interested in their elderly friend.

David gestured toward the man. "Charlie, do you know that man over there?"

Charlie looked, then shrugged. "I don't think so."

"Well, he's interested in you," said Kade.

When the man noticed them looking his way, he approached them. He smiled at David and Kade but looked straight at Charlie.

"Arthur? Arthur Burns?"

Charlie blushed. "Names Charlie. Charlie Cox."

The man sat in an empty seat in front of Kade and turned to speak to Charlie. He turned around and then looked back again. "Come on, man. I'd know you anywhere." He snapped his fingers. "Wait a minute! You died! I mean, Arthur died. Yes, I remember now. You drowned. I mean, Arthur drowned. That was--uh--at least twenty-five years ago." He frowned. "You sure you're not Arthur? You sure do look like him. Maybe a little more gray, but identical, I'd say." He stood when Charlie kept shaking his head. "I'm sorry, man. I sure thought you were Arthur."

Charlie smiled. "I've always heard everyone has a twin somewhere in the world. I guess Arthur was my twin."

The man returned to his seat but stared at Charlie until the ballgame ended. As they were leaving, the man followed them to the vehicle.

"Look," he said. "You're not fooling me, Arthur. I thought

something was fishy about you drowning. I know how good of a swimmer you are."

When Charlie didn't respond, he continued. "If you don't want to admit it, I understand. You know who I am, and you know you can trust me. If I were in your shoes and had the nerve, I'd have done the same thing."

Charlie stared at the man and finally nodded. "Okay, Frank." He rubbed his head. "I'm sorry for all the trouble I caused back home."

"You had a great funeral," Frank said. "Abigail cried her eyes out, and everyone sympathized with her. Arthur, you sure had a lot of friends. The lodge was never the same without you."

"Yeah. The lodge."

"I'm sorry about Abigail and Heath. She shouldn't have done that to you. It was bad enough for her to cheat on you, but man, with the lodge president—your business partner and friend. That was low-down and dirty. Then, for her to clean out your bank account, too. She did a great job of stabbing you in the back."

"It's okay, Frank. It's over and done. I've forgiven them both, and my life is good now. I'm happy."

"But, Arthur, she took everything. Even your inheritance." He looked sideways at Charlie. "You could have beat her, you know. Why didn't you try?"

Charlie stared off into space and pulled his earlobe. "It just wasn't worth it. I never liked to fight, especially with Abigail."

"But, Arthur, she stripped you. How could you let her do that?"

Charlie looked at Frank a while before he answered. Then he lowered his head and his voice. "You know how much I loved her, Frank. More than life itself. That's why I left. If I died, she would be free to do whatever she wanted without guilt or shame. You knew what she was doing, but most people didn't, so they would support and help her. Isn't that what happened?"

Frank sighed. "Yes, that's what happened. She mourned for a week, I think. Then she and Heath went to Hawaii for a wedding."

Charlie laid a hand on Frank's arm. "It's okay, Frank. Don't worry about it. That was a long time ago. I hope she's happy."

Frank shook his head. "She isn't. The marriage didn't last five years. She sold everything and moved west somewhere. I haven't heard from her since."

The two men shook hands, and Charlie turned to Kade and David. "I'm ready to return to Crandall Island," he said. "Right where I belong,"

David cocked his head and stared at Charlie. "Okay, so now we know part of your story. There's just one thing I'd like to know. How do you know so much about the island and its inhabitants? You seem to know about everyone that ever lived there."

Charlie snickered. "Oh, that. I've talked to many people here and elsewhere and read and studied everything about the island I could find. I'm a history buff, you know. You can tell I like to talk, but I also like to listen."

By the time they reached the parking lot, it was almost empty. Kade went to the driver's side of their rented car. "Aww, man! A flat tire!" He kicked the tire, and David moaned.

Charlie leaned over to look. "This tire was slashed," he said. The rest of the tires looked fine. "Now, who would want to slash our tire? You boys got someone mad at you?"

They glanced around to see if anyone was watching them. A dark gray SUV was parked on one side of the parking lot, and a navy four-door truck on the other. They both appeared to be empty.

Kade popped the trunk to get the spare and jack, but it was empty. "Now, why would a rental car not have a jack and a spare?" he said. "David, do you have the number of the rental company?"

David dialed, then shook his head. "No one is picking up. I guess they've closed already." He dialed again. "A taxi is coming."

They watched the SUV and truck leave and discussed the game until a taxi arrived. David and Charlie crawled into the back seat, and Kade in the front.

"Where to?" the driver asked.

When Kade looked at the man, he blinked. The man's bulbous nose was pierced with a chain that ran from his nose to his eye, then across to his ear. Tattoos covered him like nothing Kade had ever seen. A rope tattoo surrounded his neck, and snakes ran down both arms with their heads covering his hands.

David spoke from the back seat. "To the Holiday Inn on Union," he said. He snickered at Kade's wide eyes. "Hey, man, you okay?"

Kade blinked again. "Sure, I'm fine. Just thinking about that rental. We can't return it before we leave."

"No problem," David said. "I'll call Pruitt. He'll settle it with the rental company in the morning. We can't do anything about it tonight, and I'm ready to go home."

"Yeah." Kade looked back at the driver. "Driver, forget the hotel. Just take us to Riverside Drive. I'm ready to get home, too." He turned to look at Charlie. "Aren't you, Charlie?"

Charlie nodded and continued to stare out the window.

Meanwhile:

"Mama, can I go for a walk by the river?" Ruby pointed to a member of the shelter staff. "She said I can find some pretty flowers a ways down the path."

Nancy was busy putting clothes in the washing machine. "Uh huh," she murmured. "Just don't go too far and get lost. And stay away from the riverbank. I don't want you to fall in."

Ruby grabbed a basket and a pair of scissors and went out the back door. Soon, she was cutting wildflowers and putting them into her basket. A boat came alongside the bank near her, but she paid no attention. She hummed as she worked, moving down the path. Seeing a black-eyed Susan blooming further down, she waded through the weeds to reach the flowers.

In the laundry room, Nancy finished folding the towels and wiped her brow. She started up the stairs to put the towels away. "Ruby? Come help me, girl." Then she remembered. Her eyes grew round, and she ran out the door.

"Ruby! Where are you?" she yelled. What was she thinking to have let that child go off alone? Lord only knows what danger lies along the shoreline. She ran down to the river and looked along the banks. She ran down the river path, yelling for her daughter.

She rounded a curve just in time to see a man exiting a boat. There was Ruby with her basket of blossoms. The man walked toward the girl, and Nancy screamed. Ruby turned and ran to Nancy. The man grinned at them.

"Hello," he said. "It's been a while since I've seen you, ladies. I've missed you so much. Nancy, why did you leave me?"

Nancy spoke through gritted teeth. "You stay away from me and my child."

The man crept closer. "Oh, my. You seem unhappy with me. Didn't I give you everything you needed? You had good food and clothes. I was generous with you, wasn't I?"

Nancy pulled Ruby to her side, and together, they backed away. "We don't want your kind of generosity. Come on, Ruby."

The man reached out a hand. "Why don't you get into my boat, and we'll go for a little ride?"

"You stay away from us, Drax," Nancy said. "We want no part of you. Leave us alone."

He jumped forward to grab her arm, but she shoved Ruby aside and whirled, kicking with all her might. Her kick landed in his groin, and he doubled over. She grabbed Ruby's hand, and they fled back toward the shelter. She was thankful for the self-defense classes the shelter provided.

THIRTY-EIGHT

David spoke on the phone. "Sadie? Hey, we're heading home. What? They did what? Are they okay? Don't worry. We'll be home soon."

"What's wrong," Kade asked.

"Someone attacked Nancy and Ruby on the riverbank," David said. "Some guy in a boat tried to get them."

"Did they know who he was?"

"Nancy said it was the guy who was trafficking them. She said he would have grabbed Ruby had she not gotten there when she did. Sadie said we'd get the full story when we get home." He poked the driver in the back. "Hurry up, driver."

The driver glanced into the rearview mirror and smirked. David frowned. What was that look on the guy's face? He looked down the street. "Hey, this isn't the way to Riverside Drive."

Kade's head jerked around. "Say, buddy, where are you taking us? We told you Riverside Drive."

The driver shrugged. "This is a shortcut."

Kade grabbed the guy's arm. "This is no shortcut, man. We know where we are, and we told you where to take us. Now, turn this rig toward Riverside Drive. Now."

The driver pulled the cab over and jumped out. They were in a secluded area. He pulled a gun from his pocket. "Now get out — all of you," he said.

David crawled out with his hands up. Kade got out of the passenger side, and Charlie slid out, but he kept low to the ground.

"You..." the driver pointed his gun toward Kade. "Come over here. And don't try anything."

Kade edged around the back of the car and stood close to David. "Look," he said. "If it's our money you want, take it." He reached into his back pocket and pulled out his wallet. David did the same. "Just don't do something stupid like shoot us."

To distract the man, Kade talked louder. "If you want to rob us, that's fine. Just don't add murder to your crime."

David understood Kade was keeping the man's attention away from Charlie, so he raised his voice and joined in. "Yeah, that would be stupid. Murder will get you in way more trouble than robbery."

"Why are you yelling?" the man asked. "I'm not deaf."

"Oh, you're not? I thought maybe you were," David yelled.

"My grandma is deaf," yelled Kade. "This is how we talk to her. I guess it's a habit."

"Yeah," yelled David. "Both my grandparents are deaf. They can't hear anything."

"Even their pet parrot yells," said Kade. "And their dog barks really loud."

The man looked confused. Kade kept yelling random things while David edged around the driver. Charlie had moved around the front of the cab, and he and David jumped the man at the same time. Kade grabbed the gun, and Charlie held the man on the ground. David called for law enforcement, and soon, the man was sitting in the back of a police car, cuffed.

The first officer talked to David, Charlie, and Kade while the other checked out the cab driver. "Hey, there's a warrant for this man's arrest," the second officer said. "Carp Dixon. He's wanted in three states, once for murder."

"We'd better check out this cab." The men looked inside, then opened the trunk. Inside, the real cab driver was tied up but alive. They pulled him out, and he stumbled around for a moment.

"I oughta kill you," the cab driver sputtered as he went after Carp. The officers held him back.

"We'll need you at the station to make a statement," one officer said. "This time, we'll make sure this criminal stays behind bars. We'll need you all to go to the station."

Another police car pulled up, and the officer took David, Kade, and Charlie to the station. It was late when they returned to the boat to go home, but they were tired and ready to sleep in their own beds. A short time later, they arrived at the shelter.

The following day after breakfast, the clients who gathered in the lounge gasped as they listened to Charlie tell the story. David and Kade intervened only when he omitted some minor detail.

After that, Nancy and Ruby relayed their scary experience. "It was Drax," Nancy said. "I thought I'd never see him again. It was like he knew we would be there, but that's impossible."

"How did you happen to be there?" asked David.

Nancy said she was busy and distracted when Ruby asked to go down the shoreline to pick flowers.

"Why did you want to go along the river?" David asked. "All kinds of flowers are on the other side of the shelter property. In fact, why didn't you pick some from the backyard?"

"Wren said if I'd go beside the river, I could find lots of black-eyed Susans. Those are my favorites."

David looked over at Wren. "Why would you tell her that? You know these children shouldn't be near the water."

She shrugged. "She said she loves those flowers, and I saw some there the other day. How could I know she would take off by herself to pick them?"

David scowled. "We adults must constantly watch these kids to keep them safe," he said. Wren lowered her head and scooted down in her chair. "In fact," David continued, "the way things have been around here lately, we all need to stay away from the river unless we're in a group. We have to be cautious of our surroundings all the time."

After a hard day in the garden, handling clients' squabbles and dealing with calls from DHS, Sadie and Sophia sat on the shelter patio watching Ruby, Sage, Elfi, and Jamie play on the playground with Benji. Birds chirped in the trees, and squirrels played under them in the shady backyard while Baby Jonathan slept in his playpen. The ladies enjoyed the cool breeze blowing from the river as they drank sweet tea and chatted. The female clients and boys had walked to the Village to deliver Bella's paintings and to shop a little before the stores closed.

"Did you see Iris catch that wasp in the window this morning?" Sophia asked. "She picked it up and took it outside. I can't believe it didn't sting her."

"They never do sting her," Sadie said. "It beats all. She treats those insects like they're humans. She can't stand for one to be hurt."

Sophia slapped at a bug. "I know they are all God's creation, but they sting and bite, so I want to eliminate them."

"Me too," Sadie said. "I'll slap a mosquito before I think about it. I blame Eve for those tiny creatures being here to torture us. If she hadn't eaten that fruit in the garden, we'd be living in heaven now."

"Did you notice the fly swat missing?" Sophia giggled. "She hid it."

"That's why Tina couldn't find it yesterday. She fussed and fumed for an hour or more. Finally, she used a dishtowel to swat the two flies pestering her."

"Mrs. Sadie, look what I found over there." Elfi held out a tiny ring coated with dirt.

Sadie took the object and looked it over. "It looks like a baby ring," she said. "Let's clean it up." She wiped it clean with a napkin. "Look. It has a tiny blue stone. I guess someone lost it here a long time ago."

"May I keep it?" asked Elfi.

"You found it, so it's yours. Want me to hold it for you so you won't lose it in the yard?"

Elfi agreed and ran to play with Benji.

"He loves her so much," Sadie said as she watched them play. "She's a good little babysitter."

"She's such a little dear," Sophia said. "So bright. Juliet says she does great in school. She's one of her top students." She leaned forward. "Look! She's teaching him his letters."

"She sure is," Sadie said. "I wondered how he could spell his name. The other day, David was playing with him, and he spelled B-E-N. I thought David taught him, but he said he didn't. I guess I know now who is teaching him."

Later, Sadie showed the ring to Jesse and Kathleen when they visited. "You know," Jesse said, "years ago, there was a house here on this spot. A man moved his family here to work for Mr. Crandall, Oliver's dad. He had a bunch of kids. Must have been one of theirs."

Kathleen looked closely at the ring. "This looks like real gold," she said. "I believe that's a real gem. A sapphire, maybe. Why don't you let me take it to the city and have it appraised?"

A few days later, Kathleen returned with the ring. "It is gold with a sapphire. The jeweler said it's very old and quite valuable. You'll want to keep it somewhere safe."

Sadie talked to Grace, and they agreed to lock it up until Elfi was old enough to keep it. An excited Elfi told everyone about her find, and Grace allowed her to show it around at supper.

The next day, Charlie came, and Elfi wanted to show him the ring. She ran to find Sadie in her office and asked about it. When Sadie went to get it from the safe, it was gone.

The safe was still locked, and there was no evidence it had been forced open.

"Maybe Mr. David put it somewhere else," Sadie told her. "Don't worry, we'll find it. Just be quiet and don't say anything to anyone about it. It'll be our secret."

"I've been watching the camera upstairs," Officer Jason said when Sadie notified him. "Someone is going in and out, but I never can identify the person. Seems like whoever it is always wears a hoodie or something to hide her face. I think we need a better camera."

While everyone was having lunch, Jerome went to look in the room. Sure enough, the little ring was lying on a piece of cotton in a small bowl on top of a dresser. He adjusted the camera and took the ring. Maybe whoever it was would reveal themselves when they looked for it.

When the meal was over, David, Officer Jason, and Jerome met in David's office to watch what happened in the spare room. It didn't take long. The door opened, and a female entered. She went to the bowl and gasped when she saw the ring missing. She looked under the bowl, around the dresser, and on the floor.

"Can you zoom in?" asked David. Officer Jason moved the cursor to zoom in the camera lens about the time the woman turned to face it.

"Jiminy Cricket!" Jerome said. "What's she doing in there?"

The three men looked at each other as recognition dawned on their faces. Could it be? David ran his fingers through his hair as he paced. "I'll talk to her," he said.

"Let's not confront her right now," Jason suggested. "Let's wait and see what she will do about the missing ring."

"It makes no sense," said David. "How could she be the one causing all the problems around here? That is if she's guilty of everything. The kidnapping. The flooded sinks. The thefts."

"Yeah, and the rumors." Jerome shook his head. "It certainly doesn't make sense. I can't believe she's guilty of all that."

They agreed to keep an eye on her the next day.

Meanwhile:

"Paul, someone took the ring." The young woman wrung her hands and paced when she met Paul down by the river around midnight. "I put it in the room. I didn't think anyone ever went in there."

"Maybe one of the kids found it," Paul suggested. "Didn't you say you found a doll in there one day? Then one of the little girls probably has the ring."

"They know about it," she said. "Elfi showed it to everyone. If one of the others found it, they would surely take it to her."

She pushed her hair back from her face. "I don't mind telling you I'm nervous about this. What if Mr. David or Officer Jason went in there and found it?"

"Nah, not likely. It had to be one of the kids or maybe one of the ladies. Just keep an eye out. If someone found it, they'll probably tell someone or act funny."

"Yeah. I'll watch them tomorrow."

THIRTY-NINE

The girl showed up late for breakfast the following day. When she appeared, she looked like she hadn't slept. She almost dropped a plate of pancakes and slipped when she poured a glass of milk, spilling it on the table. As the clients came in and sat around the table, she could hardly eat because she was watching everyone else. When David came in, Sadie pulled him into the hall.

"She is so nervous," she said. "Look at her. She's watching everyone like a hawk. There's definitely something going on with her."

"I'm going to talk to Louisa," he said. "She's working in the kitchen this week. Louisa would notice if she were acting different."

Louisa mopped her brow and shook her head when David talked to her. "Good Lord!" she said. "That gal is nothing but a bundle of nerves. I don't know what's going on with her, but something sure is. She spilled pancake mix and burned the bacon. I had to give her errands to run, or breakfast would've never been ready this morning."

During breakfast, she excused herself and left through the back door before everyone finished eating. Jerome followed her down the river path.

"She's calling someone." He had David on the phone. "I can't hear what she's saying. If I get any closer, she'll see me."

"It's okay," said David. "Stay back, but keep watching her. She may try to meet someone. If she does, we need to know who that someone is."

"Wait—she's running down the river path," Jerome said. "I'll try to keep up with her."

"Just don't let her see you." David waited with the phone to his ear. He could hear Jerome huffing. The whishing sound of tall weeds and bushes finished with a thud and a grunt. "Are you all right, Jerome?"

"No—I lost her. She headed through the woods towards the Craft Village."

"Well, it's okay. Just come on back. We'll have to wait this thing out, I guess."

Much later, she returned to the shelter and helped Louisa in the kitchen. She excused herself early and disappeared. David watched the camera, but she didn't go back into the spare room.

Kade ran into David's office. "David, I've got to go to the city tomorrow. One of my crew is in trouble and needs help. I need your expertise and influence." David agreed and left with Kade early the following day.

Sophia called Sadie. "Baby Jon's being a little fussy today. I think he's cutting teeth. I'm going to stay home with him. Besides, I need to clean my closet. I'm ready for some new clothes. Maybe some of the clients can wear those I'm getting rid of."

"Sure," Sadie said. "I'm sure they'd love some of your things. Just bring them over when you're done."

The day was quiet. Some ladies worked in the garden, some in the kitchen, and others cleaned. The children played in the backyard under the watchful eyes of Caroline and Wren. Sadie worked on a newsletter for donors who were faithful givers and those who had pledged to help the shelter. She went to the kitchen for a mid-afternoon snack when the phone rang. It was Sophia.

Sadie knew immediately something was wrong. "Call Jason." Sophia's voice sounded different.

"Sophia, what's wrong?" But the phone went dead. "Sophia!" Sadie punched the call button, but the phone went straight to voice mail. Sadie called Jason.

"Something is wrong with Sophia. Please go to her house."

She paced until the phone rang again. It was Jason.

"Sadie, Sophia's in trouble. Someone ransacked her house, and she is gone. Baby Jon is gone, too. You'd better call Kade and David. I'm going to find Sophia."

Sadie grabbed the phone and dialed David. He didn't answer. She dialed Kade. Silence. She had to do something. She dialed Ms. Emma at the shipping company. "They're out on the river," Ms. Emma said. "I'm sure they're busy and won't pick up. Give me a minute, and I'll call them on the two-way radio."

Sadie drummed her fingers on the table. She ran her fingers through her hair. *What is taking so long?*

"Sadie? David says he'll call you back as soon as he has time," Ms. Emma said.

"No!" Sadie yelled. "Sophia is in trouble. Someone took her and baby Jon. Please tell him that he and Kade must come home at once."

Ms. Emma gasped. "Well, why didn't you say that in the first place? You okay, honey? I'll tell them at once."

Sadie paced until David finally called. "What happened?" he asked. "We're headed for the dock now to get our boat."

"Oh, David." Sadie burst into tears. "Jason says someone has been in Sophia's house, and she and the baby are gone."

"Calm down, sweetheart. Get yourself together. We must be strong to get her back. It may be nothing, but it could be bad."

"Oh, David, how could this happen? Please hurry."

Kade filled Sadie in on his talk with Jason when they arrived at the dock. Jason said her purse, phone, and diaper bag were gone. Almost as if she had prepared to be gone. But it didn't make sense that someone ransacked her house or she never answered her phone. Jason had called mainland law enforcement for help. Two officers had arrived, and they were waiting for more.

Jason met them at the dock. He and Jerome had solicited help from the islanders, and they were scouring the island. "They must have gone off the island," Jason said. "Most likely, it is someone from the mainland."

While they were talking, Kade's phone rang. "Kade, boy," a rough voice said. "I have your pretty little wife and that sweet little boy of yours. Guess you want them back." The speaker snickered. "Well, come and get them. Oh, wait. I guess you don't know where they are." The sound of a boisterous laugh came through the phone.

"Who is it?" Sadie's voice was a whisper. "Who would take Sophia? And why?"

David's Adam's apple bobbed up and down as he watched Kade's ashen face. "I don't know, but we'll find them," he said.

"And when we do, they'll be sorry." Kade slammed his fist against a tree, and blood oozed from his knuckles. Sadie wrapped his hand with a tissue from her pocket.

One of the officers from the mainland stepped up to the group. "Excuse me," he said. "I'm Officer Dinkins. Officer Conners and I have worked on cases similar to this before. Almost always, the perpetrator will expose himself. He'll reveal where he is eventually, but try to keep you guessing. He wants you to chase him. That's how he gets his kicks."

"That's right," said Officer Conners. "We have to listen closely to the clues he gives. Hopefully, before too long, he'll give himself away. Do you know anyone with a vendetta against you or your wife? It would help if we had some idea who it might be."

"The clients at Willow Grove Shelter have husbands, exes, and other family members that may want to do damage," said David. "Other than that, the only one I know who has reason to hate us is in prison."

"Who is that?" Officer Dinkins asked.

"Cosmos Rouge." Kade rubbed his head. "He does have a beef with us since we closed down his trafficking and gambling ring a while back."

"Cosmos Rouge?" Officer Conners rubbed his nose. "I think I've heard of him."

"How well do you know this Rouge?" asked Officer Dan. "Where is he from?"

Kade's face reddened. He stomped toward the river. David stepped up to answer the question. "He's from here," he said. "He was born and raised on this island. We went to school together. He left to play football and returned when he was injured. That's when he started an organized crime ring here on the island."

"Oh, well, that may explain his motive." Officer Dinkins looked toward Kade, who was staring out over the river. "But you said he's in prison."

"Yes. Locked up tight. I hope he stays there a long time."

"Then who could it be?" Sadie asked. "Someone is sure messing with us."

Officer Conners cocked his head and looked at her. "Something has been going on?" he asked.

"Well, we've had so many things happen lately. Like, I was attacked in my house. And someone kidnapped Marleigh's baby."

"We have had a lot of situations," said David. "Things stolen from the Craft Village and from clients here. A baby snatched while we were at the zoo. Kids kidnapped by grandparents who should not have known they were here." He scratched his head.

A police boat pulled up, and several officers jumped out. One gestured to the group. "Let's go," he yelled. "We can't waste any time."

David's boat and the police boat pulled out of the dock, loaded with men and weapons. They had to win this war no matter who the perpetrator was.

Meanwhile:

A young woman ran down the path by the river until she came
to a spot where the island jutted out into the water. She stopped
there and listened. Sure enough, a boat was coming. Fast. She
sheltered her eyes with her hand and watched until she could see
the red speedboat zooming toward her. She waved both arms. The
boat slowed and pulled up to the shore. A man inside motioned to
her, and she waded to the boat. He reached out to help her
aboard.

She leaned over and peered below the deck where a woman
lay tied up on a bed. A child slept beside her.

FORTY

"We don't even know what the boat looks like," said David. "How can we look for it? There are boats everywhere. It could be any of them."

Officer Dinkins looked around at him. "We pretty much keep up with the boats on the river. We'd recognize an unfamiliar one. Of course, if the perpetrator is a regular, we wouldn't know. Then we have the good ol' boy system. We can talk to the boaters around here, and they will tell us if there is someone who can't be trusted."

They were passing the island's south end when Officer Conners yelled something to Officer Dinkins, who slowed the boat, turning it toward the island. The officers on board used binoculars to look for movement in the trees along the shoreline. They steered the craft toward the chute when a red speedboat shot out from the chute into the river. The officers turned the boat back toward the main river to chase the speedboat.

Kade scrambled to the front of the boat, but one of the officers pushed him back. "I know you're anxious to find your wife," the officer said, "but we must keep you safe. We have no idea if that's the boat we're looking for, and if it is, we can't anticipate what they'll do. You'll be no help to her if you are hurt."

Kade sat down. He popped his knuckles and pulled his earlobe. David moved to sit beside him. "Hey, we're going to find them," he said. "We're trusting God to help us."

Kade nodded. He buried his hands in his dark hair. A long sigh escaped his lips. "I know. It's times like these my faith is stretched to the max, but I know He's with Sophia and Jon. He'll keep them safe."

"Yes," said David. "No matter what happens, we know it'll end up okay."

The boat suddenly veered to the right, throwing David and Kade to the floor.

"Are you guys okay?" asked Officer Dan.

They pulled themselves up. "What happened?" asked David.

"Look!" One of the officers pointed. The red speedboat had docked at a small pier by some trees. Some people were running up an embankment toward an old building.

"It's them," shouted Kade. "Look! That man is carrying Jon. Dang! They're dragging Sophia. I'll kill them!"

As soon as they docked, the officers jumped out, followed by David and Kade. They ran to a grove of trees near the building.

"Stay back," ordered Officer Dan. "We don't know if they're armed."

It didn't take long to hear shots fired from the building, sending them diving for cover.

"I was afraid of that," said Officer Dan. "We can expect guys like these to be armed. They are criminals and only care about getting what they want no matter the price." He turned to the other officers. "I counted three men."

"Yeah," one said. "There are three. They shouldn't be hard to take."

"Let's go." Officer Dinkins gestured to the other men. They ducked down and ran to surround the structure.

"Please watch out for my family," Kade pleaded.

"Oh, that's our first concern," Officer Dinkins said. "These men know what they are doing and will take all precautions to see that the woman and child aren't hurt."

The building was an old barn with a loft filled with hay.

Windows on both sides and a large open door on each end allowed the officers, David, and Kade, to see inside. Two men stood on each side of the front door facing toward the river. The other one was guarding Sophia and Jon. He had them pushed back against some hay bales. Sophia looked scared, but she cuddled and comforted baby Jonathan.

"Careful, guys," Officer Dinkins ordered. "Watch out for Sophia and the baby." He peered through the window. "Do you recognize any of them?" he asked David and Kade.

Kade looked in. "Look!" he said. "It's the guy who drove the taxi the other day. The one who held a gun on us."

David rose to see, then ducked back down. "It sure is. I wonder who he is. And how'd he get away from the police?"

"He held a gun on you?" Officer Dinkins asked. "When was that?"

They explained what happened in the city. "I thought he'd be locked up," said Kade. "The officers arrested him."

Officer Conners rolled his eyes. "Yeah, that happens. We arrest them, and the system lets them go. It seems useless sometimes to risk our lives to catch the bad guys."

"Pssst." One of the officers gestured for Dan. "There're some loose boards over here," he said. "I think I can crawl through it if someone distracts them."

The boards were positioned behind the hay where Sophia lay. The loose nails could easily be removed. Getting Sophia and Jon out would be easy if they could lure the man guarding them away.

"Kenny and I will go to the front and cause a commotion," Officer Dinkins said. "That should cause the three of them to come to the front. Then you can get inside. Just be careful, Steve."

He motioned for the other officers to surround the place and keep their eyes open. He suggested David and Kade stay near the rear, where they would get Sophia out. Kade rubbed the back of his neck.

"Stay calm," David said. "Let them do their jobs."

Staying out of sight behind the trees, Officers Dinkins and Conners circled to the front of the barn. The other officers surrounded the place, also staying out of sight. Steve waited beside the loose boards, ready to move. When someone signaled that everyone was in place, those in the front started shooting and yelling.

Watching through a window, David saw all three men run to the front and start firing their weapons. He motioned to Steve, who jerked the boards loose and ducked inside. He grabbed Sophia and pulled her toward the hole when a shot inside sounded. Steve fell, and another shot rang out. Sophia stumbled and fell against the wall, holding Jon against her chest. Kade ran to the hole, ducked in, and grabbed baby Jon while David dragged Sophia out. Three officers ran to the spot while those in the front continued to shoot. One officer entered to get Steve while the others poured shots into the barn through the windows and doors.

"We got one, but the other two are still alive," said Kenny.

Kade looked up from where he knelt beside Sophia. "Three," he said. "There's another. The one who shot my wife and Steve."

David took the crying baby from him. "Did you know who it was?"

Kade grimaced. "No, I didn't see him." He leaned over Sophia again. "She's breathing." An officer called for an ambulance.

Officer Dinkins ran around the building. "What happened? I thought we had them all in the front returning our fire?"

Kade held Sophia's head and stroked her hair. "Stay with me, sweetheart. Please don't leave me. Help is coming." He looked up at Dan. "I was afraid something like this would happen."

Sirens screamed as an emergency vehicle came down a dirt road to stop beside the barn. The EMTs loaded Steve and Sophia into the back of the ambulance. Kade crawled in beside the driver, and David handed Jon to him.

"They're getting away," an officer shouted from the front of the barn. David and Sadie ran around the building.

"What happened?" asked David. "How did they get out? I thought y'all had the doors covered."

"They were. There's another door we didn't know about." The officer pointed. "They ran through the woods back toward the river."

The other officers were already running toward the river. Soon, they were all loaded on the boats, racing back toward the island. The red boat had circled the end of the island and headed down the chute. The first police boat shot down the river to try to cut it off at the other end of the island, so the others went down the chute. When they saw the boat at the shore, they docked beside it. The passengers were far enough ahead to be out of sight.

"They went over there," shouted an islander as they passed his house. He pointed to an old house built at the water's edge. One side had stilts to hold it above the river. Rickety steps led up to a porch that was half fallen. A round face topped with red hair peeped out from a broken window.

David gasped. "It's Cosmos! He must have escaped from prison."

Officer Dinkins grabbed his phone and soon confirmed it was true. He had escaped.

Meanwhile:

"What are you doing in here? And why do you have that?" Loreen stood in the upstairs room doorway where someone had been hiding things. She looked at the young woman who held a gold necklace. "I know that belongs to Mrs. Sadie. What are you doing with it?"

"Uh—Mrs. Sadie gave it to me." The young woman put her hand behind her and blushed.

"I don't think so." Loreen took the necklace from her. "What else do you have there?" She moved around the young woman. On the bed lay piles of jewelry, gold pieces, and some bags of something. "Marijuana? You're doing drugs? Look at all this stuff. I know all this doesn't belong to you." She turned, but the young woman had fled. Loreen ran out the door and down the stairs. The woman was running out the back door.

"Stop her," Loreen shouted. Charlie and the kids were on the patio, and Charlie grabbed the woman by the arm.

"Here. Where are you going so fast?" he asked.

"Looks like she's the one who's been taking our stuff," Loreen said. "I caught her upstairs with a bunch of things that have disappeared lately. And with this." She held up Sadie's necklace.

"That's Mrs. Sadie's," said Elfi. "I saw her wear it. She said Mr. David gave it to her as a birthday gift."

"That isn't all," said Loreen. "There are bags of marijuana on the bed. Guess she's been doing drugs. Or selling them. She knows better than that."

"Well, well," said Charlie. "Looks like we need to find David and report this."

"David is gone," said Loreen. "I don't know when he'll be back."

"No problem," said Charlie. "I happen to know where he is." He pulled the young woman along to the Ranger. "Get in and don't try anything," he ordered.

FORTY-ONE

The Ranger pulled up at the old house. Law enforcement surrounded the place. David ran to meet Charlie. "What's going on, Charlie?" he asked.

"Oh, just a little problem back at the shelter." Charlie pulled the young woman out of the Ranger. "Seems like this girl has been up to trouble. Loreen caught her red-handed with stolen goods. And to top that off, she has bags of drugs."

David stared, mouth open. "Wren? You're the one…."

Wren's blush deepened, and she smirked. "Yeah, so what?"

A voice yelled from the building. "Wren, is that you? I told you to stay away."

"Cosmos? You okay?" Wren yelled back.

David looked at Wren and then toward the building. "You're helping Cosmos? You have been helping him all along?"

Wren snickered. "Me and Cosmos go way back. He needed help, so I obliged."

David frowned and shook his head. "You mean all those things that happened—baby Aiden…."

She laughed. "Oh, yeah. I've been pretty busy wreaking havoc around that place. Flooding the upstairs bathrooms. Spreading rumors. It was kinda fun turning people against each other. I almost got baby Beula. If I had, you wouldn't have got her back like you did Aiden. She would have been gone for good in just a few hours."

David's face almost matched his red shirt, and he

grimaced. "I won't consider it fun, but you'll pay now for what you've done. I'm disappointed in you, Wren. I would never have thought you'd turn out like this."

"Oh, yeah, Mr. Goodie-Two-Shoes. I'm sure you can't believe someone like me can be so bad. After all, every person can be redeemed, right? That's what you and Mrs. Sadie preach all the time." She turned to Sadie, who had been standing, mouth open, by David. "I guess you won't think so now, huh?"

Cosmos yelled from the window. "Wren, get out of here."

She turned to look at him. "Baby, I'm staying here with you as long as it takes."

An officer moved to cuff her when chaos broke out in the building. Someone threw a smoke bomb inside, and the occupants ran out with their hands up. All except Cosmos. He came out shooting. Officers returned fire from behind trees until he went down. Wren jerked away from the officer and threw herself on top of him.

"You've killed him!" she yelled. "How could you kill him?" She screamed and cried until an officer pulled her off. Another officer checked his vitals. He was dead.

"I guess that's over," said David.

"You monster! You don't even care," shouted Wren.

David went to her. "Wren, I do care. I wish this hadn't happened. And it wouldn't have if he had made the right choices. He had a chance to rehabilitate, but he didn't. You can change and make a better life for yourself."

"We do care, Wren," said Sadie. "We want you to make the right choices."

She snarled. "You'll have me thrown into prison. How does that give me a chance for any life?"

Charlie stepped forward. "Wren, you kidnapped a baby, and you'll suffer the consequences for that and other things you've done. Accept what the law gives you. Then change. Do your time. But choose to change."

An officer cuffed a weeping Wren and led her to the

police boat. With a promise to go to the police station the next day, David and Sadie returned to the shelter with Charlie.

At the shelter, clients and staff surrounded them. Louisa made them some supper while they answered questions until Louisa chased everyone out. "They'll answer your questions later when they finish eating," she said. She cried when she learned about Wren. "I love that girl," she said. "She has a special talent. I hope she's able to develop it someday. She'll make an excellent chef."

After they ate, everyone gathered in the lounge. The clients wanted to know everything that had happened and were sad to hear about Wren.

"You mean the police 'rested her?" asked Brent.

"Yes," replied David. "They took her to the police station because she broke the law."

"When will she come back home?" asked Elfi. "I like to play with her. She tells good stories."

Sadie pulled the little girl close. "We don't know, but we hope it won't be long."

"She was a good jump rope thrower," said Ruby. "She could beat anyone jumping."

"Yeah." Jamie sniffed. "She knew how to make really good mud pies. Almost good enough to eat." Jax giggled.

"She helped Louisa make our turtle soup," said Randall. "She really liked it, too."

"Why did she do bad?" Sage wiped her eyes. "Did she want to hurt us?"

Sadie and David looked at each other. They knew the truth was best. They knew they were responsible for these clients and Wren, even though she wasn't a client.

"Sometimes people do bad because they think they will be rewarded for it. Maybe Wren thought Cosmos would like her better if she helped him. They have been friends for a long time, and she wanted to make him happy."

"Did it make him happy?" Sage asked.

"Yeah, but now she's not happy." Elfi wiped her eyes.

"Even if bad things make someone happy, that happiness doesn't last long," explained David. "Aren't we happy when we do good things? When we are kind to others?"

The children all nodded.

"Now, off to bed with all of you," said Sadie. "We're all tired. We'll feel better in the morning."

The next day, when David, Sadie, and Charlie arrived at the police station, they were confronted by a group of people. When they saw David approaching the building, they shoved the door open. The men surrounded David and Sadie, shaking their fists and cursing while the women cried.

"You took my son's life," a rough-looking man shouted. "First, you ruin him by locking him up, but that wasn't enough. You had to take his life."

"Mr. Rouge, I assume?" David said.

"Yes. Cosmos, the boy you killed, is my son," Mr. Rouge said. "He didn't deserve to be locked away, and he sure didn't deserve a bullet."

"Sir," David said, "your son is responsible for ruining his life. He's the one who broke the law." David tried to go past him, but Mr. Rouge pushed him against the door frame.

"He was a good boy until he went to the city. If you had been a better friend, you would've talked him out of that. You would've got him to stay on the island."

David raised his eyebrows. "Mr. Rouge, I'm sorry about how things turned out with your son. You did a good job raising him. The wrong choices he made aren't your fault, sir. He chose to break the law."

Mr. Rouge broke down. He turned to his wife, and together, they cried as they walked away. David and the others pushed through the group to enter the police station. But a man grabbed David's arm and held him back.

"Aren't you David Kingston? The one who runs Willow

Grove Shelter?" a man asked.

"I am. This is my wife, Sadie, and Charlie Cox. May we help you?"

"I'm Wren's dad, Richard Yarrow. This is my wife, Melissa. They tell me you are the cause of our daughter's arrest."

David shoved his hands through his hair. "Sir, did you know your daughter was accompanying and aiding a man who escaped prison?"

A young man in the group stepped forward. "You high and mighty Kingstons think you can do what you want. I'm here to tell you no matter how much money you have. You ain't all that."

"Shut up, Paul," Mr. Yarrow said. He turned to David and scoffed. "You mean Cosmos Rouge? Why, they've been friends since birth. He's the one who committed the crimes, not Wren."

"Yes, sir, but she had been helping him all the while he was locked up."

"How is that possible? She's been here the whole time. Ain't she been living at your shelter, working for you?"

"She has. But somehow, she has communicated with him. I don't know who helped her, but I'm sure these capable officers will find out."

Two men in the group whispered to each other until Mr. Yarrow turned to face them. "You boys need to hush," he said. "I'll handle this."

"Ah, Pa, me and Sully can take care of this bunch," one said.

"I'm sure you can, Jase, but it's better if I get matters straight. You boys go to the boat before you say something I'll regret."

The boys kicked the dirt and scowled as they walked away.

Mr. Yarrow turned back to David's group. "Now, back to business," he said. "We don't appreciate the trouble you've got our daughter into. She may be a little rowdy sometimes, but she's a good girl."

"You betcha, she is," Mrs. Yarrow said. "A hard-working girl. She ain't never been in trouble before she got mixed up with you."

"Ma'am," Sadie said. "She is a hard-working young woman. She's a good cook, too. The shelter cook says she could be a great chef someday. She's also good with children, and they love her. Did you know that?"

Mrs. Yarrow's mouth opened, and her eyebrows puckered. "She is? I ain't never seen her with kids. She's our youngest, so she ain't never been around kids that I know of." She snickered. "I know she's a good cook. She does all our cooking when she's home. It ain't easy making enough food to satisfy our boys. Yep, she's good in the kitchen. But kids? Humphf. Who'da thought it."

"I know she has done wrong things, but she has potential if she will make better choices," Sadie said.

"Exactly what wrong things has she done?" asked Mr. Yarrow.

Sadie looked at David, eyebrows raised. David nodded. "Like I said before, she has been communicating with Cosmos, and it appears he has been getting her to do things for him. For instance, she kidnapped a baby from the shelter. We found the child, but we don't know what she had planned if we hadn't."

Mr. Yarrow pooched out his lips. "And you know for a fact she did it? Maybe it was someone else."

"She admitted she did it," David said. "She also stole several things from the clients at the shelter. We caught her with those things. And she admitted to other minor things that caused us aggravation and made trouble for us."

"My, my, my." Mr. Yarrow smirked. "Lord help if you had a little trouble and aggravation." He leaned toward David. "Boy, our little girl ends up in prison, you'll need the Lord's help for sure." He whirled around, then back around to grab his wife's arm. Together, they stomped off.

"Oh, David," said Sadie. "I don't like the sound of that."

Charlie agreed. "That sounded like a threat to me."

David waved his hand in dismissal. "Never mind. They're all talk." They went inside and gave their statements before boating back to the shelter.

Meanwhile:

"I can't take being locked up." Wren paced the floor when Paul visited her in jail. "I have to get out somehow."

Paul shook his head. "No, Wren. Your dad says you'd best stay put. Just wait and see what they say to you. Maybe since this is your first offense, you'll get off with nothing. Or, at most, a suspended sentence."

"I don't know. They assigned me a lawyer, and he says I might get some prison time." She twisted her fingers together. "I can't take it. You guys have to figure out a way to get me out. I can hide on the island where they'll never find me."

"I don't know. That island ain't all that big."

"Come on. I did this for you, Jase, and Sully, as well as for Cosmos. I just did what you guys told me. I wouldn't be in trouble if I hadn't listened to y'all."

"I'll talk to the others. We'll see what we can do."

"You'd better. Y'all promised me nothing bad would happen. Now look. Cosmos is dead, and I'm locked up."

FORTY-TWO

Every day, the ladies at the shelter worked to keep the kids from thinking about Wren, but they didn't play long until one of them mentioned her. Angie and Lyric spent more time with them, helping them with crafts and other projects. They made designs in jars and on paper plates using lentils and rice. When they cut paper designs and pictures for cards, Elfi suggested they send cards to Wren.

"We can cheer her up," she said. "We need to let her know we love her and haven't forgotten her."

Sadie agreed that might be a good idea. It was a small jail in a small town, so they might allow her to have them.

When David and Sadie were ready to go in a few days, Tashina asked to go along. Then Louisa wanted to go.

"I'll tell you what," said David. "You ladies go, and I'll stay here. I have some things I need to do anyway."

The ladies packed a basket and boated to the town to visit the jail. When they arrived, the officers at the jail looked through the basket and allowed them to see Wren in a visiting area. At first, she withdrew, but the cards from the children made her smile. Soon, she was laughing and talking with Louisa and Tashina while Sadie looked on. She wanted to know about each of the kids and asked about some recipes Louisa had mentioned.

"I'm sorry about all the trouble I caused," she said. "I wish I could have a redo. A lot of things would be different."

"Girl, we're all there," said Tashina. "We've all made

mistakes we wish we could fix. But we can't. The only thing left is to start now doing the right thing."

Louisa nodded. "Ain't that the truth? We all have things in our past that we'd like to forget. But life ain't like a computer. You cain't just delete something and go on. You have to start now making things better for yourself."

"If I ever get out of here, I want to get away from my family, especially my brothers. They're always getting me into trouble." She fiddled with the tie belt on her jail uniform. "I — they — Dad...." She looked from one to the other.

"What is it, dear?" Tashina asked. "You can tell us. What's bothering you?"

"I — uh — oh, never mind." She waved her hand when the guard called for her to return to her cell. She ran to hug each of them and wiped tears as she left.

Afterward, Sadie took Tashina and Louisa to a local restaurant. While they were eating, Sadie noticed a couple watching them. She ignored them, but when she paid the bill and started to leave, the man stopped her.

"Ain't you the Kingston woman who runs the shelter on Crandall Island?"

"I'm Sadie Kingston. I work at the shelter. Is there something I can do for you?"

"Yeah. You can tell your husband if he knows what's good for him, he'll leave the Yarrows alone. He's caused enough trouble, and we ain't havin' it."

"I'm sorry you feel that way," Sadie said. "I'll give him your message." She pushed the door open, then turned. "I'll tell you something, though. If you're defending the Yarrows, you must be one of them. If the Yarrows commit crimes, they'll be turned over to the law. And that includes you."

She told David about the encounter that night. He hugged her. "Be careful, Sadie. I have a feeling that bunch can be mean. I'm starting to wonder if they aren't hiding something. This may go much deeper than what we know."

The next day, David got a call from an officer at the jail.

Wren had escaped.

"What?" Sadie gasped. "Yesterday, she was all about changing and making the right decisions. What happened?"

"Did she say she wanted to change?"

"Well, she said she wished she could have a redo. She said she was sorry for all the trouble she caused. Sounds to me like she wanted to change. Guess that went out the window."

"Who knows? She must have changed her mind."

Sadie shrugged. "She did say something that bothers me. She said her brothers are always getting her into trouble — that she wants to get away from her family, especially them. I think she was trying to tell us something when the guard came to get her. I have a feeling something bad is wrong in that family."

"From what we saw at the station, you're right. Seemed to me like a lot of anger and displacement of guilt. Some people refuse to accept responsibility for their actions."

They heard nothing else for the next few days. Then, a banging at the door woke Tashina in the middle of the night. Looking at the security camera, she could see a hooded figure.

"Who's there?" she called. Another bang. "Who's there? Show your face."

A face showed up on the system. It was Wren.

"Please, Tashina, let me in. Hurry."

"Are you alone?" Wren moved so Tashina could see the area, and then Tashina opened the door. She hurriedly closed it after the girl.

Tashina gasped. "What happened to you? Who did this to you?" Wren was bruised and bleeding. Both eyes were black.

"My dad," she sobbed. "He got mad because I escaped jail. I wouldn't have done it, but Sully and Jase busted me out and told me I had to go with them." She wiped her nose on her shirttail. "I didn't want to do it, Tashina. They made me."

"Then why did your dad beat you?"

"They lied to him. They told him I got out and asked them to hide me." She sobbed harder. "That isn't the truth, Tashina.

I swear."

Tashina led her to the clinic and doctored her cuts. "I'll have to call Officer Jason and David," she said. "They'll know what to do." She made the calls as soon as she stopped most of the bleeding. The two men burst through the door in a few minutes.

Wren told them the story, and Jason called the jail. They said one of the guards saw some men and the girl running into the woods. The officers gave chase but weren't able to apprehend them. "They have a manhunt now," the jailer said. "Guess maybe they'll have to look on the island."

"Yes, those people live here," David said. "We'll keep the girl here until you guys come for her. Maybe you'll find her brothers soon."

"Can you describe them? That would help if you could."

David described the men who had accosted him at the station. When Tashina had cleaned the girl up, Jason took her upstairs to the spare room and sat on guard outside the door.

The next day, police boats surrounded the island, and officers combed through the small piece of land. Louisa took food up to Wren, and the clients stayed indoors. Two officers guarded the shelter in case Jase and Sully showed up there.

Sadie and David went upstairs to talk to Wren.

"Sophia's a lawyer, right?" Wren twisted a lock of hair. "Think she could help me when she gets better?"

"We'll have to wait until she's well. Then she'll have to answer that," Sadie said. "First, why don't we learn some things about you?"

"Okay," Wren said. "That information I gave when I came here isn't right. I lied. I'm sorry."

Sadie wrote down Wren's personal information and asked about her family. At first, Wren was hesitant to say anything about her dad, but she finally admitted he beat her mom and molested her. With the admission, tears flowed.

"He's so mean," she said. "He drinks a lot, and so do my brothers. They're mean to me, too."

"Has this just started?" asked David. "I've never seen you bruised up before now."

"Yeah. My brothers have always been mean to me, but my dad has never beaten me until now. I think because I saw some stuff I wasn't supposed to. Dad was mad."

"What did you see?" asked Sadie.

"Drax and another guy brought some girls by the house last night. Sully and Jase treated them awful. Dad yelled at them for bringing them by. He said they were supposed to take them to the old Weeks place. I think he meant where we were when Cosmos was — you know —. He said I'd better not say anything, or he'd beat me."

"Did you say something for him to beat you tonight?"

"No, but the boys lied on me. That's why." Pleading eyes searched the faces of David and Sadie. "Please help me. I don't want to go back home, but I don't want to go back to jail either. What am I going to do?"

David rose. "Sadie, I've got to make a call. Meet me in my office when you've finished here." He put a hand on Wren's shoulder. "We'll do what we can, Wren. I don't know what will happen. I can't make any promises except we'll do our best to help you. Okay?"

She nodded. David called Jason. "It's more than we thought," he said over the phone. "Cosmos and his accomplices kept the trafficking ring alive. Looks like the Yarrows are running it for him now. Have the guys check the old house where they got Cosmos."

He ran to the dock and yelled for Jerome. "We need to get to the old Weeks place. They may be holed up there."

Jerome ran to the dock. "With all the traffic on the river, maybe we should take the Ranger."

"Good idea." They jumped in and slowed when they saw the building. They stopped short and hid in the bushes. Before long, they saw movement through one of the windows.

"Look," said Jerome. Several boats pulled to the shore, and David went through the bushes to meet the officers.

"Did Jason tell you what we just learned?" he asked. Grim-faced officers nodded.

"We thought we got rid of that bunch of crooks," one officer said.

Keeping behind trees and bushes, they surrounded the building. Someone produced a bullhorn and called out. "Come on out, Yarrow. Bring your boys with you. We have you surrounded."

"You bunch-a skum-sucking, muck-raking, flat-bellied lizards!" Yarrow shouted. "you'll have to come in and git me." He used several other choice words.

"That will be our pleasure," yelled the officer. A chemical smoke bomb flew into the window. Smoke bellowed out every opening, and with it came Yarrow, his sons, Drax, and another guy.

While the other officers handcuffed the younger men, David took down Yarrow. He put a knee on his neck. "Where do you have the girls?" he asked.

Yarrow sputtered. "I don't know what you're talking about."

"You'd better tell me if you don't want your head buried in this mud. Now, where are they?"

Jason stood above David, his gun pointed at Yarrow. "You'd better tell us now," he said, "before David gets really mad."

"Just tell him, Pa." Sully yelped when an officer twisted his arm behind him.

"Yeah, tell him!" yelled Jase. An officer forced his arm upward. Drax moaned and yelped as officers pressured him to reveal the location of the trafficked females.

"I'll tell 'em," yelled Drax.

"Boy, you'd better be quiet," said Yarrow. David shoved his face further into the mud. The man struggled until David pulled his face up so he could breathe, then shoved it down again. A few more times of that, with Yarrow spitting and sputtering, he yelled. "Okay. I'll tell."

David pulled him up so he could talk. "Where are they?"

"They're over at Ashport in an old barn right off the river," he said. Then he snickered. "Doubt you'll get there in time to save them. A boat will land shortly to pick them up. Then they're gone for good."

David shoved his face back into the mud before an officer took over and cuffed him. David, Jerome, and two officers loaded into a boat and sped over the water to Ashport.

They pulled into a dock near the small town and jumped ashore. They had located an old building as they pulled into the dock, so they ran in that direction. When they arrived, they saw someone holding a rifle standing by the door. They ducked down and waited. After a brief conference, they slipped around the building surrounding it.

"I'll cause a distraction," said Jerome. "Then you can move in." He threw a rock against the building close to the man. When the man jerked in that direction, Jerome threw another rock, causing the man to run around to the side of the building. Two officers ran inside, and one waited for the man to return. He jumped him from behind, and all the officers ran into the building. David and Jerome followed.

They looked around behind bales of old hay, hay rakes, and other farm equipment. Nothing. David found a ladder leading to the loft and climbed up. Across one end, a large tarp divided the room. He could hear coughing and sniffing from behind it. The big, scared eyes of children and women looked at him when he pulled back the tarp.

"Shhhh. It's okay. I won't hurt you." He spoke softly to calm the frightened girls. Three women hovered over the small ones.

"Who are you?" one asked.

"I'm David," he said. "We have come to take you home."

The women looked at each other in disbelief. "You're going to take us home?"

Jerome and an officer stepped up beside David. "Yes," an officer said, "we're taking you home. You want to come with us?"

The females looked at one another and arose. One little girl ran to David and threw her arms around him. He patted her on the head and then wiped his cheeks.

Gunshots sounded outside, and David pushed the girls back behind the tarp. "Stay down," he ordered. "Don't move."

The officers had stayed out of sight when they saw a boat pull into the dock. Sure it was the men who came for the girls, they waited, ready.

"Are you the only one here?" one man from the boat asked the guard outside.

"Yeah, it's just me. The girls are inside."

"We're in a hurry," the man said. "Go get them."

When the guard entered the barn, an officer grabbed him and held his mouth so he couldn't yell out.

"What's taking him so long?" The man pushed another one toward the barn. "Go see what's keeping him."

An officer grabbed the second man. After a while, the leading man entered. He found himself looking into the barrels of several guns.

The officers helped the victims down the ladder and guided them to the boat. One woman ran over to the handcuffed guard and kicked him in the shin.

"You're evil, Paul, just like the Yarrow bunch you hang with," she said.

Meanwhile:

A woman stumbled through the trees that separated the shelter from the rest of the island. She could hardly walk from the beating she had suffered. One of the officers guarding the shelter ran to help her.

"Who are you?" he asked.

"Melissa Yarrow." She wiped the blood from her nose with her shirttail. "I need help."

The officer helped her to a bench and motioned to another officer. "Get Ms. Tashina," he said. "Be careful. This is Mrs. Yarrow. It may be a setup."

The officer ran inside and returned with Tashina. She took one look at the woman and ordered the men to get her inside to the clinic.

"What happened to you?" Tashina asked.

"My husband. He went crazy. He's a monster when he drinks." She sniffed. "And that's pretty much all the time anymore. Ever since he brought that Drax fellow home with him."

"Who is Drax?"

"He's some guy Richard met a while back. Richard thinks we can make a lot of money helping Drax deliver drugs for some guy on the mainland. He says the island is a good place to cook and hide drugs."

"Oh. That's interesting." Tashina continued treating the woman's wounds. "Where are they doing that?"

"There's an old shed near the landing by Weeks place," she said. "Ouch!" She winced. "Bushes and briars bury it. You can't see it 'til you're right on it."

"Really. Here, lift your chin. I need to bandage the wound on your neck."

"I don't want Richard to be involved in that kind of stuff," Melissa continued. "I never wanted my boys to do drugs. I wanted them to go to college in the city and make something of themselves. They're all smart, you know."

"I'm sure they are." Tashina cleaned the blood from Melissa and removed her gloves. "I'm sorry your husband hurts you and Wren. You deserve better."

"Can I stay here? I hear you help women in this place."

"You can stay until Mrs. Sadie gets back. She'll get your information and talk to you about your intentions. We need to know you intend to work with the team here and not involve your family with us."

FORTY-THREE

The Willow Grove family gathered in the lounge at the end of the day. The children played on the floor while the adults talked about the recent events.

"I heard that Officer Steve had surgery, but he is doing well," said Jerome.

Sadie nodded. "Yes, Officer Dan gave an update on his condition."

"We're happy that Sophia is recovering," David told them. "She will be home in a day or two. She says to give you all her love."

"We miss her." Mandy rocked her baby in the corner while her husband watched.

"What will happen to Wren?" Juliet asked.

"That depends on a lot of factors," David said. "With Sophia on her side, she has a chance to get off light."

Sadie agreed. "Because her dad and brothers manipulated her, she might. And this is her first offense."

"More like forced," said Tashina. "I don't think she had much of a choice."

"If she had told us what was going on, we could have helped her," said David. "We could have protected her."

"That sounds easy, but it's a hard thing." Iris brushed her hair back from her face. "When a man manipulates a woman, she's scared to go against him. And her dad and brothers lorded it over her. It's hard to go against one, but wow! She had three threatening her."

"I'm sure that's true," Sadie said. "Bless her heart. I hope they give her mercy. She deserves a break."

Nancy pursed her lips. "I hope they put those guys away for good. Those poor women. And what that man did to his wife. What a monster."

"Most of us can relate to her," said Marleigh. "I'm glad she's with us now."

"Where is she?" asked Grace.

"She's resting upstairs," answered Tashina. "She will be ready to join us in a day or two. It takes time, you know. We're all new to her."

Elfi scooted over to Tashina and laid her head on her knee. "We'll help her," she said.

"Yes." David stood. "Willow Grove is a place of refuge for the hurting. A shelter for those who are scared and wounded. Right?"

Heads nodded. The children looked at David with big eyes, and the adults looked at each other. Each one had a story. Some had been wounded because of the decisions of others, and some because of their own choices. No one placed blame. They all knew that grace came from God. They all realized the sacrifices made by others for them to have a place to work to better their lives. They were all grateful.

David held out a hand to Sadie. She rose and stood beside him. "Sadie and I are thankful for all of you," he said. "Without you, there would be no Willow Grove."

"You mean you're glad we are all here?" The question came from Brent.

"Yes, little man." David rubbed the boy's head. "We liked the turtle soup and all the adventures in the woods. And we hope we never get chiggers again."

Jax and Randall jumped around, scratching themselves while everyone laughed. Brent jerked up his shirt. "Wanna see my red spots?"

THE END

MORE BOOKS BY THIS AUTHOR

Life in the Leaves series
Whip or Rill
Hannah Hummingbird
Beatrice Blue Jay
Morey Mockingbird

Life in the Trees series
Rusty Rabbit's Conundrum
Rowdy Ryker
Missing Grandma

Other Children's books:
> Brave Buster
> Thin Girl
> Kind Korie
> Benny Shares
> A Prince Needs a Princess
> Rocking Ages

Novels:
> Modified
> Rectified
> Pepper
> Where the River Goes
> Willow Grove
> Reluctant Queen

Nonfiction
> It Pays to be Picky
> Who Am I

To contact this author: mjauthor5@gmail.com
mjwriter.com

Made in the USA
Columbia, SC
22 May 2024